PROPHECY

OF THE

SISTERS

PROPHECY
OF THE
SISTERS

MICHELLE ZINK

SCHOLASTIC INC.
New York Toronto London Auckland
Sydney Mexico City New Delhi Hong Kong

ISBN 978-0-545-29360-0

12 11 10 9 8 7 6 5 4 3 2 1   10 11 12 13 14 15/0

Printed in the U.S.A.   23

First Scholastic printing, September 2010

Hand-lettering and interior ornamentation by Leah Palmer Preiss
Book design by Alison Impey

 *To my mother, Claudia Baker.*
For betting on me.

1

Perhaps because it seems so appropriate, I don't notice the rain. It falls in sheets, a blanket of silvery thread rushing to the hard almost-winter ground. Still, I stand without moving at the side of the coffin.

I am on Alice's right. I am always on Alice's right, and I often wonder if it was that way even in our mother's womb, before we were pushed screaming into the world one right after the other. My brother, Henry, sits near Edmund, our driver, and Aunt Virginia, for sit is all Henry can do without the use of his legs. It was only with some effort that Henry and his chair were carried to the graveyard on the hill so that he could see our father laid to rest.

Aunt Virginia leans in to speak to us over the drumming rain. "Children, we must be going."

The reverend has long since left. I cannot say how long we

have been standing at the mound of dirt where my father's body lay, for I have been under the shelter of James's umbrella, a quiet world of protection providing the smallest of buffers between me and the truth.

Alice motions for us to leave. "Come, Lia, Henry. We'll return when the sun is shining and lay fresh flowers on Father's grave." I was born first, though only by minutes, but it has always been clear that Alice is in charge.

Aunt Virginia nods to Edmund. He gathers Henry into his arms, turning to begin the walk back to the house. Henry's gaze meets mine over Edmund's shoulder. Henry is only ten, though far wiser than most boys of his age. I see the loss of Father in the dark circles under my brother's eyes. A stab of pain finds its way through my numbness, settling somewhere over my heart. Alice may be in charge, but I am the one who has always felt responsible for Henry.

My feet will not move, will not take me away from my father, cold and dead in the ground. Alice looks back. Her eyes find mine through the rain.

"I'll be along in a moment." I have to shout to be heard, and she nods slowly, turning and continuing along the path toward Birchwood Manor.

James takes my gloved hand in his, and I feel a wave of relief as his strong fingers close over mine. He moves closer to be heard over the rain.

"I'll stay with you as long as you want, Lia."

I can only nod, watching the rain leak tears down Father's gravestone as I read the words etched into the granite.

Thomas Edward Milthorpe
Beloved Father
June 23, 1846–November 1, 1890

There are no flowers. Despite my father's wealth, it is difficult to find flowers so near to winter in our town in northern New York, and none of us have had the energy or will to send for them in time for the modest service. I am ashamed, suddenly, at this lack of forethought, and I glance around the family cemetery, looking for something, anything, that I might leave.

But there is nothing. Only a few small stones lying in the rain that pools on the dirt and grass. I bend down, reaching for a few of the dirt-covered stones, holding my palm open to the rain until the rocks are washed clean.

I am not surprised that James knows what I mean to do, though I don't say it aloud. We have shared a lifetime of friendship and, recently, something much, much more. He moves forward with the umbrella, offering me shelter as I step toward the grave and open my hand, dropping the rocks along the base of Father's headstone.

My sleeve pulls with the motion, revealing a sliver of the strange mark, the peculiar, jagged circle that bloomed on my wrist in the hours after Father's death. I steal a glance at James to see if he has noticed. He hasn't, and I pull my arm further inside my sleeve, lining the rocks up in a careful row. I push the mark from my mind. There is no room there for both grief and worry. And grief will not wait.

I stand back, looking at the stones. They are not as pretty or bright as the flowers I will bring in the spring, but they are all I have to give. I reach for James's arm and turn to leave, relying on him to guide me home.

☙

It is not the warmth of the parlor's fire that keeps me downstairs long after the rest of the household retires. My room has a firebox, as do most of the rooms at Birchwood Manor. No, I sit in the darkened parlor, lit only by the glow of the dying fire, because I do not have the courage to make my way upstairs.

Though Father has been dead for three days, I have kept myself well occupied. It has been necessary to console Henry, and though Aunt Virginia would have made the arrangements for Father's burial, it seemed only right that I should help take matters in hand. This is what I have been telling myself. But now, in the empty parlor with only the ticking mantel clock for company, I realize that I have been avoiding this moment when I shall have to make my way up the stairs and past Father's empty chambers. This moment when I shall have to admit he is really gone.

I rise quickly, before I lose my nerve, focusing on putting one slippered foot in front of the other as I make my way up the winding staircase and down the hall of the East Wing. As I pass Alice's room, and then Henry's, my eyes are drawn to the door at the end of the hall. The room that was once my mother's private chamber.

The Dark Room.

As little girls, Alice and I spoke of the room in whispers, though I cannot say how we came to call it the Dark Room. Perhaps it is because in the tall-ceilinged rooms where fires blaze nonstop nine months out of the year, it is only the uninhabited rooms that are completely dark. Yet even when my mother was alive, the room seemed dark, for it was in this room that she retreated in the months before her death. It was in this room that she seemed to drift further and further away from us.

I continue to my room, where I undress and pull on a nightgown. I am sitting on the bed, brushing my hair to a shine, when a knock stops me midstroke.

"Yes?"

Alice's voice finds me from the other side of the door. "It's me. May I come in?"

"Of course."

The door creaks open, and with it comes a burst of cooler air from the unheated hallway. Alice closes it quickly, crossing to the bed and sitting next to me as she did when we were children. Our nightdresses, like us, are nearly identical. Nearly but not quite. Alice's are made with fine silk at her request while I prefer comfort over fashion and wear flannel in every season but summer.

She reaches out a hand for the brush. "Let me."

I hand her the brush, trying not to show my surprise as I turn away to give her access to the back of my head. We are

not the kind of sisters who engage in nightly hair brushing or confided secrets.

She moves the brush in long strokes, starting at the crown of my head and traveling all the way down to the ends. Watching our reflection in the looking glass atop the bureau, it is hard to believe anyone can tell us apart. From this distance and in the glow of the firelight, we look exactly the same. Our hair shimmers the same chestnut in the dim light. Our cheekbones angle at the same slant. I know, though, that it is the subtle differences that are unmistakable to those who know us at all. It is the slight fullness in my face that stands in contrast to the sharper contours of my sister's and the somber introspection in my eyes that opposes the sly gleam in her own. It is Alice who shimmers like a jewel under the light, while I brood, think, and wonder.

The fire crackles in the firebox, and I close my eyes, allowing my shoulders to loosen as I fall into the soothing rhythm of the brush in my hair, Alice's hand smoothing the top of my head as she goes.

"Do you remember her?"

My eyelids flutter open. It is an uncommon question, and for a moment, I'm unsure how to answer. We were only girls of six when our mother died in an inexplicable fall from the cliff near the lake. Henry had been born just a few months before. The doctors had already made it clear that my father's long-desired son would never have the use of his legs. Aunt Virginia always said that Mother was never the same after Henry's birth, and the questions surrounding her death still linger. We don't speak of it or the inquiry that followed.

I can only offer her the truth. "Yes, but only a little. Do you?"

She hesitates before answering, the brush still moving. "I believe so. But only in flashes. Little moments, I suppose. I often wonder why I can remember her green dress, but not the way her voice sounded when she read aloud. Why I can clearly see the book of poems she kept on the table in the parlor but not remember the way she smelled."

"It was jasmine and . . . oranges, I think."

"Is that it? The way she smelled?" Her voice is a murmur behind me. "I didn't know."

"Here. My turn." I twist around, reaching for the brush.

She turns as compliant as a child. "Lia?"

"Yes?"

"If you knew something, about Mother . . . If you remembered something, something important, would you tell me?" Her voice is quiet, more unsure than I've ever heard it.

My breath catches in my throat with the strange question. "Yes, of course, Alice. Would you?"

She hesitates, the only sound in the room the soft pull of the brush through silken hair. "I suppose so."

I move the brush through her hair, remembering. Not my mother. Not now. But Alice. Us. The twins. I remember the time before Henry's birth, before Mother took refuge alone in the Dark Room. The time before Alice became secretive and strange.

It would be easy to look back on our childhood and assume that Alice and I were close. In the fondness of memory, I recall her soft breath in the dark of night, her voice mumbling into the blackness of our shared nursery. I try to remember our proximity as comfort, to ignore the voice that reminds me of our differences even then. But it doesn't work. If I am honest, I will admit we have always eyed each other warily. Still, it was once her soft hand I grasped before falling into sleep, her curls I brushed from my shoulder when she slept too close.

"Thank you, Lia." Alice turns around, looking me in the eyes. "I miss you, you know."

My cheeks are warm under the scrutiny of her stare, the closeness of her face to mine. I shrug. "I'm right here, Alice, as I've always been."

She smiles, but in it is something sad and knowing. Leaning in, she wraps her thin arms around me as she did when we were children.

"And I as well, Lia. As I've always been."

She stands, leaving without another word. I sit on the edge of the bed in the dim light of the lamp, trying to place her uncommon sadness. It is unlike Alice to be reflective, though with Father's death I suppose we are all feeling vulnerable.

Thoughts of Alice allow me to avoid the moment when I will have to look at my wrist. I feel a coward as I try to find the courage to pull back the sleeve of my nightdress. To look again at the mark that appeared after Father's body was found in the Dark Room.

When I finally pull back my sleeve, telling myself that

whatever is there is there just the same, whether or not I look, I have to press my lips together to keep from crying out. It isn't the mark on the soft underside of my wrist that is a surprise, but how much darker it is now than it was even this morning. How much clearer the circle, though I still cannot decipher the ridges that thicken it, making the edges seem uneven.

I fight a surge of rising panic. It seems there should be some recourse, something I should do, someone I should tell, but whom might I tell such a thing? Once, I would go to Alice, for whom else might I trust with such a secret? Even still, I cannot ignore the ever-growing distance between us. It has made me wary of my sister.

I tell myself the mark will go away, that there is no need to tell someone such a strange thing when surely it will be gone in a few days. Instinctively, I think this a lie but convince myself I have a right to believe it on a day such as this.

On the day I have buried my father.

2

The thin November light is spreading its fingers across the room when Ivy pads in carrying a kettle of hot water.

"Good morning, Miss." She pours the water into the basin on the washstand. "Shall I help you dress?"

I lift myself up on my elbows. "No, thank you. I'll be fine."

"Very well." She leaves the room, empty kettle in hand.

I throw back the covers and make my way to the washstand, swirling a hand in the basin to cool the water before I wash. When I am finished, I dry my cheeks and forehead, peering into the glass. My green eyes are bottomless, empty, and I wonder if it is possible to change from the inside out, if sadness can radiate outward, through the veins and organs and skin for all to see. I shake my head at the morbid notion, watching my auburn hair, unbound, brush my shoulders in the looking glass.

I take off my nightdress and pull a petticoat and stockings from the bureau, beginning to dress. I am smoothing the second stocking up my thigh when Alice sweeps in without knocking.

"Good morning." She drops heavily onto the bed, looking up at me with the breathless charm that is uniquely Alice.

It surprises me still, her effortless swing from barely concealed bitterness to sorrow to carefree calm. It should not, for Alice's moods have always been mercurial. But her face bears no trace of sadness, no trace of last night's melancholy. In truth, other than her simple gown and lack of jewelry, she looks no different than she ever has. Perhaps I am the only one to change from the inside out after all.

"Good morning." I hurry and fasten the stocking, feeling guilty that I've lazed in my room for so long when my sister is already up and about. I move to the cupboard, both to find a gown and to avoid the eyes that always seem to look too deeply into mine.

"You should see the house, Lia. The entire staff is in mourning clothes, on Aunt Virginia's orders."

I turn to look at her, noticing the flush on her cheeks and something like excitement in her eyes. I push down my annoyance. "Many households observe the mourning period, Alice. Everyone loved Father. I'm sure they don't mind paying their respects."

"Yes, well, now we shall be stuck inside for an interminable time, and it is so very dull here. Do you suppose Aunt

Virginia will allow us to attend classes next week?" She continues without waiting for an answer. "Of course, you don't even care! You would be perfectly happy to never see Wycliffe again."

I do not bother arguing. It is well-known that Alice yearns for the more civilized life of the girls at Wycliffe, the school where we attend classes twice a week, while I always feel like an exotic animal under glass. I steal glimpses of her at school, glittering under the niceties of polite society, and imagine her like our mother. It must be true, for it is I who finds pleasure in the stillness of Father's library and Alice alone who can conjure the gleam of our mother's eyes.

We spend the day in the almost-silence of the crackling fire. We are accustomed to the isolation of Birchwood and have learned to occupy ourselves within its somber walls. It is like any other rainy day save for the lack of Father's big voice booming from the library or the smell of his pipe. We don't speak of him or his strange death.

I avoid looking at the clock, fearing the slow passing of time that will only seem slower if I watch its progress. It works, in a manner of speaking. The day passes more quickly than I expect, the small interruptions for lunch and dinner easing me toward the time when I can escape to the nothingness of sleep.

This time I don't look at my wrist before climbing into bed. I don't want to know if the mark is still there. If it has changed.

If it is deeper or darker. I slip into bed, sinking toward darkness without further thought.

I am in the in-between place, the place we drift through before the world falls away into sleep, when I hear the whispering. At first, it is only the call of my name, beckoning from some far-off place. But the whisper builds, becoming many voices, all murmuring frantically, so quickly that I can only make out an occasional word. It grows and grows, demanding my attention until I cannot ignore it a second longer. Until I sit straight up in bed, the last whispered words echoing through the caverns of my mind.

The Dark Room.

It is not entirely surprising. The Dark Room has been at the forefront of my mind since Father's death. He should not have been there. Not in the one room that would invoke the memory of my mother, his beloved dead wife, more than any other.

And yet, in those last moments, as life slipped from his body like a wraith, he was.

I slide my feet into slippers and make my way to the door, listening a moment before opening it and looking down the hall. The house is dark and silent. The footsteps of the servants cannot be heard in the rooms above our own or in the kitchen below. It must be quite late.

All this registers in seconds, leaving only the faintest of impressions. The thing that gets my attention, the thing that makes the small hairs rise on my arms and the back of my neck, is the door, open just a crack, at the end of the hallway.

The door to the Dark Room.

It is strange enough that the door to this, of all rooms, should be open, but stranger still that there is a faint glow leaking from the small gap between the frame and the door.

I look down at the mark. It shadows my wrist even in the darkness of the hallway. *It is this I've been wondering, is it not? I* think. *Whether or not the Dark Room holds the key to Father's death or the reason for my mark?* Now it is as if I've been summoned to that very place, called to the answers I have sought all along.

I creep down the hallway, careful to lift my feet so the bottoms of my slippers don't scuff along the wood floor. When I reach the door of the Dark Room, I hesitate.

Someone is inside.

A voice, soft but urgent, comes from within the room. It is not the same frantic murmur that called me here. Not the disjointed voices of many. No. It is the voice of one. A solitary person whispering inside.

I don't dare push open the door for fear it will creak. Instead, I lean toward it, peering through the opening into the room beyond. It is difficult to get my bearings through such a small crack. At first everything is only shapes and shadows. But soon I make out the looming white sheets of the covered furniture, the dark mass I know is the wardrobe in the corner, and the figure sitting on the floor, surrounded by candles.

Alice.

My sister sits on the floor of the Dark Room, the glow of many candles casting her body in soft yellow light. She is

muttering, whispering as if to someone very near, though from my vantage I see not a soul. She sits on folded knees, her eyes closed, arms at her sides.

I scan the room, careful not to touch the door lest it should spring to life and glide open even farther. But there is no one else there. No one but Alice, murmuring to herself in a strange sort of ceremony. And even this, this dark rite that sends tendrils of fear racing through my body, is not the strangest thing of all.

No, it is that my sister sits with the rug pulled back, a large well-worn rug that has been in the room as long as I can remember. She sits, as naturally as if she has done it countless times before, within a circle carved into the floor. The angles of her face are nearly unrecognizable, almost harsh, in the candlelight.

The cold from the unheated hallway seeps through the thin fabric of my nightdress. I step back, my heart beating so loudly in my chest that I fear Alice will hear it from within the Dark Room.

When I turn to make my way down the hall, I have to resist the urge to run. Instead, I walk calmly and step into my room, closing the door behind me and climbing into the safety and comfort of my bed. I lay awake for a long time, trying to force from my mind the image of Alice within the circle, the sound of her murmuring to someone who wasn't there at all.

The next morning, I stand in the clear light streaming through the window, sliding the sleeve of my nightdress up and over my wrist. The mark has become darker still, the circle thicker and more prominent.

And there is something else.

In the stark light of day, it seems quite obvious what it is — the thing that encircles the circle itself, making the edges less clear. I trail a finger across the surface of the mark, raised as a scar, following the lines of the snake that coils itself around the edges of the circle until its mouth is eating its own tail.

The Jorgumand.

Few girls of sixteen would know it, but I recognize the symbol from Father's books on mythology. It is at once familiar and frightening, for why should such a symbol rise from my skin?

I only briefly consider telling Aunt Virginia. She has had her share of grief and worry over Father's death. Our well-being is now left to her, our only living relative. I'll not add another worry to the ones she already has.

I chew my lower lip. It is impossible to think of my sister without remembering her posture on the floor of the Dark Room. I resolve to ask her what she was doing. And then I will show her the mark.

After dressing, I step into the hall, preparing to search for Alice. I hope she is not walking the grounds as she has since she was a child. Locating her as she takes sun in her favorite spot on the patio will be considerably easier than searching the fields and forests surrounding Birchwood. As I turn away from my chamber, my eyes slide to the closed door of the Dark Room. From here, it looks as it always has. It is almost possible to imagine that Father is still alive in the library and that my sister has never knelt on the floor of the forbidden room in the mystery of night. And yet she has.

My mind is made up before I fully realize it. I make my way swiftly down the hall. I don't hesitate on the threshold of the room. Instead, I open the door and step through it in seconds.

The room is just as I remember it, the curtains drawn against the daylight, the rug back in place over the wood floor. A strange energy pulses through the air, a vibration that seems to hum through my veins. I shake my head, and the sound almost disappears.

I move to the bureau and open the top drawer. I should not be surprised to find my mother's things there, but somehow I am. Most of my life, she has been no more than an idea. Somehow, the fine silk and lace of her petticoats and stockings make her seem very real. I can see her suddenly, a flesh-and-blood woman, dressing for the day.

I force myself to lift her underthings, looking for anything that might explain Father's presence in the room at the time of his death — a journal, an old letter, anything at all. When I find nothing, I do the same with the other drawers, lifting and searching to the very back. But there is nothing there.

Nothing but the paper drawer liner that long ago lost its scent.

I lean lightly against the dresser, surveying the room for other possible hiding places. Crossing to the bed, I kneel and lift the ghostly coverlet, peering beneath the bed. It is spotless, doubtless cleared of dust and cobwebs only during the maid's latest round of cleaning.

My eyes settle on the rug. The image of Alice within the circle is etched in my mind. I know what I saw, but I cannot keep myself from looking. From being sure.

I move toward the rug and am at its edge when my head begins to buzz, the vibration closing in on my thoughts, my vision, until I think I might faint. The tips of my fingers become numb, a prickly tingling beginning at my feet and radiating upward until I fear that my legs will give out altogether.

And then the whispering begins. It is the same whispering I heard last night before coming to the Dark Room. But this time it is threatening, as if warning me off, telling me to go back. A cold sweat breaks out on my brow, and I begin to tremble. No, not tremble. *Shake.* I shake so violently my teeth clatter together before I sink to the floor in front of the rug. A small voice of self-preservation shouts at me to leave, to forget the Dark Room altogether.

But I *must* see for myself. I must.

My hand weaves and shakes in front of my eyes, reaching for the edge of the rug. The whispering grows louder and louder until the great buzz of many voices becomes a shout within my head. I will myself not to stop, grasping the corner of the rug with fingers that can hardly close around the fine weave of the carpet.

I pull it back, and the whispering stops.

The circle is there, just as it was last night. And although the whispers are silent, my body's reaction to the circle only becomes more violent. I think I may be sick. Without the cover of darkness, I see that the gouges are fresh where the wood has been dug away to form the circle. This is no remnant from my mother's time in the Dark Room but an addition much more recent.

I pull the rug back over the carving, rising on wobbling legs. I will not let it drive me from the room. My mother's room. I force myself to the wardrobe as I had planned, though I must step around the rug, for my feet cannot, *will not*, allow me too close.

Flinging open the wardrobe doors, I perform a quick search, knowing it is not as thorough as it could be and knowing just as well that I no longer care. That I really must leave the room.

In any case, there is nothing of note in the wardrobe. Some old gowns, a cape, four corsets. Whatever drew Father to this room is as inexplicable as the reason for Alice's presence here last night and the thing that draws me to it now.

I step around the rug, making my way to the door as swiftly as possible without actually running. The more distance I put between myself and the rug, between myself and the circle, the better I feel, though still not well.

I close the door behind me more loudly than I should, leaning against the wall and forcing down the bile that has risen in my throat. I don't know how long I stand there, catching my breath, forcing my physical symptoms into submission, but all the while my mind is full of fierce and frightful things.

3

The day is like a diamond, all beautiful warmth on the outside but without any heat to accompany it. Henry is sitting in his chair by the river with Edmund. It is one of Henry's favorite places, and though I was young, I remember well the construction of the smooth stone pathway that winds almost to the water's edge. Father had it built when Henry was but a babe who loved the sound of stones thrown into the water. Edmund and Henry can often be found near the terrace on the banks of the rushing water, skipping stones and placing the small secretive wagers that are forbidden but overlooked by Aunt Virginia.

I circle the house and am relieved when Alice comes into view on the patio outside the sunroom. Next to the wide open spaces surrounding the house on every side, the glass-enclosed conservatory is her favorite, but it is closed off from November to March due to the cold. During those months, she can often be found on the patio, wrapped in a blanket and sitting on one of the outdoor chairs even on days that I find uncomfortably cold.

Her legs are stretched out in front of her, the stockings at her ankles showing enough to be considered inappropriate anywhere but within the confines of Birchwood Manor. Her face, soft and round again in contrast to the harsh angles of night, is tipped to the sun, her eyes closed. The shadow of a smile toys with her lips, and they curve upward in an expression that might be either sly or peaceful.

"Why do you stand there staring, Lia?"

I am startled by her voice and the way her face doesn't change at all. I have not made a sound, having stopped in the grass before stepping onto the stone that would announce my arrival. And still she knows I'm here.

"I was not *staring*, Alice. I was only watching you. You look so happy." The heels of my boots click on the patio as I walk toward her, and I try to hide the note of accusation that has crept into my voice.

"And why wouldn't I be happy?"

"I wonder why you *would* be, Alice. How *could* you be happy at a time such as this?" My face burns with anger, and I'm suddenly glad her eyes remain closed.

As if reading my mind, she opens her eyes, focusing on my face. "Father is no longer in the material world, Lia. He is in heaven with Mother. Isn't that where he'd like to be?"

Something in her face puzzles me, some shade of peacefulness and happiness that seems altogether *wrong* so soon after Father's death.

"I . . . I don't know. We have already lost Mother. I should think Father would have liked to stay and watch over us." It sounds childish now that I've said it aloud, and I once again think Alice the stronger twin.

She tips her head at me. "I'm certain he watches over us still, Lia. And besides, what is there from which we need protection?"

I feel the things she has left unsaid. I don't know what they are, but they pluck at something dark, and all at once I am scared. All at once, I know I will not ask Alice what she was doing in the Dark Room, nor will I show her the mark, though I cannot put words to a singular reason.

"I'm not afraid, Alice. I only miss him, that's all."

She doesn't answer, her eyes closed once again to the sun, the look of calm restored to her pale face. There is nothing more to say, nothing more to do but turn and leave.

When I return to the house, I follow the sound of voices in the library. I cannot make out the words, but they are the voices of men, and I listen for a minute, enjoying their baritone vibration before opening the door. James looks up as I enter the room.

"Good morning, Lia. We've not been too noisy, have we?" There is a thread of urgency under his greeting, and I know immediately there is something he wishes to tell me in private.

I shake my head. "Not at all. It's nice to hear noise coming

from Father's study again." Mr. Douglas is peering with a magnifying glass at the cover of a thick brown volume. "Good morning, Mr. Douglas."

He looks up, blinking as if to clear his vision before nodding kindly. "Good morning, Amalia. How are you feeling today?"

"I'm quite all right, Mr. Douglas. Thank you for asking, and thank you for continuing the catalogue of Father's collection. He wanted so to see it done. It would make him happy to know that the work continues."

He nods again without smiling, and the room falls still with the shared grief of friends. I am relieved when Mr. Douglas becomes preoccupied, looking away and shuffling around for something he seems to have misplaced.

"Now . . . where is that blasted ledger?" He pushes papers aside at an increasingly frenzied pace. "Ah! I think I've left it in the carriage. I'll return in a moment, James. Carry on." He turns and marches from the room.

James and I stand in the sudden quiet left by his father's departure. I have long suspected that the never-ending job of cataloging the library had as much to do with Father's desire to see James and me together as it did his constant acquisitions to the collection. As with his views on women and intellect, my father was not a conformist with regards to class. Our bond with the Douglas men was based on true affection and a shared love of old books. Though there are undoubtedly those in town who think the friendship improper, Father never let the opinions of others form his own.

James reaches out, taking my hand and gently pulling me toward him. "How are you, Lia? Is there anything I can do?"

The worry in his voice, the gruff concern, brings the prick of tears to my eyes. I am at once flooded with both sadness and relief. In the safety of James's company, I realize the strain of my constant caution around Alice.

I shake my head, clearing my throat a little before trusting myself to speak. "No. It will simply take time, I think, to become used to Father's absence." I try to sound strong, but the tears spill onto my cheeks. I cover my face with my hands.

"Lia. Lia." He moves my hands and grasps them in his. "I know how much your father meant to you. It's not the same, I know, but I'm here for anything you need. Anything at all."

His eyes burn into mine, and the tweed of his waistcoat brushes against my gown. A familiar rush of heat works its way outward from my stomach to the far reaches of my body and to all the secret places that are only a distant promise.

He reluctantly steps back, straightening and clearing his throat. "I should think there might be one day when Father would remember to bring the ledger in from the carriage, but it's a stroke of luck for us. Come! Let me show you what I've found."

James pulls me along, and I find myself smiling in spite of the circumstances, in spite of his fingers nearly touching the mark. "Wait! What is it?"

He drops my hand when he reaches the bookshelf near the window, reaching behind a stack of books waiting to be

catalogued. "I discovered something interesting this morning. A book I didn't realize your father had acquired."

"What . . ." My eyes light on the black volume as it comes into view. ". . . book?"

"This one." He holds it toward me. "I found it a couple of days ago, after . . ." Unsure how to make reference to my Father's death, he smiles sadly and continues. "Anyway, I put it behind the others so I could show it to you before it's catalogued. It was in a hidden panel at the back of one of the shelves. Father, as ever, was looking for his spectacles and didn't see it at all. *Your* father . . . Well, it's obvious your father didn't want anyone to know it was there, though I'm not sure why. I thought you might like to see it."

When I drop my gaze to the book, recognition ripples through me, though I am certain I have never seen it before in my life.

"May I?" I reach out to take it from him.

"Of course. It belongs to you, Lia. Or . . . It belonged to your father and I assume it belongs to you. And to Alice and Henry, of course."

But this is an afterthought. He is giving the book to me.

The leather is cool and dry in my hands, the cover decorated with a design I can only feel through the raised figures under my fingers. It is very old, that much is clear.

I find my voice but am too enthralled with the book to look up at James. "What is it?"

"That's just it. I'm not sure. I've never seen anything like it."

The cover sighs and creaks as I open it, little particles of leather sprinkling the air beneath the book like pieces of dust in sunlight. Oddly, there is only one page, covered in words I vaguely recognize as Latin. I am suddenly sorry I've not paid more attention to our language studies at Wycliffe.

"What does it say?"

He leans in, brushing my shoulder as he looks at the page. "It says, 'Librum Maleficii et Disordinae.'" He looks into my eyes. "Approximately? The Book of Chaos."

"The Book of Chaos?" I shake my head. "Father never made mention of it, and I know his collection as well as he knew it himself."

"I know. And I don't believe he ever mentioned it to my father, either. Certainly not to me."

"What sort of book is it?"

"Well, I remembered you have trouble with Latin, so I took it home and made a translation. I *knew* you'd want to know more." His eyes twinkle with these last words, and I recognize it as a small jibe toward my endless curiosity.

I roll my eyes, smiling if only to feign exasperation with James. "Never mind, what does it say?"

He looks back to the book, clearing his throat before beginning. "It starts out, 'Through fire and harmony mankind endured until the sending of the Guards, who took as wives and lovers the woman of man, engendering His wrath.'"

I shake my head. "Is it a story?"

He pauses. "I think so, though not one I've ever heard."

I turn the single page. I don't know what I'm looking for when clearly there is nothing else there.

"It goes on from there," he adds before I can begin asking questions, "to say 'two sisters, formed in the same swaying ocean, one the Guardian, one the Gate. One keeper of peace, the other bartering sorcery for devotion.'"

"Two sisters, formed in the same swaying ocean . . . I don't understand."

"I believe it's a metaphor. For the birth fluid. I think it alludes to twins. Like you and Alice."

His words echo in my mind. *Like you and Alice.*

And like my mother and Aunt Virginia, and their mother and aunt before them, I think. "But what of 'the Guardian and the Gate'? What does that mean?"

He shrugs a little as his eyes meet mine. "I'm sorry, Lia. I don't know about that part."

Mr. Douglas's voice drifts down the hall and we glance at the library door. I look back at James as his father's voice gets louder and nearer the library door.

"Have you translated the whole page?"

"Yes. I . . . Well, I wrote it down for you, actually." He reaches into his pocket as Mr. Douglas's voice sounds from just outside of the door, giving us fair warning of his arrival.

"Very good, Virginia. Tea would be most lovely!"

I put a hand on James's arm. "Can you bring it to the river later?" The river is our usual meeting place, though not normally for something as staid as a book.

"Well . . . Yes. When we stop for lunch? Can you meet me then?"

I nod, handing the book back to him as his father comes through the door.

"Ah, here it is! You see, James, it's just as I said — I *am* losing my wits in my old age!" Mr. Douglas waves a leather-bound ledger in the air.

James's smile is brilliant. "Nonsense, Father. You're simply too busy, that's all."

I only half-listen to their banter. Why would the book be hidden in the library? It was unlike my father to keep to himself so rare and interesting a find, but I can only assume he had a reason for doing so.

And I have reasons of my own for wanting to know more.

It cannot be chance alone that Father was found dead on the floor of the Dark Room, or that shortly thereafter I discovered the mark, observed my sister in her eerie ritual, and was given this strange, lost book. I cannot be sure what it all means or how these events work in concert, but I'm certain they do.

And I intend to find out how.

4

Henry and Edmund are no longer at the river. Edmund has always been protective of Henry, and he will doubtless be more so now that Father has passed. There is a chill in the air, a portent of the coming winter, and worrying over Henry is a habit for us all.

I follow the pathway to the terrace at its end, stepping into the woods and making my way to the boulder that sits in the shelter of a giant oak. Serenity creeps over me as I settle onto the rock that James and I call ours. It seems that nothing bad or frightening could happen here, and by the time I hear James approaching, I have almost convinced myself that everything is just as it should be.

I smile at him as he draws near, peering up at him in the sunlight when he stops in front of me. He takes my hand and pulls me to my feet with a smile. "I'm sorry. We were finishing the Religious History collection. Father wanted to complete it before stopping for lunch. Have you been waiting long?"

He pulls me toward him, but it is with newfound gentleness, as if the loss of my father has made me somehow more fragile. And I suppose it has, though I should not like to admit it to anyone. It is only James who knows me well enough, who loves me well enough, that he sees my grief though I look just the same on the outside.

I shake my head. "Not long at all. In any case, waiting for you is made easy in this place. A place that reminds me of you while I wait."

He tips his head, taking a finger and tracing my face from the loose curls at my temple, down the angular jut of my cheekbone, across the curve of my jaw. "Everything reminds me of you."

He lowers his lips to mine. The kiss is gentle, yet I don't need the hard press of his lips to feel the urgency in his body's call to mine. He pulls away, trying to protect me, trying not to push me in these days after Father's death. There is no ladylike way to tell him to push all he wants, that his mouth and body on mine are the only things keeping me from losing my hold on a reality I never questioned until these past days.

"Yes, well . . ." He stands up straighter. "Come. I've brought my notes on the book."

He lowers himself to the boulder, and I make myself comfortable next to him, the skirt of my gown crinkling as it rubs against the rough fabric of his trousers. He pulls the book from his jacket together with a folded piece of paper. Smoothing it across his thigh, he bends his golden head to the slanted hand-writing covering the page top to bottom.

"The story is an ancient one, if the book is to be believed."

"What sort of story?"

"A tale about angels or . . . demons, I think. Here, you can read it just as easily." He lowers himself to the rock once again, thrusting the book and his notes toward me.

For one brief moment, I don't want to read it. I wonder if there is a way to ignore it. To simply go on as I always have, pretending none of it exists. But it doesn't last long. Even now I feel the wheels of a great invisible machine turning all around. They will continue turning whatever I do. This I somehow know.

I bow my head to the comfort of James's handwriting, strangely matched with the terror of words that are not his.

> Through fire and harmony mankind endured
> Until the sending of the Guards
> Who took as wives and lovers the woman of man,
> Engendering His wrath.
> Two sisters, formed in the same swaying ocean,
> One the Guardian, One the Gate.
> One keeper of peace,
> The other bartering sorcery for devotion.
> Cast from the heavens, the Souls were Lost
> As the Sisters continue the battle
> Until the Gates summon forth their return,
> Or the Angel brings the Keys to the Abyss.

The Army, marching forth through the Gates.

Samael, the Beast, through the Angel.

The Angel, guarded only by the gossamer veil of protection.

Four Marks, Four Keys, Circle of Fire

Birthed in the first breath of Samhain

In the shadow of the Mystic Stone Serpent of Aubur.

Let the Angel's Gate swing without the Keys

Followed by the Seven Plagues and No Return.

Death

Famine

Blood

Fire

Darkness

Drought

Ruin

Open your arms, Mistress of Chaos, that the havoc of the Beast will flow like a river

For all is lost when the Seven Plagues begin.

My attention is drawn again to the oddity of a one-page book. I don't know as much about books as James, but even I realize that it is unusual for someone to have a book bound and printed for only one page.

"Shouldn't there be more? There's nothing here. Nothing at all after the story. It seems that there *should* be more. Something that tells what happens next . . ."

"I thought the same thing. Here, let me show you."

He brings the book closer so that it is between us, half on his legs and half on mine, and turns the single page. "Look, here." He points to the space where the pages meet the binding.

"I don't see anything."

He takes a loop from his pocket, handing it to me and pulling the pages taut. "Look closely, Lia. It's difficult to see at first."

I hold the lens of the loop over the area marked by his finger, moving my face to within inches of the page. And then I see the tear marks, so clean as to not be tear marks at all. It is as if someone has taken a razor, slicing cleanly from the book the pages that were once there.

I look up. "There *were* pages here."

He nods.

"But why would someone remove them from such an old book? Surely it's quite valuable if nothing else."

"I don't know. I've seen many strange and damaging things done to books, but cutting pages from one such as this is a sacrilege."

I feel the loss of pages I have never seen. "There must be another copy somewhere." Closing the book, I turn it to the cover and then to the binding for clues about the publisher. "Even if this is the only printing, the publisher will have a copy, will they not?"

He presses his lips together before answering. "I'm afraid it's not that simple, Lia."

"What do you mean? Why not?"

His eyes drift to the book, still in my hand, before skittering away. "I've not . . . I've not told you the strangest thing by far. About the book."

"Do you mean to say there is something stranger than the story itself?"

He nods. "Far stranger. Listen, you know from your father, from me, that books are full of clues. The typeface, the ink, even the leather used and the manner of the bindery tell us from where a book comes and how old it is. Virtually anything one needs to know about a book can be discovered with enough study of the book itself."

"And? Where *does* it come from?"

"That's just it. The typeface is very old, but one not documented as far as I can tell. The leather is not leather at all, but some other material, something I've not seen." He sighs. "I cannot find a single clue to its origin, Lia. It makes no sense at all."

James is unaccustomed to mysteries he cannot solve. I see the distress on his face but can do nothing to lessen it. I have no more answers than he.

❧

I return from the river to find Henry sitting alone before the chess board in the parlor. The sight brings a lump to my throat, and I try to compose myself before he sees me. His days will be vacant without time spent playing chess or reading with Father in front of the fire. Neither will my brother have the distraction of school, for Father took Henry's schooling upon himself, spending hours teaching him far beyond the subjects commonly deemed necessary.

In this way, Father augmented my and Alice's education as well, introducing us to all manner of mythology and philosophy. Even our attendance at Wycliffe two days a week was a compromise of sorts between Father, who believed he could do a better job all around of educating us, and Aunt Virginia, who argued that we would benefit from the social aspect of exposure to girls our own age. Of course, Alice and I have had the advantage of Father's influence for sixteen years. We can advance our education independently of Wycliffe's curriculum if we wish, but what will happen to Henry?

I swallow my fear for his future and enter the room with as much carefree briskness as I can muster. His eyes light up when I ask him if he'd like company, and we take turns reading aloud from *Treasure Island*, Ari purring against my leg as if he knows I need the reassurance. The simple pleasure allows me to forget, if only for awhile, the events taking shape around me.

It isn't late when we finish, but I am tired. I say good night, leaving Henry near the fire with his book. I am halfway up the stairs when I hear Alice's voice coming from the library. Though it is not off-limits to any, I cannot remember the last time Alice spent time there. My curiosity gets the better of me, and as I make my way there, Alice's voice is so soft that at first I think she is talking to herself. But it takes me only a moment to realize that she is not alone. Her voice is matched by the deeper timbre of a man's voice, and when I reach the

half-open door of the library, I am surprised to see James sitting in a high-backed chair near the reading table.

It is rare enough to find Alice casually about the library but rarer still to find her conversing privately with James. Certainly, they maintain a comfortable if distant friendship given the closeness of our families and the relationship between James and me, but it has never been anything more. I have never witnessed a flicker of attraction or even playful flirtation between them, yet the feeling that rises in me at the sight of them together comes perilously close to one of alarm.

I stay silent, watching and waiting as Alice walks slowly behind the chair in which James sits. She trails a finger along the high back of the chair, not quite touching the nape of James's neck.

"I think I should like to take more of an interest in the library now that Father is gone," she says, her voice a seductive purr.

James sits up straighter, staring ahead as if she is not, at that very moment, the height of impropriety. "Yes, well, it is right here under your very own roof. You can avail yourself to it any time you choose."

"True. But I wouldn't know where to begin." She stands very still behind him, her hands resting lightly on his shoulders, the bodice of her gown just behind his head. "Perhaps you can assist me in choosing material most suited to my . . . interests."

James stands suddenly, crossing to a writing table and busying himself by shuffling the papers on its surface. "Actually, I'm quite busy with the catalogue. I'm certain Lia would be willing to help you. She knows the library and its contents better than I."

James's back is to Alice. He does not see the expression that flashes across her face, but I do. I see the rage there and it matches my own. What can she be thinking? I've had enough, and I step into the room, crossing it briskly. She is surprised to see me, though not ashamed as I would have expected. James lifts his eyes as I come into view.

"Lia," he says. "I wanted to finish a few things here, but Father had another client. He should be back to retrieve me" — he pulls his watch from his pocket, consulting it before continuing — "any moment now." He flushes, though surely he has no reason to be embarrassed when it is my sister who behaves so badly.

I steady my voice before speaking. "Perfectly understandable. I'm sure my father would be pleased with your diligence." Forcing a flinty smile to my face, I turn my attention to my sister. "Really, Alice. James is quite right; if you've an interest in the collections, you need only ask. I'd be happy to help you choose something." I stop short of questioning her behavior, for I do not want to give her the satisfaction of my seeming paranoid and insecure.

She tips her head, looking into my eyes and studying my face for a moment before speaking. "Yes, well, perhaps I shall. Still, it does ease my mind to know that James, in all his expertise, is present should you ever be . . . unavailable."

"Not to worry," I tell her firmly. "I've no intention of being unavailable, to you or anyone, anytime soon."

We stand across from each other, the wing chair between us, for an awkward moment. I see James only in profile and am relieved that he remains quiet.

Finally, Alice gives me a small, tight smile. "Well, I've some things to attend to. I shall see you, both of you," she adds, looking pointedly over my shoulder in James's direction, "later."

I watch her leave but do not say anything about the altercation to James. I want to apologize for Alice's odd demeanor, but my mind is full of questions to which I am not sure I want answers.

5

The next morning, my sister is silent on the way to town. I
don't ask her why, though Alice's silences are rare. This time
her silence is an echo of my own. I sneak a glance at her out of
the corner of my eye, noting the curve of her chin and the
curls that bounce at the nape of her neck as she leans her head
toward the window of the carriage.

The carriage rattles to a stop, and Alice sits up straighter,
smoothing her skirt and looking my way. "Must you look so
unhappy, Lia? Won't it be nice to escape the gloom of Birchwood? Heaven knows the great dreary house will still be waiting for us at the end of the day!"

She delivers the words with good humor, but I feel the ten-
sion in her voice, see it on the too-careful set of her face. This
is the theatrical version of Alice, the one who has carefully
rehearsed her lines.

I smile in answer as Edmund opens the carriage door.

"Miss."

"Thank you, Edmund." I wait on the sidewalk as Alice emerges from the carriage. As usual, she does not bother speaking to him.

He turns to me before leaving. "I'll be back at the end of the day then, Miss." He doesn't often smile, but he does it now, so faintly I wonder if anyone can see it but me.

"Yes, of course. Goodbye, Edmund." I hurry to catch Alice as she heads for the steps in front of Wycliffe. "You might at least be polite, Alice."

Alice spins around, favoring me with a carefree smile. "And why is that? Edmund has worked for the Milthorpes for years. Do you think a simple 'please' or 'thank you' makes his tasks any easier?"

"Perhaps only more pleasant."

It is an old argument. Alice's treatment of Birchwood's servants is notoriously poor. Worse, her rudeness often extends to family, particularly Aunt Virginia. My mother's sister does not complain aloud, but I see the resentment pass over her face when my sister treats her like a glorified nanny.

Alice sighs in exasperation, reaching for my hand and pulling me up the steps toward Wycliffe's door. "Oh, for goodness' sake, Lia! Come along, will you? You shall make us late."

As I stumble up the stairs after my sister, my eyes drift to the Douglases' bookstore, tucked into the storefront under the school. James is three years older than I and finished with his formal schooling. I know he will be at work in the shop and wish I could open the door and call to him, but there isn't a moment left before I am pulled by Alice into the vestibule at Wycliffe. She closes the door, rubbing her gloved hands together for warmth.

"Heavens, it's getting cold!" She unties her cloak, eyeing my still fingers. "Hurry, Lia, will you?"

I cannot think of any place I want to be less than Wycliffe. But Edmund has already gone, so I force my hands to move and hang my cloak near the door. Mrs. Thomason hurries toward us from the back of the building, looking in equal parts annoyed and flustered.

"You're late for morning prayers, Misses! Now if you hurry, you might slip in without too much fuss." She gives me a little push toward the dining room, as if I somehow need it more than Alice. "And I'm most sorry to hear of your loss. Mr. Milthorpe was a fine man."

I follow Alice to the dining room, rushing to keep up with her purposeful gait. Through the doors, the voices of the other girls are strung together in eerie unison as they recite morning prayer. Alice pushes one of the heavy doors and steps through it in one motion. She doesn't even try to be quiet, and I have no choice but to follow meekly behind her, wondering how she holds her head so high and her back so straight while making a spectacle of us both.

Miss Gray's voice falters as Alice marches in, causing most of the girls to peek at us from behind closed lids. Alice and I slide into our seats at the table, mumbling the words along with the other girls. When everyone has said "Amen," thirty

pairs of eyes open to survey us. Some do it in a way they must think is careful, but others, like Victoria Alcott and May Smithfield, do not bother to hide their curiosity.

"Alice, Amalia. So nice to have you back with us. I know I speak for everyone at Wycliffe when I say that we are most sorry for your loss." Miss Gray remains standing before the table as she delivers her practiced speech, sitting only when we have murmured our thank-yous.

Emily and Hope, the girls on either side of me, avoid my eyes. I have never been a skilled conversationalist, and death undoubtedly makes for awkward company. I study the napkin on my lap, the silver sparkling next to my plate, the butter congealing on my toast. Anything but the uncomfortable glances of the other girls. They avoid my eyes.

All but one.

Only Luisa Torelli looks at me candidly, offering a small smile that I feel as condolence even from across the table. Luisa always sits alone, the seats on either side of her empty whenever the girls at Wycliffe can arrange it. The other girls whisper about her because she is Italian, though with her raven curls, cherry-stained lips, and exotic dark eyes, jealousy is the more likely culprit. That I am now set apart for something even simpler — the novelty of being an orphan who has lost both parents to a bizarre set of circumstances — doesn't seem to matter. All at once, it seems we are more the same than different, and I wonder if perhaps Luisa and I were meant to be friends all along.

Mr. Douglas has acquired an old French text, and we are divided into two groups and sent to the Douglases' bookstore as part of our translation studies. I should like to have a quick word with James about the book, but he is at work in the back with his father, the other girls, and Mrs. Bacon, our chaperone.

In no time at all, I've completed my assigned passages and am standing at the bookcase nearest the window, browsing the new arrivals from London, when I hear hushed conversation coming from one of the other shelves. Leaning back, still hidden in the shadow of the towering bookshelf, I see Alice speaking in an urgent whisper to Victoria. Alice sets her mouth into the hard line that means she has made up her mind and will not change it no matter what is said, and with that, they look around and slip from the shop as if it is the most natural thing in the world.

It takes me a moment to realize what they have done. When the force of it hits me, I'm both relieved and oddly hurt not to have been included in whatever scheme they have planned.

It doesn't take as long as it should to come to a decision that could land me in such trouble. Were it any other chaperone I might think twice, but Mrs. Bacon can be counted on for one thing above all others — her propensity for falling swiftly and deeply asleep on almost every occasion that Wycliffe's girls are in her charge.

I move to the door with quiet purpose, trying to behave as if

I have every reason to leave the bookstore. The soft clearing of a throat sounds behind me as the cold knob turns in my hand.

"A-hem."

I briefly close my eyes, hoping it is James who has caught me sneaking away, for he will surely not tell. But when I turn, it is Luisa Torelli, leaning against one of the shelves and staring at me slyly from beneath the fringe of her inky lashes.

"Going somewhere?" she asks softly, eyebrows raised.

There is no menace in her face, only excitement barely concealed under the smile teasing her mouth. I should probably think through the decision to include her, but Alice has gone, and I don't want to lose track of her while I stand about trying to make up my mind.

"Yes." I tip my head to the door. "Are you coming?"

A brilliant smile breaks across her face as she nods, springing to the door as if she has been waiting years for the invitation. She is bolder than I, out of the shop and trotting down the walk while I pull the door shut quietly behind me. She is waiting, halfway to the corner, when I reach her.

She resumes walking, her eyes focusing on my sister's retreating back, Victoria beside her. "I assume we're going that way?"

I nod as the magnitude of our infraction begins sinking in.

Luisa seems oblivious. "Where are they going?"

I look over at her and shrug. "I have no idea."

Her laugh is musical, ringing through the air as a passing gentleman turns to stare. "Wonderful. It's a proper adventure, then."

I fight a smile. Luisa is nothing like I imagined. "Yes, one that will land us in a heap of trouble if we're caught."

Her mouth widens in an impish grin. "Well, at least we shall take Victoria Alcott with us."

Alice and Victoria have come to a building not unlike the one that houses Wycliffe. They stop on the walk, conversing as they steal glances at the door at the top of the steps. I have not given thought to Alice's reaction when she realizes we've followed her, but there is nothing to be done and nowhere to hide. Her mouth drops open as Luisa and I approach.

"Lia! What . . . Whatever are you doing here?"

Quiet fury washes over Victoria's face.

I lift my chin, refusing to be intimidated. "I saw you leave. I wanted to know where you were going."

"If you tell," Victoria threatens, "you will live to regret it. You —"

Alice casts Victoria a silencing glare before looking at me. "She shan't tell, Victoria. Will you, Lia?" It is not a question that requires an answer, and she continues. "All right, then. Come along. We haven't all day."

They don't give Luisa a glance. It is as if she isn't there at all. As we follow them up the steps, I realize Alice did not answer my question. She does not break stride until we reach the top of the steps, leaning in to beat an enormous lion knocker against the carved wooden door. We shift nervously on our feet until we hear the sound of approaching footsteps.

Luisa tugs on Alice's sleeve. "Someone's coming!"

Victoria rolls her eyes. "We can hear that, Luisa."

Luisa's onyx eyes flash in anger, but before she can defend herself the door is pulled open. In almost the same moment, we are met with a dark stare from the woman standing on the threshold.

"Yes?" She levels each of us with her gaze, as if to see who among us is sure to be the troublemaker. I should like to point her in Victoria's direction, but I don't have the chance or the nerve.

Alice pulls herself up straight, putting on her haughtiest air. "Good morning. We have come to see Sonia Sorrensen."

"And who, may I ask, is calling. And for what purpose?" The woman's skin is the color of dark caramels, her eyes a shade lighter, almost amber. She reminds me of a cat.

"We would like to pay her for a sitting, if you please." Alice's manner is imperious, as if the woman has no right to question her, though Alice is a mere girl who should not even be on the streets without a chaperone.

The woman's eyebrows rise ever so slightly. "Very well. You may step into the foyer. I shall see if Miss Sorrensen has time for visitors." She holds the door open as we file in, our skirts rustling and crowding around our legs in the small entry. "Please wait here."

She ascends a simple wooden staircase, and we are left in a perfect silence broken only by the ticking of an unseen clock in a room beyond the parlor. The desire to flee presses upon my chest as I realize we are standing in a strange house with who-knows-who upstairs and not a soul in the world to know where we are.

"What are we doing here, Alice? What is this place?"

Alice's smile is cold and hard. In it I see the pleasure she finds in knowing things other people do not know. "We are here to see a spiritualist, Lia. Someone who can speak to the dead and see the future."

I do not have time to ponder Alice's reasons for wanting to know the future. Voices drift from the room above us, and we look to each other in the crowded vestibule. Our eyebrows lift in silent question as heavy footsteps rattle the floorboards over our heads.

The woman peers down the steps, beckoning us up the staircase. "You may come."

Alice pushes to the front. Victoria and Luisa follow her up the stairs without hesitation. It is only when Luisa reaches the third step and turns to me that I realize I haven't moved.

"Come on, Lia. It's all in good fun."

I swallow my sudden fear and smile a response, following her up the narrow steps and through a door at the right of the landing.

The room is dark, the shades drawn over the windows so that only the faintest whisper of light lurks about the edges of the frame. But the girl sitting at the table is full of light, surrounded by candles flickering gold against her creamy skin. Her hair shimmers even with the meager glow from the covered windows, and although the room is full of shadows, I can see the curve of her cheek and am sure even from the doorway that her eyes are blue.

"Miss Sorrensen is a touch under the weather." The woman who brought us to the room glances accusingly at the girl. "She can only offer you a brief sitting."

"Thank you, Mrs. Millburn." The girl's voice is a murmur to the older woman, who closes the door behind her without reply. "Please sit down."

Alice and Victoria move cautiously toward the table, taking the chairs opposite the girl. I, on the other hand, am so drawn to her that I take the seat to her right. Luisa sits next to me, closing our mismatched circle.

"Thank you for coming. I am Sonia Sorrensen. You've come for a sitting, then?"

We bob our heads, unsure what to say. No social lesson at Wycliffe has prepared us for such an outrageous occasion.

She meets our eyes, one at a time. "Is there someone with whom you'd like to make contact, a message you hope to retrieve?"

Only Victoria speaks. "We would like to see what you know about the future. Our future." She sounds impossibly young, and I wonder if I might remember her shaking voice to call upon the next time she is mean at Wycliffe.

"Well . . ." Sonia looks at each of us again before settling her eyes first on Alice, and then me. "Perhaps I shall have a message for *you*."

Alice's eyes find mine through the dark. For a moment, I think I see cold fury there, but I quickly discount it. I am not thinking clearly. The forbidden outing and strange house, a house likely *made* strange as a way to make Sonia's task easier, has loosened the strings of reality. I take a deep breath.

"Let us join hands." Sonia holds her hands out to either side. Hands are clasped until it is only mine that is left to be joined with Sonia's to complete the circle. When I reach out, careful to conceal my wrist, her hand is cool and dry in mine. "I must ask for silence. I never know what I will see or hear. I work at the will of the spirits, and sometimes they have no will to join me at all. You must not speak unless directed." Her eyelids flicker and then close.

I peer at the faces, distorted and shadowed, around the table. In them I see remnants of the girls I know, but here no one is as they seemed in the sunlit street. With nothing to do but stare at Sonia, they close their eyes one by one. Finally, at last, I close mine as well.

The room is so completely sealed that I do not hear a sound — no horses' hooves or shouts from the streets below, not even the ticking clock in the house below us. Only the whispery in and out of Sonia's breathing. I settle into it — *in, out, in, out* — until I am not sure if it is her breathing or my own pacing the seconds and minutes.

"Oh!" The sound bursts forth from the seat next to me, and I jump as my eyes fly open to Sonia's face. Her eyes are already open, though she seems very far away. "There *is* someone here. A visitor." She looks at me. "He's here for you."

Alice looks around, wrinkling her nose. I smell it a moment

later. Pipe smoke. Just the memory of it, really, but a memory that my soul knows no matter what my mind says.

"He wants to tell you that everything will be all right." Sonia closes her eyes for a moment, as if trying to see something that cannot be seen with them open. "He wants you to know that . . ." And here she stops. She stops and opens her eyes wide in surprise, staring at me before turning her gaze to Alice and then back again. Her voice is the murmur of whispered secrets. "Shhhhh . . . They know you're here."

She begins to shake her head, muttering as if to herself or someone else very near, though it is quite clear she is not speaking to us. "Oh no . . . Oh no, oh no, oh no. Be gone, now," she says softly, as if negotiating with a wayward child. "Go on. It is not me. I am not the one. I didn't summon you." Her voice, held in quiet calm until now, cracks with the strain of her false demeanor. "It is no use. They will not listen. They've come for . . ." She turns to me, lowering her voice to a whisper as if afraid someone might overhear. "They've come for you . . . for you and your sister." She is perfectly lucid, looking directly into my eyes with such clarity that it is impossible to think her mad, though her words should make it easy to believe.

The room grows quiet. I don't know how long we sit in the surprised silence before Sonia finally blinks, looking around her as if realizing where she is for the first time. When she sees me she sits up straight, fixing me with a stare filled with accusation and fear.

"You shouldn't have come."

I shake my head. "What . . . What do you mean?"

She looks into my eyes, and even in the flickering candle-light I see that they *are* blue, just as I thought. Not the saturated ocean blue of James's eyes, but a blue as brittle as the ice that forms on the deepest parts of the lake in winter.

"You know," she says softly. "You must know."

I shake my head, not wanting to look at the other girls.

"Please, you should go now." She pushes back from the table so fast her chair tips to the floor.

I look up at her in shock, frozen in my seat.

"Well, if this isn't a load of poppycock!" Alice rises, her voice breaking through the awed silence. "Come, Lia. Let's go."

She marches over, pulling me up from my chair and turning stiffly to Sonia, who still stands with such horror on her face that I'm almost immobilized all over again. "Thank you, Miss Sorrensen. What is the fee for the sitting?"

Sonia shakes her head, blond curls bouncing. "Nothing . . . Just . . . Please do leave."

Alice pulls me toward the door. She does not have to say a word to Victoria, who is already making her way out of the room. Luisa waits for Alice and me to leave. I hear her footsteps on the floor behind us, an unfamiliar comfort as we make our way from the room.

I hardly know what I am doing as Alice leads me down the stairs, past the woman called Mrs. Millburn, and out the front door. I have the vague sensation of pressed bodies and swishing skirts as Victoria and Luisa work their way out around me.

Otherwise, it is nothing but a dream as we hurry down the street in awkward silence.

The cool afternoon air, together with the possibility of being caught having taken our leave from the bookstore, should be enough to force me back to reality. But somehow it isn't, and my earlier unease with my sister is forgotten as I stumble through the streets with my hand in hers as though I am a child. Victoria walks a few steps ahead, while Luisa trots alongside, saying nothing.

When Mr. Douglas's shop comes into sight, I see Miss Gray, standing outside and speaking harshly to James and Mrs. Bacon. They turn their eyes to us as we come into view. I avoid looking at Miss Gray's face. If I do, I shall know for certain how very much trouble we are in. Instead, I focus on James. I stare intently into his face, creased with worry, until it is only him I see.

6

Alice and I pull on our coats in silence, Miss Gray's reprimand ringing in our ears. Luisa's stricken face as she was sent to her room is still fresh in my mind, making it impossible to feel sorry for myself.

It is only Miss Gray's pity for our recent loss that has saved us from a report to Aunt Virginia, and by the time we close Wycliffe's door behind us, it is near enough to dismissal that Edmund is already waiting, standing tall beside the carriage. Alice marches down the walk and is already settling into the darkness of the carriage when I hear the voice behind me.

"Excuse me, Miss! Miss?"

It takes a moment to find the person belonging to the voice. She is so small — only a child — that I look around and above her before coming to the conclusion that it is, in fact, the little girl who is speaking to me.

"Yes?" I look back toward the carriage, but Alice is hidden inside and Edmund is bent over, inspecting one of the spokes with both hands and singular concentration.

The child walks toward me, golden ringlets gleaming and a confidence in her step that makes her seem older than she probably is. She has the face of an angel, plump and pink at the cheeks.

"You've dropped something, Miss." She bows her head a little, holding out her hand, her fingers closed into a fist so that it is impossible to make out the thing she holds.

"Oh no. I really don't think so." I look down at my wrist, noting the small bag still swinging there.

"Yes, Miss. You have indeed." She meets my eyes, and something there makes me hold very still. My heart beats hard and fast in my chest until I look more closely at her small hand. The white teeth of my small ivory hair comb are revealed in the girl's fingers, and I exhale a breath I did not realize I was holding.

"Oh my goodness! Thank you ever so much!" I reach out and take the comb from her hand.

"No, thank *you* ever so much, Miss." Her eyes darken, her small face sharpening as she dips in a curtsey every bit as odd as her gratitude. She turns and skips away, her skirts swishing behind her, a childish hum fading with her footsteps.

Alice leans forward in her seat, calling to me from the open door of the carriage. "Whatever are you doing, Lia? It's positively freezing, and you're letting all the cold air into the carriage."

Her voice shakes me from my position on the street. "I dropped something."

"What is it?" She surveys me from the cushioned seat near the window as I climb in beside her.

"My comb. The one Father brought me from Africa."

She nods, turning to stare out the window as Edmund closes the door to the carriage, wrapping us in muffled silence.

I am still clutching the comb, but when I open my hand it isn't the ivory comb that gets my attention but a loop of black velvet that trails from behind it. Something cold and flat lies in my palm behind the comb, within the velvet, but I do not dare unravel it for fear of Alice discovering it at the same time.

The teeth of the comb bite into the soft flesh of my palm as I close my fingers around it, and it is then that I remember. Reaching back, I touch my hair, recalling my rush to get ready for Wycliffe this morning. I didn't have time for coffee, and in my hurry I barely managed to pin my hair into place.

But I *had* used the pins — it was the comb I'd skipped in my rush to leave the house. I can still see it, sitting on the dressing table as I rushed out of my room a few hours before. How it traveled from my chamber at Birchwood all the way to town and into the little girl's hands is another mystery I cannot begin to solve.

❧

In the safety of my room, my hands tremble as I pull out the comb, studying it as if it might have changed during the hours spent inside the darkness of the velvet bag.

But no. It is just the same.

The same comb Father brought back from Africa, the same comb I have put in my hair almost every day since, and the very same comb given to me by the girl on the street. I set it aside. Whatever answers I need are not to be found in its soft sheen.

When I reach into the bag again, my hand finds the whispery ribbon and with it the hard thing I felt in my palm in the carriage. I spread the velvet out until the black ribbon snakes across my white nightgown.

It's a necklace of some sort, I think. The black velvet surrounds a small metal medallion, suspending it between two lengths. I think it a choker, but when I lift it to my neck, I find it is not nearly long enough to go all the way around. My eyes are drawn to the pendant hanging from the ribbon. It is featureless — nothing but a plain, not-very-shiny gold disc. I rub two fingers against the cool surface on either side, feeling a ridge on the back. When I flip it over, there is a dark outline shading the surface of the circle. The darkening room forces me to lean in, the outline slowly coming into focus.

I take the tip of a finger and run it along the edge of the design in the circle, as if this will make real the image I see there. My finger sinks into the etched circle, its surface slightly indented in opposition to the one on my wrist.

And yet it is nearly the same. The only difference is the letter C in the center of the pendant. I turn my wrist over, looking from the cold circle in my hands back to the mark. Now there is something else, something called forth by the medallion in my hand. The smudge inside the circle of my wrist seems to clarify, becoming clearer by the moment until I am sure the unknowable shape inside the circle will soon become the letter C just as on the pendant.

And now I know.

I'm not sure how, but somehow I know what the velvet ribbon is for, where it belongs. Wrapping it around my wrist, I am not surprised that it fits perfectly or that, when I close the clasp, the black ribbon lies snug and flat against my skin. The medallion sits atop the matching circle on the inside of my wrist. I can almost feel the raised skin of my wrist nestle into the engraved circle of the pendant. A wave of terrifying belonging ripples through me.

It is this that most frightens me — the call of my body to the medallion. It is this inexplicable affinity for the thing that feels as if it has always been mine, though I have never seen it before today, that makes me remove the bracelet. I open my bedside drawer and push the coil of velvet to the very back.

I am profoundly tired. Lying back against the pillow, I fall into a sleep that is sudden and complete. The blackness that smothers me is total, and in the moment before everything falls away, I know what it feels like to be dead.

I am flying, up and out over my body. My sleeping form lies below, and a surge of exhilaration takes hold as I move freely away from it and straight through the closed window.

I have always had strange dreams. My earliest memories are not of flesh-and-blood things, not of my mother's voice or my father's boot steps in the hall, but of mysterious, unnamable shapes and my own swift escape through wind and trees.

Even still, until Father's death, I had never had a flying dream that I could clearly remember. But I have had them almost every night since and am not surprised to find myself floating over the house, the hills, and the road leading away from our property. Soon enough I am over the town itself, and I marvel at how different it appears in the haze of my dream, the mystery of night.

Making my way past Wycliffe and the bookstore, past the house where Sonia Sorrensen lives, I leave the town behind for the blackness of sprawling fields. The sky above me, around me, glows. It is not the black sky of night, but a deep and endless blue with the hint of violet somewhere in its depths.

Soon, I am over a larger city. Buildings rise toward the sky, and great factories spit clouds of smoke into the night, though I cannot smell a thing. I come to the edge of the city, and for a split second, an ocean stretches before me as far as the eye can see, and then, gloriously, I am over it.

And *this* I can smell.

The briny moisture fills my nose, and I laugh aloud at the wonder of it. A humid wind blows my hair, and in this moment I would be content to fly forever, to give myself over to the indigo sky through which I travel.

I move farther and farther out over the water until the city is not even a speck in the distance. As the water rushes below, a small voice cautions me to go back, whispering that

I've gone too far, but it is only the shadow of a warning. I ignore it, reveling in the utter abandon of my journey, allowing myself to swoop past the waves and fall farther into the mysterious sky.

But the warning grows louder and more insistent until it is more than a whisper, until it is an actual voice I hear. The voice of a girl.

"Go back!" The voice calls to me, muffled and broken. "You've gone too far. You must go back!"

Something about it makes me stop, and I am astonished to find myself hovering, not quite flying, but not sinking into the sea of my dream either. And then I feel it. Something ominous roaring behind me, coming at me with a speed that finally prompts me to move.

I push myself through the sky, back toward the area I think is land. The fantastical ability to control my speed and direction has grown stronger during my brief flight, and even through the fear my body hums with this new knowledge, this new power.

But under my elation, terror builds by the second as I speed toward home, the forbidding thing sounding nearer and nearer, swift on my heels. There is still a long way to travel, though it seems I cover the miles as if they are merely feet.

The thing behind me now has a noise, a shrieking howl that fills me with a panic so debilitating that my pace slows just when I need it the most. I can see the dark outline of town in the not-so-very-far distance. I am close, and yet I'm pulled backward both by my pursuer and my own fear. I might stop altogether, if not for the figure sweeping toward me from the direction of town.

At first, it is a pale glimmer in the distance, but soon she is right in front of me, and it takes only a moment to realize that she is the spiritualist, Sonia Sorrensen.

"Come! Come! There's no time to waste! Oh, why did you have to go so far?" She no sooner says it than she is waving me forward. "Go! Go back as fast as you can. I'm right behind you!"

I do not stop to wonder how or why Sonia Sorrensen has appeared in my dream. I hear the panic in her voice, and I fly. She follows on my heels until we come to the town.

"I cannot risk going with you. It's not safe." She is already drifting away from me. "Become one with your body as quickly as possible. Do not allow yourself to be detained. Not for any reason."

"What about you?" My voice is distant and small. I cannot feel its vibration in my throat.

Her eyes meet mine. "It's not chasing *me*."

Her words move me forward. I fly over the fields, the road to Birchwood, and up the face of the house. When I reach the window to my room the snarl of the thing behind me grows angry, hissing words I cannot quite understand.

Guard the . . . Mistress. . . .

I stop unwittingly, trying to decipher the strange message.

It is a delay I cannot afford.

The dark being snarls and snaps, close enough that I could

touch it if I had the courage to reach out a hand. I cannot see anything within the black mass, but I sense thundering hooves and a great many wings, all beating in a timeless rhythm that is at once familiar and terrifying. I have a flash of panic before a peculiar resignation settles into my bones.

I am too late. It is too close. I am frozen, unable to move with the apathy that has seeped into every cell of my body.

And yet it cannot touch me.

It hovers around the periphery of a barrier I cannot see. The whispering that at first was so near, so immediate, now seems muffled and distant. The great wings that were before so close now seem to beat from behind a blanket of thick velvet. The thing howls in anger, but it is a useless show of frustration, for I remain behind an invisible shield of safety.

My lethargy shakes loose, and I push through the window, stopping over my sleeping body for a mere second before dropping into it.

It is a strange sensation, feeling my soul click into place like the piece of a puzzle and knowing for certain it was not a dream.

7

When I come down the stairs, Henry is sitting in his chair by the window in the parlor. *Treasure Island* lies open in his lap, but he is not reading. Instead, he stares out at the grounds on the other side of the window pane.

I don't bother trying to silence my footfall as I approach. I know well what it is like to be so deep in thought, and I've no wish to startle him. Even still, he takes no notice of me until I speak.

"Good morning, Henry."

He looks up, blinking as if I've woken him from a trance. "Good morning."

I tip my head, looking deeper into his eyes and trying to define the expression I see in their brown depths. "Are you all right?"

He stares at me a long moment and is opening his mouth to

speak when Alice rounds the corner into the room. We both turn to look at her, but when I return my eyes to Henry, his gaze does not leave Alice's face.

"Henry? Are you all right?" I repeat.

Alice raises her eyebrows as she looks quizzically at our brother. "Yes, Henry. Is everything all right?"

It takes him a moment more to answer, but when he does, his response is given to Alice, not to me. "Yes. I'm only reading." A note of defensiveness has crept into his voice, but before I can think more about it Aunt Virginia enters the room, stealing our attention.

"Lia?" She stands in the doorway, an odd expression on her face. "Someone is here to see you."

"To see me? Who is it?"

Her eyes skip nervously from my face to Alice's and back again before answering. "She says her name is Sonia. Sonia Sorrensen."

⚜

Sonia and I don't speak on our way up the hill to the cliff overlooking the water. In the vacuum of the words we do not say, I focus on the sky, an endless sapphire that goes on and on. I can almost see the curve of the horizon, and I wonder how anyone could have thought the Earth flat when faced with this kind of sky.

I try not to think of Alice, of her barely concealed fury at the mention of my visitor. I was both relieved and surprised when she left the parlor before Sonia was escorted in by

Aunt Virginia. It saved me from having to come up with an explanation, but I am under no illusions; Sonia's arrival and Aunt Virginia's presence only bought me a little time with my sister. Alice will not let so curious a caller go unquestioned.

By the time Sonia breaks our silence, my nerves are taut with unspoken words.

"You mustn't go so far, Lia." Her gaze remains fixed in the distance as if nothing was said at all.

A swift and forceful anger fills my chest. "Tell me, how does one measure 'far,' Sonia? Perhaps you can tell me how to measure distance when I am flying out of my body in the middle of the night."

She takes a minute to answer, her profile as clear and beautiful as the marble statues we sketch at Wycliffe. "Yes. It must be confusing. If you've never done it before, I mean." Her voice is a murmur.

"If I've never . . . Well, of *course* I've never done it before!" I stop, tugging on her arm so that she must stop, too. "Wait! Are you saying *you* have done it before?"

She looks into my eyes, shrugging and pulling her arm away. Turning, she continues to climb the rise leading to the lake. I hurry to catch her and am breathless when I finally reach her side.

"Won't you answer?"

She sighs, looking over at me as we walk. "Yes, all right? I've done it before. I've been doing it since I was a child. Some people do it without realizing it, thinking they are dreaming,

69

for example. Others can do it on command. Many, actually. Many people in my world anyway."

She says this as if we are not walking side by side on the very same ground, as if she occupies some strange corner of the universe, invisible and unreachable to me.

"In your world? Whatever do you mean?"

She laughs a little. "Are we not from different worlds, Lia? You live in a grand house, surrounded by the family and things you hold dear. I live in a small house governed by Mrs. Millburn, with only the company of other spiritualists and those who pay us to describe the things they cannot see."

Her words silence my questions. "I . . . I'm sorry, Sonia. I suppose I didn't realize it wasn't your home, that the woman, Mrs. . . . uh, Mrs. Millburn was not your . . . relative."

Even from her profile, I see the flash of anger in her eyes. "For goodness' sake! Don't pity me! I'm quite content with the way things are."

But she does not sound content. Not really.

We finally reach the rise, that last invigorating moment when we step onto the top of the hill making me feel, as always, that I have stepped into the sky. Despite all that has happened on this ridge, it is impossible not to appreciate the majesty of the view.

"Oh! I didn't know there was a lake here!" In Sonia's voice is the awe of a child, and I realize she mustn't be much older than I. She takes in the view — the lake, shimmering below us, the trees swaying in a breeze too soft for autumn.

"It's well hidden. Even I don't come here much, actually."
Because my mother fell from this cliff, I think. *Because her broken body lay on the rocks of the lapping lake below. Because I simply cannot bear it.*

I gesture to a large rock set back from the edge. "Shall we sit?"

She nods, still unable to remove her eyes from the call of the water below. We settle side by side on the boulder, the hems of our skirts touching over the dusty ground. I have questions. But they are unfathomable things, dark shapes that swim just below the surface of my consciousness.

"I knew you were coming." She says this simply, as if I should know exactly what she means.

"What? What do you —"

"Yesterday. At the sitting. I knew it would be you."

I shake my head. "I don't understand."

She looks right into my eyes in the way that only Alice ever has. As if she knows me. "Lately, when I try to hold a sitting, I close my eyes and all I see is your face. Your face and . . . well, many strange things I don't usually see."

"But we have never seen each other before yesterday! How could you possibly see my face in your . . . in your visions?"

She stares toward the lake. "There is only one reason I can think of. . . . Only one reason why I would see you, why you would come."

She turns her face from the lake, looking down and avoiding my eyes as she removes the glove covering her left hand.

She lays the glove across her lap, pulling the sleeve of her gown up over her wrist.

"It's because of this, is it not? Because of the mark?"

It is there. The unmistakable circle, the slithering snake. Just like mine. Just like the one on the medallion.

Every cell in my body, every thought in my mind, the very blood in my veins, seems to go still. When everything begins moving again, it is in a great rush of shock.

"It cannot be. It . . . May I?" I reach a hand toward her.

She hesitates before nodding, and I take her small hand in mine. I turn it over, knowing without looking a second longer that the mark is the same. No, not quite the same. Her mark is not red, but one shade lighter than the rest of her skin. It is raised, just as mine is, as if it is an old scar.

But that is not all. That is not the only difference.

The circle is there, and the winding snake, but that is the end of Sonia's mark. The C does not appear on her wrist, though it is otherwise an exact replica of mine and the one on the medallion.

I return her hand carefully, as a gift. "What is it?"

She chews her lip, before tipping her head toward my hand. "First let me see."

I thrust my wrist toward her. She takes it, tracing with her finger the outline of the C in the middle of my circle. "Yours is different."

My face burns with shame, though I've no idea why. "Yes, a little, though we might just as well say *yours* is different. How long have you had it?"

"Forever. Since I was born, I've been told."

"But what does it mean?"

She breathes deeply, fixing her gaze into the trees. "I don't know. Not really. The only mention of the mark, the only one I know of, comes from a little-known legend told in the circles of spiritualists and others interested in the Watchers. And in the lesser known pieces of their story."

"The Watchers?"

"Yes, from the Bible?" She says this as if I should know, as if I should have an intimate understanding of the Bible when our religious upbringing has been haphazard at best. "They were angels, you see, before they fell."

A tale about angels or . . . demons, I think.

Cast from the heavens . . .

She continues, unaware of the recognition firing through my mind. "The most accepted version is that they were cast from heaven when they married and had children with the women of Earth. But that isn't the only version." She hesitates, bending to pick up a stone and rubbing it clean with the hem of her skirt before returning her eyes to me. "There is another. One far less told."

I fold my hands in my lap, trying to calm the rising unease thrumming through my mind. "Go on."

"It is said the Watchers were tricked into their defiance by Maari."

I shake my head. "Who?"

"One of the sisters. One of the twins."

The sisters. The twins.

"I have never heard of a twin by that name in the Bible. Of course, I'm no scholar, but even so . . ."

Sonia worries the stone, round and flat, between her fingers. "That is because it isn't found in the Bible. It's a legend, a myth, told and passed down through the generations. I am not saying it's true. I'm only telling the story as you asked."

"All right, then. Tell me the rest. Tell me about the sisters."

She settles farther back on the rock. "It is said that Maari began the betrayal by seducing Samael, God's most trusted angel. Samael promised Maari that if she gave birth to an angel-human, she would receive all the knowledge denied to her as a human. And he was right.

"Once the fallen angels, or Watchers, took the humans as wives, they imparted all manner of sorcery to their new partners. In fact, some of the more . . . enthusiastic members of our society believe that is where the gifts of the spiritualists originate."

"So then what? What happened after the Watchers took their human wives and shared their knowledge?"

Sonia shrugs. "They were banished, forced to wander the eight Otherworlds for all eternity until the Doom of Gods, or as Christians call it, the Apocalypse. Oh yes, and after that they were not called the Watchers."

"What were they called?"

"The Lost Souls." Her voice drops, as if she is afraid to be heard uttering the words aloud. "It is said there is a way for them to return to the physical world. Through the sisters, one the Guardian and one the Gate."

My head snaps up. "What did you say?"

She shakes her head. "Just that there is a way —"

"No. After that. About the sisters."

But I know. Of course I do.

A small line forms on the bridge of her nose as she remembers. "Well, the way I've heard it told, sisters of a certain line continue the struggle, even today. One remains the Guardian of peace in the physical world, and the other the Gate through which the Souls can pass. If the Souls ever make their way to our world, the Doom of Gods will begin. And the Souls will fight the battle with as many lost souls as they can bring back from the Otherworlds. Only . . . I've heard there is a catch of sorts."

"What sort of catch?"

Her brow furrows. "Well, it is said the Souls' Army cannot commence the battle without Samael, their leader. And Samael can only make his way through the Gate if he is summoned by the sister destined to call him forth. It is said the Army accumulates, passing into our world in great numbers through the Gates, waiting . . ."

"Waiting for what?"

"For Samael. For the Beast, known to some as Satan himself."

She says it simply, and I realize I am not even surprised.

8

The world goes still. There is no room in my mind for the wind in the trees or the lake lapping the shore below. No room for anything, really, except the tendrils of the prophecy twisting itself into something that is only a seed of reason.

But Sonia isn't privy to my thoughts, and she continues as if my world is not, at this very moment, turning in on itself. "The only reason I'm telling you the story at all is because of the mark. It is said, you see, that the Souls are symbolized by the Jorgumand."

I try to keep my face impassive. If I let my resistance fall, if I let her see the depth of my panic, the little reason I have left will surely desert me. "All right, then. We both have the mark. I still don't understand what part we could play in such a bizarre tale."

She sighs in resignation, standing and pacing in front of me. "I don't, either. But I'm tired of fearing it alone. *I* don't have a sister. I hoped . . ." Her voice softens as she stops to look at me. "Well, I suppose I hoped I was right; I hoped that you *did* have the mark and that we might find the answer together."

"All right." I tip my head, challenging her with my eyes. "Then let's go back to last night. You can start by telling me what I was doing falling through the sky."

She closes the small distance between us, stopping and grasping my hand with something like a smile. "You were only traveling the Plane, Lia. Wandering. Have you really never done it before?"

I shake my head. "Not that I remember. And whatever is the Plane?"

"It is an amazing place," she breathes. "A sort of . . . gateway to the Otherworlds. A place where anything is possible."

I remember my exhilaration as the earth passed beneath me, the sky as deep and endless as the sea. And then I remember something else. "But what of the . . . the thing? The dark thing."

She grows serious, the light leaving her eyes. "The walls are thin between the physical world and the Otherworlds, Lia. It is the very thing that makes it possible to do such wondrous things and the very thing that makes it so dangerous. What was following you last night . . . Its strength was like nothing I've ever encountered, and I have chanced upon many beings in my travels, both good and evil."

"Do you think it has something to do with the mark? With the prophecy?"

She chews her lip again. "I don't know, but the ways of the Otherworlds are complicated. You must learn its nature to safely explore its terrain."

My anger resurfaces. "And how am I to do that? How am I to learn such an odd thing? Surely Miss Gray and the instructors at Wycliffe would think me mad were I to ask!"

She giggles behind the glove of her hand. "No, it would be ill advised to seek such instruction at Wycliffe. But your strength will grow as you become accustomed to travel, and you already have some form of authority, whether or not you realize it."

"What do you mean?"

"That . . . thing. That . . . being. I think it wanted your soul."

I cover my alarm with a brittle laugh. "My soul?"

But she isn't laughing. "Listen, Lia. There is something you should know about traveling the Plane. The soul can be free of the body for only so long before the astral cord, the thread connecting body and soul, is severed. Once that happens, the soul can never return."

"Do you . . . do you mean that one's body would be left empty, as if it were dead?" My voice is shrill as a rising tide of hysteria fills my throat.

She holds up a hand, trying to calm me. "It doesn't happen often, all right? There are not many in the Otherworlds with strength enough to separate a soul from its living body. But it *can* happen." She swallows, and though she tries to hide it, I see her fear. "I . . . I have heard of a place, an awful place, called the Void. A place where displaced souls are banished. A place between life and death. I think that is where the dark thing meant to take you. To the Void."

"Do you mean to say that one's soul would be stranded there forever?" My voice is a squeak.

"Those who are banished to the Void are lost for eternity." Her eyes are haunted. "Listen, Lia. I don't know all the ways of the Otherworlds, all right? But the dark thing wanted you, and I have never seen something so powerful fall short of its mark. Yet . . .

"For some reason, it couldn't reach you. I've no idea what it was that protected you from the full measure of its force, but it would be wise to avoid travel until we find out — or until you can be certain you will have the same protection next time."

❧

We walk back to the house in silence. When Birchwood comes into view, Sonia puts a hand on my arm, looking upward. I follow her gaze to see Alice watching us from an upstairs window.

"Do be careful, Lia," Sonia says. "Be careful until we find some understanding."

My sister is too far away for me to see her expression, but even still, I feel the cold fingers of fear at the sight of her shadowy figure in the window.

Sonia and I continue to the courtyard, and I watch as she

leaves in her hired carriage. I wait for it to disappear down the tree-lined path before turning away from the house. I don't wish to speak to Alice about Sonia. Not yet.

I hear the rush of water before I come to the riverbank. Last week's rain has filled the river to the brim, causing it to race over the rocky bottom at a furious pace. Stepping off the stone terrace, I head into the sheltered copse of evergreens, maples, and oaks. It is almost lunchtime, and I wonder if James will be waiting.

"James?" My voice would be quiet in any other setting, but here it resonates among the serenity of the riverbank. "Are you here, James?"

Strong arms grab me from behind, lifting me off my feet. A squeal escapes my throat, and I kick my feet in blind instinct to free myself from the steely grip. As I lift my fists, preparing to pummel my unseen assailant, I am turned around to face my captor. Warm lips close on mine, his hands loosening their grip on my shoulders and finding their way into my hair instead.

I lose myself in the kiss, feeling as if the river rushes through me, all the way from the hair on my head to the soles of my feet.

Then I shove and step away.

"Ugh! Goodness, James! You gave me such a fright!" I favor him with a childish and ineffective punch to the shoulder. "Someone might have come upon us!"

He laughs, covering his mouth with a palm as if to compose himself. His face becomes more serious when he sees the

expression on my face. "I'm sorry, Lia. Really. But who else would grab you so?"

There is still a trace of amusement in his eyes, and I glare at him in the hopes of removing it.

He comes closer, looking around and pulling me taut against him. "I didn't mean to frighten you. I'm only happy to see you. It takes such effort to see you in the library in front of my father, to see you on the street with Alice, to see you anywhere at all and not do this."

He pulls me closer for an instant, and I feel the length of his body against mine. It steals my breath, and for a moment there is no prophecy, no book, no mark.

Only James's warm body against mine.

I am embarrassed at the effect of his touch. I don't want him to feel my heart striking against the bodice of my gown or to hear my catching breath, so I pull away, eyeing him playfully.

"You've grown bold," I tease.

He laughs then, and the birds in the trees above us take flight, frightened by the exuberance of it. "Me? Bold? That's quite funny coming from one of Wycliffe's rogue young ladies!"

My cheeks become hot at the mention of our escape yesterday from Wycliffe. There wasn't time to tell James of our visit to Sonia Sorrensen's. Not in the chaos that ensued after our return. And I am grateful for the reprieve, if the truth is told. Sonia's behavior during the sitting so unnerved me that I hadn't decided how to explain it to James. He knows only what we told Miss Gray — that we fancied a bit of fresh air and took an impromptu stroll. Now, after my discussion with Sonia over the lake, I am quite certain that it is best for all concerned if that remains the story of record.

"Besides," James continues, oblivious to my turmoil, "I might say you *make* me bold, and what of it? Why else do we come to our favorite place, to the shelter of the tree and the comfort of our rock?" He sits on the rock then, as if to demonstrate its comfort, grimacing in play at its hard surface. "All right, then. Perhaps the rock isn't as comfortable as I remember. . . . Or perhaps it is only more comfortable when you are near." He lifts his eyebrows, patting the spot next to him and grinning wickedly.

I smile at his attempt to get me closer, making my way to the rock and dropping next to him. "Actually, there's something I should like to tell you. Something I think may have to do with the book you found in Father's library."

His grin fades. If there is one thing that might take James's mind off the less virtuous reasons for our meetings by the river, it is discussion of a rare book. "What is it?"

Drawing a deep breath, I take the smallest possible step forward. That is how the telling will have to be done. "I believe I understand the reference to the Guardian and the Gate, however much one *can* understand such a thing."

"Really? But it sounds like such gibberish!"

I look down at my skirt, smoothing it across my lap while I begin. "Yes, well . . . I might have agreed only a couple of days ago, but now . . . well, now I know there *is* a story . . . a story about sisters, actually. Twins, like Alice and me."

He listens mostly in silence, interrupting once or twice to clarify parts of the story he doesn't understand. But his questions are those designed to further the scholarly pursuit of knowledge. They are not questions in the true sense, not in the sense that he actually believes the story is real. Instead, he listens as if to a fairy tale. I tell him everything save mention of the mark. When I am finished, silence fills the space around us as full as any words.

He finally speaks, his voice gentle, as if not wanting to hurt my feelings. "But . . . Why have I never heard this tale, Lia? Certainly, as a bookseller, as one who assists serious buyers in the amassing of their collections, I would have heard of it if it had any merit."

His doubt raises doubt of my own. Doubt that the prophecy might be believable to anyone but those of us with the irrefutable proof of the mark.

I shrug. "I don't know, James. I wish I could answer you, but I cannot."

This is the point at which I should show him the mark. It is well hidden beneath the long sleeve of my gown, but I can almost feel it burning, a silent reminder that there is one important detail I have omitted from the story.

But I don't tell him. I would like to say it is because I'm afraid he won't believe me, or that it is because I want to keep him from becoming involved in something so dark. But the truth is I feel the mark as a scar. It brands me as damaged, unclean.

And I cannot bear for James to know. Not yet.

Going to bed is not as easy as it once was. I lie there, trying to force my mind to the blank page that will allow me to sleep.

But the words of the prophecy, the shadow of my sister in the upstairs window, the mark naming me as a thing I scarcely understand — they all conspire to keep me from rest. I finally rise and cross the room to my writing table.

How is it that the legend Sonia told me by the lake is the same as the one in Father's ageless book? And how have I come to share virtually the same mark with someone like Sonia? A spiritualist, no less. I *feel* the questions trying to make sense of themselves, trying to fit together into something solid, something I can hold with both hands and begin to understand.

Opening the book, I remove James's translation and read the prophecy, trying to make sense of the senseless. A cold chill runs up the fine bone of my back as I read again about the sisters. But it is after the tale of the twins that the prophecy leaves me behind.

If I am the Guardian and Alice the Gate, what part does Sonia play in this strange story? And what of the Angel? If I am unable to decipher the identity of so central a figure as the Angel, how am I to understand how to fulfill my role as Guardian? How might I foil Alice's role as Gate?

I bend my head back to the book, reading the prophecy again until I come to the mention of the keys.

Let the Angel's Gate swing without the Keys, followed by the Seven Plagues and No Return.

I reread the line, willing my mind to find the answer. Even in my current state of ignorance, it is quite simple; without the keys, something terrible will happen. Something that cannot be undone.

If Alice and I are on conflicting sides of the prophecy, the keys would almost certainly be dangerous in her hands, which means I have to find them.

And I have to do it before my sister.

9

Alice does not mention Sonia on our way to Wycliffe the next day. I have spent the time since Sonia's visit avoiding my sister, hoping to put off her inquiry. I imagine my reprieve over and brace myself for Alice's questions, but she remains silent. It is as if she already knows everything. And the knowledge she has she intends to hold dark and close.

Our return to school is far from celebrated. Whether because Victoria blames Alice for the forbidden outing to Sonia's or resents us for not having to submit to a more severe punishment, she and her closely guarded circle of friends greet us with icy stares. Only Luisa seems happy to see us, me in particular.

She leans toward me during breakfast, having taken the seat next to me as if she has been sitting there all along. "Are you all right?"

I nod. "Oh, but I *am sorry*, Luisa! Did you get in a lot of trouble?"

She smiles. "Some, but it only made things more interesting. I don't regret a thing!"

After breakfast we are led through our paces in music, literature, and language. The day passes in a haze of whispered innuendo and mean-spirited laughter. By the time we file outdoors for the last lesson of the day, Landscape in Art, I cannot help noticing the stillness of Alice's expression or the way she holds her head too high, her back too straight. She avoids my eyes. For Alice, isolation is preferable to pity.

The easels are set up in the courtyard, facing the modest garden that is all but dead with the coming winter. Though the sun shines, the air is frigid with cold, and I realize this will likely be one of our last outdoor lessons of the year.

"Lia! Over here!" Luisa calls, her breath a puff of smoke, waving to me from an easel near the brick wall.

Making my way to Luisa, I am grateful and surprised all over again at her clear offer of friendship.

"I saved you an easel." She waves to the empty easel on her right, smiling up at me from her stool, paintbrush already in hand.

"Thank you. What object shall I torture today?" I am not well known for my artistic ability.

Luisa laughs. Not the polite giggle I am accustomed to from the girls at Wycliffe, but a full-fledged, joyous laugh. "I don't know. Perhaps you should choose something that's already dying." Her eyes drift to Mr. Bell, our art teacher, as he stands before us on the stone walkway that winds through the gardens.

Mr. Bell is not dapper, exactly, his face slightly too long and narrow and his hair carefully combed to hide the emerging bald spots, but he is otherwise quite normal. It is not his looks but his status as bachelor that is much discussed and wondered about among the girls at Wycliffe. Wycliffe's students, particularly those who live there, are carefully sheltered from the attention of men. Any man of marriageable age who is, in fact, not married is worthy of speculation, thinning hair or no.

"Ladies, as you know, autumn will soon be behind us. Today you will choose an artist from those we have studied, and using that artist as a guide, you may paint any scene from the garden that you wish. Given the cold, we will only have a few days to finish, so please work quickly and with focus. That is all."

Luisa is already absorbed in her painting, the beginnings of color taking shape on her canvas. I scan the dying garden for something worthy of my almost certainly doomed efforts. Dismissing anything too vibrant or complicated, my eyes light on a pointed purple flower, dark as a plum. It is a simple arrangement, one even I may be able to replicate. *Good enough*, I think.

I am determined to do my utmost when something catches my eye. It is Luisa, her hand poised over the canvas, the tip of her brush stroking an area of barren purity.

But not just Luisa. Her hand, her wrist, peeking out from her red velvet cloak and the silver bracelet loosely covering the white of her skin.

And the Mark. Sonia's Mark. *Mine*.

It is only a sliver, only the smallest of outlines, but I would recognize it anywhere.

"Whatever is the matter? Lia? What is it?" Luisa's brush drips emerald paint, her eyes full of concern.

"Your . . . The . . . Where did you get that?" I cannot take my eyes from her slender wrist.

She follows my gaze, looking down at her hand, eyes wide with panic. Her brush clatters to the ground as she pulls the sleeve of her cloak down over her wrist.

"It's nothing. Only a scar." She bends to pick up her brush from beneath the easel, her face white.

"I don't . . ." But I am unable to finish. Mr. Bell has suddenly appeared behind us.

"Miss Milthorpe, Luisa. What seems to be the problem?" He surveys our canvases with a critical eye, avoiding our faces entirely. Even with the questions beating through my brain, I am angry that he has addressed Luisa by her first name, saving the more respectful "Miss" for me.

"No problem at all, Mr. Bell. I'm quite clumsy today, that's all. I dropped my brush, but I have it now." Luisa waves it in front of him, as if to prove that she does, indeed, have the brush.

"Yes, everything is splendid, Mr. Bell. *Miss* Torelli and I are working with as much focus as we can muster."

"I see." He rocks on his heels, likely trying to decide how to handle my subtle breach of respectful conduct given that Father was a well-known benefactor of the school. "Carry on, then."

We exhale in unison when he is out of earshot.

I pick up my brush, leaning toward Luisa while I make shapeless strokes on the canvas. "Where did you get it, Luisa? You *must* tell me!"

She stiffens next to me, dipping her brush back into the green paint. "I don't know why you should care. It's nothing. Really!"

I sigh, taking only a moment to think. We do not have much time. Mr. Bell is leaning toward the girls at the far end of the row, engrossed in the canvas of one of the more artistic students. Setting my brush into the wooden recess of the easel, I hold my hand in the folds of my skirt and begin rolling up my sleeve as I speak, my voice just above a whisper.

"There is a very good reason why I should care, Luisa." When my wrist is exposed just enough for the medallion to show, I push it aside, turning my palm up so she can see. "You see, I have one as well. And it is almost exactly like yours."

She stares at my wrist for a long time, her brush still in her hand. I don't know how long we sit that way, but Landscape in Art is soon over and there is no privacy to be had as we put away the paint and carry our canvases to the art room amid the bustle of the other girls. Luisa's eyes follow me as I put away my materials, but I need time to think, to figure out what it all means, and this makes me grateful for our forced silence.

We are washing our brushes in a basin of water when she finally speaks. "I don't understand, Lia. How can this be?"

I keep my eyes on the water, murky with rinsed color. "I'm not sure. Something is happening, but I don't understand it any more than you. Not yet."

She shakes her head, loose tendrils of dark hair curling around the sweep of her neck. "Why would we both have them?" she whispers. "We have hardly spoken before this week, and yet I've had this mark for all my life."

I meet her eyes over the smell of turpentine and paint. "I don't know, Luisa, all right? Just . . . Please. Give me time to sort through everything I know."

"Oh, how I wish it weren't Thursday! Now I'll have to spend a long weekend waiting and wondering!" She is jumping out of her skin with anxiety, coiled so tightly I can nearly see the sinew of her muscles under her pale skin like one of the skeletons in Father's medical books.

I shake my brushes, placing them in a tin cup by the sink to dry before I turn to her once again. "Wait for my word. I shall get to you somehow."

Alice maintains her regal posture until Edmund closes the carriage door. But once we are alone in the semi-darkness of the gathering winter afternoon, she crumples, her shoulders sagging, her face a mask of resignation.

I put a hand on hers. "Are you all right?"

She nods, pulling her hand from mine in one quick motion without meeting my eyes. In the moment before she tucks the hand into her lap, my gaze is pulled to the smooth skin of her wrist. It is just as I suspected. The skin there is as unblemished as that of her cheek. I am the only marked sister.

She turns away from me to stare sullenly out the window,

and I am grateful for her silence. I haven't the energy or inclination to soothe her.

I sigh deeply, falling back into the comfort of the padded seat. When I lean my head back and close my eyes, all I can see is the mark on Luisa. On Sonia. On me.

It is beyond imagining that all three of us should have the mark, nearly identical and all in the same town. And yet nothing this careful, this sinister, can be so random. The belief that it *must* make sense is the only way to make sense of it at all.

Alice and I pass the ride home without speaking, coming to a stop in the front courtyard as darkness settles its hand across the sky. Edmund is not even at the door to the carriage when Alice exits like a caged animal set free, turning away from the house and toward the path leading to the lake. I don't try to stop her. After all that has happened, all that is happening even now, I still feel the pain of her humiliation at the hands of Wycliffe's self-proclaimed royalty. It is like seeing one of Father's beautiful thoroughbreds trained. It is all well and good that the horse can be ridden and contained, but I can never shake my sadness that such spirit should be broken.

I am halfway up the stairs when Aunt Virginia's voice comes to me from the foyer.

"Lia?"

I turn to face her. "Yes?" She stands at the foot of the stairs, looking up at me with a strained expression.

"Is something wrong?" Small wrinkles form at the corners of her eyes as she studies my face.

I hesitate, wondering to what she is referring. "No. Of course not. Why do you ask?"

She shrugs her slim shoulders. "You seem as if you have something on your mind. And Alice seems distraught as well."

I smile to ease her worry. "Girls of our age — bored, wealthy girls — are not always kind, you know."

Her own smile is small and sad. "Yes. I believe I remember that."

"Alice will be fine. She's simply tired and still grieving, as we all are."

She nods. I believe I've made my escape when she stops me again.

"Lia? Will you come to me if there is anything you need? Anything I can do to help you?"

I am quite sure there is something there, some trace of a message I haven't the knowledge to decode. For one half-mad moment I contemplate telling her everything. I contemplate asking her how I am to maintain my role as Guardian, how someone as confused as I should manage to protect the world from something I don't even understand.

But in the end, I say none of this, for if I am the Guardian and Alice the Gate, who is Aunt Virginia? Which role did she play in the prophecy's past?

I smile in answer to her question. "Yes. Thank you, Aunt Virginia."

I make my way up the stairs before she can say anything more.

Once in my room, the fire stoked and roaring, I sit at the

writing table and consider my options. I stare down at the book. The book with no origin, no markings, no birthplace.

A book as old as time.

James's notes peek out from behind the thin page of the prophecy. All that is left of *The Book of Chaos*. I want to solve its riddle alone, without involving anyone else, but I have come to a dead end in my understanding of its words.

Sometimes one must ask for help, however much one may not want to do so.

I take out a quill and bottle of ink from the drawer. Pulling two sheets of thick writing paper toward me, I begin to write.

Dear Miss Sorrensen,

Miss Lia Milthorpe requests the honor of your presence for tea . . .

With my invitations to Sonia and Luisa written and a reckless desire to ignore the book for just a while, I entice Henry into an evening of games. His eyes are still shaded with sadness, and truth be told, I could use the distraction from the many questions waiting for answers. They will still be waiting, whatever I do to pass the time.

On the way to the parlor, I pass the glass doors of the conservatory, a figure within catching my eye. It is Alice, sitting with Ari on her lap in a large wicker chair by the window. Though I stand in the warmth of the hall, it is plain to see that

the conservatory is frigid with cold. Starbursts of frost dot the glass, but Alice stares out the window into the darkness with only a blanket wrapped around her shoulders as if she is in a room no draftier than the fire-lit parlor. She pets the cat in a rhythmic motion not unlike the one she used to brush my hair. Even from my vantage point, I can see the vacant expression in her eyes.

I am preparing to announce myself, to open the glass doors and step onto the tiled floor of the conservatory, when something stops me cold. It is Ari, moaning and trying to rise off Alice's lap. The cat is partially blocked by the wicker chair, and I tip my head to get a clearer view. When I do, when I find a position that allows me to see more fully what Alice is doing, my skin crawls with disgust and dismay.

It is Alice, holding down the cat. Not petting his fur. Not stroking him as she was only moments ago. No. She holds a small tuft of his hair, twisting it, twisting it until the cat hisses in pain and scrambles to escape her grip. But it is her face that frightens me most. It remains impassive, the dazed expression still written there as if she is contemplating the weather. Her grip on the cat must be ironclad. He cannot escape no matter how he arches and turns.

I should like to say that I stop her at once, but I am so shocked that I have no idea how many seconds pass before I am spurred to action. When I finally fling open the door, she releases her grip on Ari without the slightest change in expression. He scrambles from her lap, shaking his body and running from the room with a speed I've not seen him display since he was a kitten.

"Oh. Lia. What are you doing here?" She turns as I enter the room, but she does not look ashamed or in the least bit concerned.

"I was coming to see if you want to play cribbage with Henry and me in the parlor." My voice is hoarse, and I have to clear my throat to continue. "What were you doing?"

"Hmmm?" She is back to staring out the window.

I make my voice stronger. "A moment ago. With Ari."

She gives a small, distant shake of her head. "Nothing. Nothing at all."

I contemplate pressing her, forcing her to confess, but what would be the purpose in it? I saw her. I know what she was doing, whatever she might say.

And though the moment may seem small, it is the knowledge behind it that fills me with dread. Because while I have never denied that Alice can be careless . . . self-centered . . . even spiteful, it has never occurred to me before today that she might actually be cruel.

10

Henry and I play game after game of cribbage and even manage to entice Cook into making popcorn and chocolate, two of Henry's favorite indulgences. As the hours pass, we move into chess. Henry beats me time and time again, having spent years as a student of Father's able strategy. We both laugh, but it is not the easy laughter of times past. Now, there is an undercurrent of sorrow coupled with a fear that is all my own. I try to lose myself in the simplicity of the hours with my younger brother, but it is Alice's blank face I see when I stare into the fire while waiting for Henry to make his move.

"Lia?" Henry's voice breaks into my thoughts.

I look up from the chess board. "Yes?"

"You should be careful."

The words send a chill up my spine, but I force a laugh. "Whatever do you mean, Henry?"

He looks away, gazing into the fire a moment before turning back to meet my eyes. "Father told me oftentimes things are not what they seem."

"Henry." I favor his seriousness with a gentle smile. I do not want to patronize him when he seems so intent on passing along his cryptic message. "To what are you referring?"

"Just . . ." He takes a deep breath as if summoning his courage, but in the end, he lets it out in a resigned sigh. "I don't know what I mean to say, Lia." He smiles, but it is a shadow of his normal grin. "Just promise you'll be careful, will you?"

I nod slowly, still trying to puzzle out the meaning in his words. "Of course."

We spend another twenty minutes playing chess, but our movements are half-hearted. Henry is yawning when we finally put the game pieces away and Aunt Virginia comes to help him to bed.

As Henry says good night, his eyes are dark with worry and something I cannot help but think resembles fear. "Thank you, Lia. Ever so much."

"Of course. I shall be happy to beat you anytime," I tease, trying to lighten his mood. I lean over and drop a kiss on his smooth cheek. "Good night. Sleep well."

"Sleep well, Lia."

Aunt Virginia wheels him around, turning to me as she passes. She smiles in silent thanks.

"Good night, Aunt Virginia."

I stand in the quiet room after they leave. Moving to the large window in the parlor, I stare at the black night as Alice

did, wondering what she saw in the emptiness beyond the conservatory windows. I look and look, the crackle of the fire the only sound in the room behind me. But I do not see a thing. Not the beautiful sky of my night dreams nor the answers I need.

Only darkness.

Later, as I ascend the stairs to bed, I hear something coming from the library. It is the sound of shuffling, of things being moved to and fro, and I turn on the carpeted steps and make my way toward the noise.

When I reach the library door, I see Alice, bent over and pulling books from the shelves. I watch for a minute, wondering why I feel alarmed when the books in the library belong as much to Alice as to me. I suppose it is because she has never been interested in Father's collection, and he long ago gave up trying to share his passion for books with Alice.

She must feel me standing there, because she turns before I say a word. Bright spots of color rise to her cheeks. I cannot remember the last time I've seen Alice blush.

"Oh! Lia! What are you doing here?" She straightens, smoothing her skirt and tucking a loose tendril of hair behind her ear.

"I saw the door open. What are you looking for?"

A blanket of calm drops over her features. "Something to read before bed." She waves at the shelves as if dismissing them. "I've not been sleeping well of late."

"Yes, I know what you mean." I tip a head to the shelves. "You need only ask if you'd like a recommendation."

She looks at me, her face turning to stone. "I shall do that. If I cannot find something on my own, that is."

We stand there, staring at each other. It is clear she doesn't mean to leave, and I have no jurisdiction over the room.

"Good night, Alice." It is not easy to turn, but I do it nonetheless, leaving her in the sanctity of the room I shared so often with my father.

I make my way back to the stairs, a mixture of fear and anger coursing through my veins. I don't know why I should want to keep the book from Alice, but I am suddenly very, very glad it is hidden in the wardrobe in my chamber.

11

It is two days later when I watch from the large window in the parlor as the carriage rounds the bend in the drive. Despite the unusual reason for my tea with Luisa and Sonia, I am excited at the prospect of their company. The child in me wants to run down the stone steps and fling open the door of the carriage. Instead, I force myself to stand slowly, straightening the folds in my skirt and walking with decorum to the foyer. Aunt Virginia looks up from her sewing by the fire and puts aside her needle to join me as I make my way down the stone steps.

I have never had anyone to tea. Aunt Virginia was understandably surprised when I told her about my plans to host my two peers, but she did not object. Birchwood is, after all, my home. I have not made a point of divulging my plans to Alice, though it is difficult to believe she doesn't know about them given the added activity in the house. Still, she has made herself scarce, something for which I am grateful whether due to avoidance or ignorance.

Aunt Virginia and I gather in front of the walkway where the carriage stops with a crunch on the gravel. Edmund opens the door, reaching in to provide assistance to its occupants. A gloved hand emerges first, and I know that it is Sonia's. A hand so childlike can only be hers. She steps from the carriage, her face full of uncertainty.

"Sonia! I'm so glad you could come!" I reach out to take her hand.

She smiles, looking from me to Aunt Virginia. "Thank you for inviting me." Her face is unreadable, but I see the careful way she chooses her words and realize she fears making a poor impression.

I look to Aunt Virginia and make the introduction. She smiles warmly. "I'm most pleased to see you again, Miss Sorrensen."

Luisa ignores Edmund's hand, bounding from the carriage in one swift motion, her smile casting a glow over us all. "Oh, thank you ever so much for inviting me, Lia!" She wraps me in a quick embrace, her cheeks glowing like ripe apricots against her dark skin. "I've never been invited to tea. Not once since I've been at Wycliffe! You should have seen the other girls' faces when the invitation arrived!"

She hardly stops to breathe, and I place a hand on her arm, if only to find a place to make introductions. "Aunt Virginia, Luisa Torelli. Luisa, Virginia Spencer."

"I'm most pleased to meet you, Miss Torelli." Aunt Virginia's green eyes sparkle.

"Oh yes! Most pleased to make your acquaintance, Miss . . . er . . . Mrs. Spencer." I stifle a smile as Luisa fumbles over my Aunt's marital status.

"You were quite right the first time, Miss Torelli. I've never married."

"Oh, that is most bold of you, Miss Spencer," Luisa breathes. "I do so admire the independent women of today!"

I know I must stop her or we shall still be standing on the gravel at suppertime, Luisa prattling away as if no time has passed at all. "Shall we go in, then? The fire is warm, and the table is set."

I loop one arm in Luisa's and the other in Sonia's. We will enjoy our tea. And then we will try to find the dark thread that binds us together.

✑

"I don't believe it." Luisa is nearly speechless. Nearly, but not quite. "And to think that all this time I thought I was the only one."

"So did I." Sonia's words are a whisper. "Well, and then Lia, after I found her." She cannot take her eyes off our wrists, thrust forward over the bales of hay on which we sit. The marks, all three of them, are proof that whatever is at work is at work in us all.

I have brought them to the stables in search of privacy from the prying eyes and big ears of the house. It is late enough that

the stable boys have all gone home, and our only company is the soft nickering of the horses and the sweet smell of hay.

I relax my arm, pulling it back toward me. "We cannot deny it. Not now. Whatever it means, we shall have to figure it out together."

Sonia shakes her head. "But how? I've told you all I know, Lia. There isn't a thing I've left out."

"What? What do you know?" Luisa narrows her eyes at us.

I sigh, making my way to a soft leather bag hanging from a peg on the stable wall. Dipping my hand into the bag, I pull out a fistful of dry, crumbly oats and make my way to the first stall.

"Sonia told me about a story, a legend really, involving twin sisters and angels who —"

Luisa makes her way to the feedbag. "The story of Maari and Katla? Of the Watchers?" She asks the question as if it is the most obvious in the world.

In my surprise, I ignore the black horse in front of me. He nudges my shoulder with his nose, and I open my palm absently. "You've heard it?"

She shrugs. "My grandmother used to tell it to me when I was small. But what does it have to do with us? With the mark?" She walks to the stall ahead of me, sticking her hand through the opening without hesitation.

I brush my hands against my skirt, reaching into the drawstring bag and pulling the book from it as Luisa watches with interest. Sonia has made no move toward the horses, remaining on the bale of hay as if there is no question of her feeding the large, shuffling animals. I sit next to her, placing the book in my lap and folding my arms over it. It is not yet time. First we must begin from the same place.

I turn to Luisa. "Tell us what you know about the sisters."

Her eyes meet mine with unspoken questions. And then she speaks. At first, her words are halting, but she warms to the details as she recalls the story from the soft, blurred edges of childhood. When she is finished, we are silent.

I run my fingers along the cover of the book, Luisa's words still sounding in my ears. Words that are the same as Sonia's on the hill over the lake. The same as those translated by James from the book.

Sonia shakes her head. "I thought it was only people like me — spiritualists and gypsies and such — who knew of the prophecy."

Luisa shrugs, giving us a rueful smile as she brushes her gloved hands together to dust off the remaining oats. "My mother was English. There were rumors that she came from a long line of heathens. All nonsense, I'm sure, but I suppose Grandmother's story comes from them."

Sonia eyes the book with hunger. "Are you going to tell us what that is, Lia?"

"My father was a collector of sorts. A collector of rare books." I hold the book out toward them. "After his death, this was found hidden behind a secret panel in the library."

Luisa closes the distance between us in a few quick steps, taking the book and dropping next to us on the hay. She opens it, turning the pages carefully but quickly before closing it with

a snap. "I cannot read a thing, Lia. It's in Latin! I can barely speak my native tongue of Italian after all these years! How do we know this has anything to do with the mark if we cannot even read it?"

Sonia takes the book before I can answer. She gives it a more thorough inspection, but her time inside it is short as well, and she closes it much as Luisa did, shrugging and looking at me over the cover.

"I'm afraid I don't read Latin, either, Lia."

I pull James's folded notes from the silken fabric of my bag. "My grasp of it is no better, but I happen to be acquainted with someone who knows it quite well."

I pass them the translation, giving them a moment to read, to pass it to one another, to ponder the words written in James's careful handwriting.

When she is finished reading, Sonia lowers the paper to her lap, her expression blank. Luisa chews her full lower lip before pulling a piece of straw from the bale. She stands and paces the floor, her footsteps ringing through the empty stable as she begins to speak.

"All right, then. Let's think this through, shall we? If the legend is true and if the mark has something to do with it and if you and Alice are the sisters —"

"That is a lot of ifs, Luisa." I don't mean to contradict her. She doesn't say anything I have not thought myself. Still, it seems important to give voice to reason even as it spins out of my reach.

Luisa nods. "Perhaps. But if we put together the book and

the legend and you and Alice and the mark . . . Well, the most important similarity between the prophecy and the three of us is you and Alice, Lia. You are twins. That cannot be sheer coincidence." She stops walking and shrugs. "Well, it could, but let us assume for the moment that it isn't, all right? Let's see where that train of thought takes us."

I nod, relieved that someone else is willing to shoulder the burden of the prophecy for the moment.

"All right, then." She resumes pacing. "You are the Guardian, your sister the Gate. It makes sense. Your mark is different, and you've already said that Alice doesn't have one at all. Besides, let us be honest, it is difficult to imagine her as guardian of anything save her own best interests." She flashes me a rueful smile. "No offense."

Once, I would have taken offense. I would have sided with my sister. But I cannot refute Luisa's perception of Alice, and deciphering the prophecy and my place in it is suddenly more important than loyalty to a sister I am becoming more and more certain I hardly know.

I shake my head. "No offense taken."

Luisa smiles kindly. "Good. So it must be you, then. You must be the Guardian. And if you are the Guardian, then Alice is the Gate."

I nod, surprised and grateful that it is that simple to her. That Luisa believes so easily the thing logic has tried to deny me time and again. "Yes. At least, I believe so. But how are we to figure the rest of it?"

" 'Cast from the heavens, the Souls were lost until the Gates

summon forth their return or the Angel brings the keys to the abyss.' " Sonia's voice drifts across the darkening stable. "That's the next piece of the prophecy. The piece after the sisters. Maybe that is our next clue."

Luisa leans back on the wall, arms folded in front of her. "I think you're right, Sonia. We must identify the Angel and find the keys. Perhaps they will lead us to an understanding of the rest."

"Yes, only . . ." Sonia's voice trails off as she bites her lip.

"Only what?" Luisa asks.

Sonia's eyes flicker to the shadowed corners of the stable. "What if Alice finds them first? Assuming they unlock the riddle of the prophecy, won't she be looking for them as fervently as us?"

Sonia's mention of Alice makes my breath feel tight in my chest. I cannot say aloud the thing I feel — that Alice's strange behavior has made me fear my own sister. That I fear not only her finding the keys before we do, but the things she might do in the meantime.

I push the thoughts aside. "I have the book. Without it, Alice may not know the breadth of the prophecy. She may well be as confused in her role as I am in mine. If I can keep the book from her, perhaps it will buy us enough time to find the keys and figure out how to use them."

Sonia nods thoughtfully. "Perhaps . . ."

The heavy silence of shared secrets fills the stable. I think about the endless questions before us, the seeming impossibil-

ity of finding their answers, and it brings me to a thought entirely new.

"Luisa?"

She is leaning against the stable wall, chewing the end of the straw she has been twisting in her fingers. "Hmmm?"

"Do you travel as well? At night, I mean? Do you have the strange traveling dreams?"

She hesitates, shifting nervously on her feet before answering. "Well, everyone has dreams, Lia. . . ."

Sonia rises, idly inspecting the saddles and bridles that line the walls. "There is no need to be afraid, Luisa. I've been traveling for years. Lia has only just begun. It would be expected that you would have the gift as well, given that we all share the mark."

Luisa shakes her head. "But they are only dreams! Only strange dreams in which I can fly. Surely many people fly in their dreams!" The words come out in a tumble, as if she has wanted to say them for a very long time.

Sonia smiles. I already recognize it as the soft smile Sonia wears when she must say something not easily understood or accepted. "Actually, it *is* possible for the soul to travel without the body, and it is not so very difficult to explain, nor difficult to become accustomed to once you understand it."

❧

Luisa leans against one of the stalls as if for support, her face a pale sheet of shock. She is well past the protestations and denial, for Sonia has too carefully and thoroughly described the sensations of travel. Travel we have all experienced and must now accept as a part of the prophecy and its mark.

Luisa stands up straighter, her face flushed with fright. "I don't want to travel any longer! Surely it must be dangerous — flying about without one's body! Suppose someone should happen upon us while we travel? We would be thought dead!"

Sonia's eyes meet mine across the darkening stable, and I know she is thinking of our conversation on the hill. Of the Void. The shake of her head is almost imperceptible, but I see it and know that she means to keep any mention of the Void from Luisa. She is terrified enough as it is.

Sonia smiles gently at her. "That would be unlikely, for the soul and the body to which it belongs share a powerful connection. There is no reason to believe you are in any danger, Luisa."

I hear the words Sonia has left unspoken: *It is Lia they are after.*

Luisa rubs her arms as if just feeling the cold that has seeped into the darkening building. The motion seems to wake her from some form of reverie, and she suddenly stands straighter. "Goodness! It's getting dark! It must be quite late! Miss Gray will be angry!"

I move toward the doors. "Aunt Virginia will write a note of apology, insisting that it was we who kept you so late. Even Miss Gray cannot be angry with Aunt Virginia, you'll see."

Closing the stable doors behind us, I fold my arms across my chest in a vain attempt to stay warm as we make our way back

toward the house. It was easy to lose track of the time in the quiet of the stables, but now I see that it is almost entirely dark. The lamps in the house are already on, blazing a welcome to us across the cold, shadowy grounds.

We stop walking as we near the patio off the conservatory. It has not been said aloud, but we are likely thinking the same thing; whatever else is spoken between us must be said before we re-enter the house.

"What shall we do, Lia?" Despair creeps into Sonia's voice. "We must find the keys, and we are no closer to understanding the passage in the book than we were before."

I touch their arms. "I shall find a way to meet you both again. In the meantime, we mustn't tell anyone about the book, the prophecy, the mark . . . any of it. Though there is no clear reason why we should keep it a secret, I feel sure we must."

Luisa gives a snort. "Why, surely there *is* a reason! Anyone would think us half-mad, would they not?"

I cannot help laughing, and I pull her into a quick embrace, followed by one for Sonia. "Oh, do take care. I wish I didn't have to bring you into this dreadful thing."

Sonia smiles. "Whatever brought us into the prophecy did so long ago, Lia. You are no more responsible than we are. Whatever comes, we will face it together."

&

Taking off my gown and changing into the soft folds of my nightdress is like shedding an old skin, and I sigh aloud as I unpin my hair and sit at the desk. I start at the beginning and reread

the prophecy, sticking again after the part about the Guardian and the Gate, the part I already know and understand.

I read it again and again, but it does me no good. I cannot make sense of it, no matter how hard I try. James's notes are fanned across the desk, mixed up now with all my shuffling. I line them up neatly, if only to give my hands something to do, and rest my head on the tips of my fingers. I have a bizarre desire to run into the fields and scream, to let loose my frustration and anger at the thing I don't understand.

I reach for the back cover of the book, ready to close it for the night, to fall without struggle into whatever dreams are waiting, when I feel the smooth lip of endpaper peeling in the corner. I smooth it down, the old habits as much a part of me as Father himself. I shall have to have the endpaper glued into place so the book doesn't further deteriorate.

But the corner does not want to smooth. The more I press it, the more it comes loose farther down, as if something is pressing against it, determined to force its way up from one place or another. Something is not right.

Smoothing my palm across the inside back cover, it is obvious that something is there. Something that doesn't belong. I don't stop to think, though tearing the endpaper off a book of this age would be reason for banishment from the library were my father still alive. Still, I pull as gently as I can and am surprised at how easily the endpaper separates from the back cover of the book. I am even more surprised, however, by what has been waiting, folded very thinly inside the book, all this time.

I pull a square of paper from the book, carefully unfolding the small package. This is no ordinary paper. Not the thick, luxurious stationery used for coveted invitations and pretentious social notices. This is as thin as onion skin, as the pages of a Bible. When the tiny bundle is at last laid flat, the drawings there take my breath away.

The first picture is a serpent eating its own tail. Underneath it is the word *Jorgumand*.

Behind it is a drawing labeled *The Lost Souls,* an army of demons riding astride white horses, blood-drenched swords raised high above their heads. This one frightens me, but not as much as the one that come next: a snake forming a circle and eating its own tail, a C at its center.

I pull it slowly from the pile, its entirety revealed an inch at a time as it emerges from the other pages of feathery drawings. When at last it is laid bare, I can only stare, my heart thudding wildly in my chest.

There is no mistaking the medallion. It is as familiar to me now as the mark on my wrist. The gold disc hangs in the center, the ribbon coiling around it. Seeing it in such vibrant detail floods me not with the fear I would expect but with a longing that is far more terrifying.

But it is the words underneath the picture that make the tiny hairs on my arms stand on end.

Medallion of Chaos, Mark of the One True Gate.

12

I shake my head at the empty room, looking down at my wrist, at the medallion lying next to the book. It is the same.

The same. The same. The same.

Medallion of Chaos, Mark of the One True Gate.

It cannot be. Logic refuses it entrance. Alice is the Gate. I *know* it. She *must* be.

But there is something primal and even welcoming that tells me it isn't true. The strange longing beating within me, answering the silent call of the medallion, of the Souls perched on the forbidding horses. It is both comforting and horrifying.

Yet it is undeniably present.

The medallion is the mark of the Gate. *The One True Gate,* though I don't know what that means. It fits my wrist perfectly.

It was given to me. It matches my mark, the mark that is different from all the others. And so, it can only be that I have been wrong all this time.

I am weary of the book and its secrets. The time has come to go to the other sister.

&

I wait until the house is silent, until the footsteps of the servants cease their movement across the floors. Then I wait awhile longer. When I am certain no one is about, I open the door and pad down the hall on bare feet. Even slippers make noise when the house is so quiet.

I knock softly on Aunt Virginia's door. For a moment, nothing happens. The house continues on its silent journey into morning. I lift my hand, ready to knock again, and the door opens, Aunt Virginia standing expectantly in its frame as if she knew it would be me all along.

"Come in, Lia." Her voice is an urgent whisper. "Quickly." She reaches out and tugs my arm, pulling me into the warmth of the room and closing the door.

"I'm sorry. I . . . I didn't think you were expecting me."

Her back is to me as she crosses the room, taking a chair by the fire and gesturing for me to take the one opposite. "On the contrary, Lia. I've been expecting you for quite some time."

I lower myself into the high-backed chair, sneaking a curious glance at my aunt. She looks different, her hair long and loose over her nightdress instead of pulled into the severe knot at the back of her neck. Now that I'm here, I am suddenly unsure how to begin. I'm grateful when Aunt Virginia saves me the trouble.

"Have you found the book, then?"

I nod, studying my hands to avoid her eyes.

She smiles sadly. "Good. He wanted you to find it, you know."

I look up from my hands. "Father?"

"Yes, of course. You don't think it was an accident that it was found, do you? That the Douglases are here cataloging the books?"

"I suppose . . . I suppose I don't know what to think anymore."

"Well, let us begin at the beginning then, shall we?" Her voice is sorrowful, and I know she does not want to begin at the beginning any more than I.

But we must. We must begin somewhere. After all, one cannot reach the end of something without the beginning.

"Yes. Let us start there."

She looks at me with silent expectation. Clearly, I am meant to divulge my secrets first. And what else is there to do? The prophecy and my place in it swirl in a cloud of confusion. Without assistance, it will be impossible to go further.

So I tell her what I know, what I *believe* I know, repeating my conversations with Sonia, my interpretations of the book. When I am finished, she speaks.

"Miss Sorrensen is quite right. The prophecy has continued for all this time, all these years, all these lifetimes. We are but one more link in the chain," Aunt Virginia says.

"I thought . . ." My throat closes around the words, and I have to clear it to continue. "I thought I was the Guardian, at first."

She looks away, into the fire. "Yes," she murmurs. "I can see why you might."

Her easy acceptance of my declaration sits so heavily on my chest I have trouble breathing. "Then it's true." It is not so easy for me, though I came to the realization myself the moment I saw the drawing of the medallion.

Her nod is almost imperceptible, as if by making her acknowledgment slight it might somehow be less true, less painful.

I am surprised at the anger that fills me in the wake of Aunt Virginia's confirmation. It pushes me to my feet, forcing me to pace the length of the room for fear I will jump out of my own skin if I remain still. "But why? Why does it have to be me?"

She sighs, a world of sadness in the soft breath that leaves her body. "Because you are the oldest, Lia. It is always the oldest."

I stop moving, stunned. That is it? The reason for my enslavement to the prophecy is something as simple, as random, as the order in which I emerged from my mother's womb?

"But I didn't ask for it. I don't want it. How can it be me if I don't want it?"

She presses her lips with the tips of her fingers. "It is a mistake, I think."

"What . . . what do you mean?" I sink back into the chair at Virginia's side.

She leans forward, looking into my eyes. "Your mother had a very difficult confinement with you and Alice. She was forced to her bed for most of it, and in the end . . ." She looks back to the fire, her eyes taking on a far-off look.

"In the end, what?"

"In the end, Alice was to be born first. Her head was down, ready to be born, while your feet were down instead, your head pointed upward. It isn't uncommon in twins, or so the doctor said. And any other time I suppose it would not have mattered. But your mother . . . she could not birth Alice. Her labors went on and on, Lia, until I thought it would kill her."

"But it didn't."

She shakes her head. "No, though I imagine not so very long ago the mother *would* have died in a birth such as yours. But your father was a very rich man who insisted on the very best for his wife and unborn children. The doctor who saw your mother, who delivered you and Alice, was trained in techniques that were, *are*, considered dangerous, including cesarean birth."

"What is that?"

Her eyes meet mine. "He cut her, Lia. He put her to sleep and he cut her. It was the only way to save her life, and perhaps the lives of you and your sister. When he opened her, instead of pulling Alice out first, he grabbed you. Alice was nearer to birth the other way, but as it turns out, you were nearer the incision made by the doctor. I don't think it was supposed to be you."

"But how do you know? How do you know any of this?"

She shakes her head. "I didn't. *We* didn't. When your mother awoke, we said a prayer of gratitude for her survival and for the survival of you and Alice, and we never spoke of it again. It was only after I began to suspect that you might be the Gate, that I thought there might be consequences to the doctor's intervention in your birth."

"But even so . . . how do you know it isn't exactly the way it was supposed to be all along?"

"Because I see the look in Alice's eyes, Lia. And when she looks at you, I'm afraid." She looks around, as if someone might have crept in on silent feet while we were sitting right there. "I see her anger, her desire, and her need. And in you . . ."

"In me what?"

She shrugs simply. "In you I see something else, something . . . *true* that has been present ever since you were a small child."

The fire has burned low, its missing warmth making the room seem more than cold, making it seem hollow, dead. It is only after a time that Aunt Virginia's gaze drifts to my hand.

"May I see it?" she asks carefully, as if she is asking to see something far more private than my wrist.

I nod, holding it out for her. Her hands are warm and dry on the tender skin of my arm as she pushes up the sleeve of my nightdress.

"Oh!" Her voice is full of surprise. "It is . . . it is different."

I look down at the mark. "What do you mean?"

"I've never seen one like this." She traces it gently with her

finger. "The Gates . . . well, they always have the mark of the Jorgumand. But I've never seen one with this C."

Her mention of the mark makes me realize that I have not yet told her about Sonia and Luisa. "There is one other thing. . . ."

"What is it?"

"Sonia and Luisa have a mark as well, only it is exactly like the one you describe. Theirs does not bear the C as mine does. What do you think it means?"

She looks into my eyes. "I don't know, but I wonder if it has something to do with the others. . . ."

Her words cause me to sit up straighter. "What others?"

"The other children with the mark. The ones your father was searching for. The ones he brought to New York."

I feel as if her words stop my heart, a ripple of intuition rippling up my spine. "I think you'd better tell me what you mean."

She nods. "It began after your mother's death. Your father began spending hours and hours in the library." Her eyes are bright as she remembers. "He had always loved the library, of course, but then . . . well, then it became his refuge. We rarely saw him, and soon he began getting strange letters, taking long trips."

"What does this have to do with the others?"

"He was working from a list. A list of names and places."

I shake my head. "I don't understand. What use could he have for such a list?"

"I don't know. He wouldn't tell me. But he brought two of them here."

"Who? Who did he bring here?"

"The girls. Two of them. One from England, one from Italy. But he would never tell me why."

There is a promise of understanding in her words, but one I am not yet ready to share. Aunt Virginia rises, trying to rekindle the dying fire as I stare at the glowing ashes, attempting to make sense of everything that has been said. Even with all I've learned, the mystery has only deepened.

But there is one puzzle that can be solved here and now.

"May I see, Aunt Virginia?"

She turns from the fire. In her eyes, I see that she knows just what I mean. She returns to the chair, sitting in it and holding out her hand without a word. When I pull aside the cuff of her nightdress I see nothing but the smooth, pale skin of her slight wrist. She bears no trace of the mark.

I nod. "I thought so." My voice is wooden in the quiet room. It is a voice that doesn't sound like mine at all.

"Lia. I'm sorry. I never wanted you to know."

She *is* sorry. I can see it in the worry lines around her eyes, the tense set of her mouth. I try to smile for her, but it doesn't feel right on my face. "It's all right, Aunt Virginia. I knew, I think. I knew it all along."

And now, at least, I need not fear my aunt. I cannot bring myself to think the other thing. The thing about my mother and her role as Gate. Instead, I focus on the things I can still change. "Where are the keys, Aunt Virginia?"

"What keys?"

I study her face, but there is no guile there. No secrets. "The keys mentioned in the prophecy. In the book. The keys to ending the prophecy."

She shakes her head. "I told you; your father was very secretive. I'm afraid I've never seen the book."

"But how did you maintain your role as Guardian without knowledge of the prophecy?"

"I was trained by my Aunt Abigail, also a Guardian." She drops her eyes to the hands clasped in her lap, before looking up at me once again. "And now it is my task to train Alice in her role as Guardian. I should already be training her, if the truth be told. But I must confess that I've done no such thing."

I shake my head. "Why?"

"I would like to say I don't know, but it would be a lie." She sighs. "I have been hoping I was wrong — that you were the Guardian and Alice the Gate, because I cannot imagine training Alice for such a role any more than I can imagine her fulfilling it."

"But . . . if you train her . . . if you teach her how to be a proper Guardian —"

She does not allow me to finish. "There is something you must understand, Lia; even among those of us who play a role in the prophecy, there are varying degrees of strength. The Guardian's ability lies both in her willingness to assume the role and in her innate power. Most desire to fulfill the role that is theirs, but some do not. Then again, some are born with

extraordinary power and others . . . others with less. I'm afraid I must count myself one of the latter. Your mother was far stronger. She was a Spellcaster, in fact, while I have little power beyond that required to travel the Plane."

I am beginning to understand, though I don't like where the knowledge leads. "So the Guardian has no guarantee of keeping out the Souls?"

"Alice's task would be great enough were she eager to assume it, but it will be impossible if she has no desire to play her part. The Guardian is simply an overseer . . . a sentinel, if you will. It is the Guardian's duty to keep watch over the sister named as Gate, to use whatever power available to deny the Souls entrance to our world and to entreat the Gate to fight against the role that is hers.

"But it is not foolproof. The Souls *have* made their way here, hundreds, perhaps thousands, of times over the past centuries. No one can say for certain how many have gathered to wait for Samael, but we do our best to limit their number. If the Doom of Gods *does* arrive, it is to our advantage to ensure that Samael fights with as few Souls as possible." She shrugs. "It is all we can do."

I'm not sure what I expected. But not this. I suppose I hoped there was some sure answer . . . some information Aunt Virginia possessed that would allow me to fight the Souls and find the keys.

But it will not be so easy. There will be no quick and simple end to the prophecy that steers my life in an ever darker direction.

My room is cold, the fire burned to a soft, orange glow. I have no idea the time; surely late enough that I should be ready for sleep. But I cannot stop thinking, cannot stop the wheels from turning over all I have learned. I let my mind wander through the darkness.

I am not the Guardian, but the Gate. Whether through fate or chance, it is something I must accept if I'm to find a way back from its bleak promise.

If I am the Gate, Alice is the Guardian.

I shake my head into the empty room, for even alone I want to protest, to cry out, *It cannot be!*

Yet I know it must.

And if I am the Gate, should I not fear finding the keys even more than Alice finding them? Perhaps it is I who might use them for harm instead of good.

I push these thoughts aside. I know my own intentions, and while it is true that I have felt the strange affinity for traveling the Plane, for the medallion that found its way to me, it is also true that I do not seek to do harm. This I know as sure as I breathe.

With this certainty, I also know that Alice does not seek to do good, whatever the prophecy may call us. Whatever names it may assign us.

My thoughts sound desperate, even to me, as if I seek to re-assure myself with false truths and empty reassurances. But there are far too many things I do not yet understand. The

prophecy is too long, too winding, to begin with those things. I shall continue instead with the ones I do.

My father began searching for something after my mother's death, compiling a list of children. Bringing them here.

One from England, one from Italy.

Sonia and Luisa.

I do not have proof. I never asked the circumstances of Sonia's coming to live with Mrs. Millburn. There has not been time. But I will wager that Sonia is from England.

Why would Father bring them here? Why would he bring them to me, for that is what it feels like — as if he brought them all this way for me, though for what purpose I cannot imagine.

At last, the call of sleep arrives. I reach to turn off the lamp, stopping before I turn the key. I *feel* the medallion in the drawer of my night table. It pulses there like a living thing, sending out a soundless but primeval signal meant only for me. Part of me believes that the medallion *belongs* to me, belongs on my wrist. But the other part, the thinking part, believes it unwise to wear it until I know what part it plays.

The will required for me to leave it takes me by surprise. I turn out the light and, all at once, my plan to leave it in the drawer is nearly overmatched by my desire, my *need*, to have it on, to feel its caress on the warm skin of my wrist. For one strange moment, I cannot remember why I should leave it off at all.

And then, from some dark recess, I find the clarity to turn away. I turn my back to the table and will myself to sleep.

My dreams are constant. I am both in them and above them, watching them unfold. There are moments when I am conscious of the feeling of flying, as if I am on one of my travels. But there are others where I know, even in the absent state of sleep, that it is a dream.

There are flashes — soundless flashes of my mother's grave, the blackness seeping from the Earth near her marker. Flashes of the cliff from which she fell, of my father and his tortured, terrified expression when we found him in the Dark Room. In my dream, the enormous winged demons chase me, but this time the army is led by something even more frightening. Its heart beats in time to my own, blocking out all rational thought as it approaches in the thunder of a thousand hooves.

Louder, louder, louder.

And then I am falling, falling through a dark and endless emptiness. At first I believe it is the hissing of the dark thing in my dream that causes me to sit up so suddenly in my bed, my breath coming fast and heavy, my heart beating ferociously in my chest. But a quick glance to the end of my bed reveals Ari, hissing at me in fear or anger. He eyes me warily, back arched and teeth bared.

And then he does the strangest thing of all.

He turns, jumping down from the bed and padding purposefully to the corner where he turns his back to me, sitting on his haunches and staring at the wall as if refusing to acknowledge my existence. I cannot take my eyes off his shadow, an ominous smudge in the corner of the room, though he is nothing but the cat I have loved for many years.

There is no light coming from the windows, and for a minute, I think perhaps it is still night. But then I hear the sounds of the servants. I remember that it is almost winter and is quite dark even when we wake.

It all moves through me in seconds — the darkness, Ari's unusual behavior, the sounds of the house slowly waking. What comes to me a moment later is the weight around my wrist. It is too dark for me to see, so I use my other hand to feel for it, just to be sure. Even that is not enough to bring belief, and I fumble for a match, lighting the bedside lamp clumsily until light bursts forth, illuminating the medallion on my wrist.

13

It takes me half the morning to escape the house unseen with the medallion.

Alice seems more watchful than usual as we eat breakfast and read, though I tell myself she cannot possibly know what I mean to do. Still, I don't take my leave until she retires to her room to work on an overdue French lesson for Wycliffe.

The wind is so cold it takes my breath away, but it does not deter me. I am already committed to the task at hand. Forcing aside my discomfort, I make my way around the house and toward the river. I will my feet forward as fast as my skirts will allow, the drawstring bag swinging from one hand as I pick up the pace. I no longer feel the cold. In fact, I don't feel or hear a thing. Everything is quiet and still as I put one boot in front of the other, as if the world itself knows what I mean to do.

When I come to the river's edge, I reach into my bag, feeling around for the medallion. I half-expect it to be gone, to have disappeared in an unreasonable bid for safety, as if it has desires all its own. But it is only a thing, after all, and it lies in the bag right where I placed it before breakfast.

All I want is to be rid of it.

I raise my arm in the air, hesitating only a second before letting go and flinging it into the river with force. A small puff of steam rises off the water where it lands. I walk as close to the river's edge as I can manage without risking a fall.

It is there, spinning downstream in the angry current, the black velvet coiling like a snake around the gold disc, glinting from the water though there is not a speck of sun in the sky.

I stay by the river awhile to gather my thoughts. I do not know how the medallion works with the prophecy, but I feel certain that it has something to do with the Souls and their pathway back. Now it is somewhere in the cold, wild waters of the river. It will sink to the bottom and lie among the rocks. I pray to a God I rarely acknowledge that no one will ever see it again.

I sit atop the dry leaves on the bank, my back against the large boulder where I pass the time with James. The thought of him brings an uneasy turn of my stomach. It is clear that if he believes in the prophecy at all, it is only as legend. Certainly, my newly revealed role as Gate would be difficult for even the most imaginative person to accept, let alone one as reasoned as James.

I attempt to envision his reaction, assuming I can summon

the courage to tell him. I remind myself that we are more than promised. We are best friends. But in the confidence of his love I also feel a deep disquiet. A small voice that whispers, *What if he doesn't want you? What if he does not wish to marry such a strange person with such a strange role in such a strange tale? He will say his love is true, but he will never look at you with the same love and trust again.* I shake my head, denying it to no one but myself.

"Why do you shake your head, though you are all alone?" James's voice startles me, and I hold a hand to the front of my cloak.

"Goodness! What are you doing here? It's Sunday!" He has appeared, leaning against a tree across from the rock, as suddenly as if I had conjured him by thought alone.

He tilts his head, a teasing smile playing at his lips. "Can't I come to call, just for the pleasure of it?"

I am torn between my desire to see him and the increasing difficulty of keeping so many secrets. "Well . . . yes. Yes, of course. I simply didn't expect you."

He walks over, his boots crunching across the forest floor. "Father didn't need the carriage, and I couldn't wait until tomorrow to see you. I hoped I might find you here." He reaches a hand down toward me, and I take it, allowing him to pull me up and against him. When he speaks again his voice is low and rough. "Good morning."

I am embarrassed by the scrutiny of his eyes on my face, though surely he has looked at me in this manner a thousand times before. "Good morning." I dip my head, avoiding his

eyes and stepping away from the warmth of his body. "And how is your father?"

It is a silly question. Of course Mr. Douglas is fine, otherwise James would not be here with me. Still, it gives me a chance to wander away from him while trying not to seem as if I want to put distance between us.

But James knows me too well. He ignores my question, making his way to me in two long strides. "What is it? What's wrong?" He takes my hand, and I feel his eyes on my face as I stare at the swirling water. "Aren't you happy to see me?"

This is it. This is where you tell him. Tell him everything. Trust in his love. It is a persistent wind that whistles through my heart but one I ignore, though reason calls me a fool.

"Of course I am." I smile, digging deeply to make it as bright and carefree as possible. "I'm . . . I'm simply not feeling myself today, that's all. Perhaps I should retire to my chamber for the afternoon."

He is disappointed. Disappointed that I shall not spend the day with him when he has come all this way. "All right, then. I'll walk you back to the house and fetch the carriage from Edmund." He covers the wounded look in his eyes with a smile anyone would believe, if only they did not know James as well as I.

❦

James and I part in the courtyard after making our way back from the river amid strained conversation. He holds my hand as he begins to walk away, as if trying to keep me from slipping further from his grasp. I watch his carriage disappear around the bend in the drive before turning toward the house.

The small voice comes from behind me as I climb the stone steps on my way to the front door. "Miss? You've dropped something, Miss."

It is the young girl from town, the one who gave me my comb with the bracelet. She wears the same sky blue pinafore, her flaxen ringlets springing around her shoulders.

I look around, struck silent by the unlikelihood of the child turning up here, so far from town. There is no sign of an adult, no carriage or horse. I descend the stairs toward her, narrowing my eyes in suspicion. It was she, after all, who gave me the medallion in the first place, never mind the innocence of her face.

"I've not dropped anything. What is your name? How did you get here?"

She ignores the question, thrusting her small hand toward me, her fingers closed into a fist. "I'm quite certain it's yours, Miss. And I've come all this way." Her hand comes toward me so quickly that it is a reflex, really, opening my palm and taking the thing from her. She turns and skips down the tree-lined drive, humming the same tune that drifted after her in town.

It is only then that I feel the water. Water that leaks from my fingers in a torrent. My hand shakes violently when I open it to see what the girl has delivered.

It cannot be.

The medallion lies in my palm, black velvet coils made all

the blacker by the water that soaks them, pouring through my fingers and onto the stone stairs. The bracelet is more than damp. It is *dripping* with water, soaked through as if it was lifted from the river only a moment before.

I have to stop the girl.

The girl, the girl, the girl.

Running down the stairs, the hateful thing I do not want clutched in my hand, I enter the darkening pathway leading to the road. I run until I am deep within the path, the trees forming a shadowy canopy that rises on either side. I stand there far longer than makes sense, staring off in the direction I saw her skip, the wind an eerie whisper in the trees overhead. But it is no use. She is gone, as I somehow knew she would be.

"Is it very cold out?" Henry asks as I come into the entry, rubbing my hands together. He and Aunt Virginia are playing cards, the fire crackling in the firebox.

"Quite. I should think none of us will be spending much time by the river until spring." I hang my cloak, turning to them with a smile that I hope hides my unease. "Who's winning?"

Henry grins, triumphant. "I am, of course!"

"Of course? Oh, you little beast!" Aunt Virginia teases. She looks over at me. "Care to join us, Lia?"

"Not just now. I'm freezing. I think I'll change into warm clothes. After dinner, perhaps?"

Aunt Virginia nods absentmindedly.

I look around the parlor. "Where is Alice?"

"She said she was going to her chambers to rest," Aunt Virginia murmurs, studying her cards with great concentration.

I head to my room to look for a blanket, a deep disquiet settling into my chest. When I come to my room and see the figure, hunched and digging through the top drawer of my dresser, I understand.

"May I help you find something?" The coldness in my voice feels unfamiliar in my throat.

Alice whirls around. She stares at me, her face an impassive mask, weighing her words before speaking as she strolls casually toward me. "No, thank you. I was looking for the brooch I lent you last summer." She stops in front of me, unable to leave the room as I stand in the doorway.

"I gave it back to you, Alice. Before school resumed in the fall."

Her smile is small and hard. "That's right. I'd forgotten." She tips her head to the door. "Excuse me."

I wait a moment, relishing her discomfort, the way she squirms under *my* gaze for once. Finally, I step aside, allowing her to pass without another word.

A half hour later, I am sitting at the writing table in my room. I have wrapped a blanket around my shoulders to stave off the chill as I brood over Alice's intentions.

The book was still in the wardrobe where I last hid it. It was not hidden so carefully that Alice couldn't have found it with a thorough search. I can only assume that she either hadn't time to search the wardrobe or that she found the book but has no use for it.

The medallion was with me all along, though I tried mightily to get rid of it. In any case, it is clear now that it will not release its hold on me so easily. With all that Alice seems to know, it is difficult to believe she doesn't realize this, if she is aware of its existence at all.

But if she was not looking for the book, and she was not looking for the medallion, what else is there?

I lower my eyes to the book, open on the table in front of me. The prophecy is so familiar that I could recite it from memory, and yet I wonder if reading it again might bring me to the thing I'm missing. I hear Father's voice, as clearly as if he is sitting beside me, saying something he so often said.

Sometimes you cannot see the forest for the trees.

Such a silly saying — a cliché, really. But I try to open my mind, to reread the prophecy as if reading it for the very first time.

At first, it is just as I remember. It is only when I come to the mention of the keys that the spark of discovery causes my breath to catch in my throat.

The keys. Alice thinks I have the keys.

The knowledge that she is searching for the keys brings me an odd kind of comfort, for it can only mean that she has not yet found them. That there is still time for me to find them first.

The door eases open with a creak, shaking me from my thoughts. I turn to find Ivy carrying a tray toward me.

"There you are, Miss. Nothing like a hot cup of tea to warm you on a cold day such as this." She places the tea on the writing table, standing awkwardly by my elbow.

For a moment, I don't understand why she has brought tea to my room unbidden or why she is standing near my chair as if expecting something more. But then I see the small piece of paper peeking from beneath the cup and saucer.

"What is this?" I turn to look at her.

She shifts from foot to foot, twisting her apron and avoiding my eyes. "It . . . It's a message, Miss. From town."

My surprise is such that I don't do the obvious thing, the simplest thing, which is simply to pick up the piece of paper and see what kind of message it holds. Instead, I ask. "A message? From whom?"

She leans in, looking around as if someone might be listening. I see from the shine in her eyes that she quite likes the bit of mystery. "From a friend of mine. A maid in the house of that girl. The strange one."

❦

Aunt Virginia is meeting with Cook and Margaret to plan next week's Thanksgiving dinner while Henry takes an afternoon rest. It is as good a time as any to make my escape in response to Sonia's message.

Edmund is in the carriage house, watching a young boy as

he polishes one of the carriages. The boy doesn't notice me, but Edmund looks up as I enter.

"Miss Amalia! Is something the matter?" I have not been to the carriage house since Alice and I were small and used it as a hiding place for hide-and-seek.

I come closer, turning my back to the boy. "I need to be taken into town, Edmund. Alone. I would not ask, except it is . . . it is important."

His gaze holds mine, and for one terrible moment I think he will refuse. For one terrible moment I think I will have to remind him that Aunt Virginia is only a guardian, that it is Alice and Henry and I who are masters of Birchwood. Thankfully, he spares me the humiliation of resorting to such a spectacle.

"All right, then. We'll take the other carriage. It's behind the stables." He turns around and heads out the door, mumbling as he goes. "Your Aunt Virginia will have my head on a platter."

14

I look at the piece of paper Ivy passed to me with my tea. I don't know what Sonia has in store, but I shall have to return the favor of trust that she has shown me. Her writing is as neat and straight as a child's.

Dearest Lia,

I have located someone who might help us in our journey. Please trust me, and come to 778 York Street at one o'clock in the afternoon.

S.S.

I have already given Edmund the address, and gather from his subsequent snort that we are not traveling to a part of town he deems appropriate. Nevertheless, he does not question me further, and I want to kiss him for his steadfast loyalty.

The carriage rumbles toward town in a series of harsh bounces and jolts across the hard-packed road. We have not had a good rain since the day following Father's funeral nine days before. I think it befitting, as if God has used all his tears on the just cause of my father's death. Even still, the lack of rain has been much discussed among the servants. They cluck their tongues and shake their heads, arguing about whether it means an especially cold winter or one especially warm.

We pass through the familiar part of town in a blink. Past Wycliffe, the bookstore, the fashionable inns and restaurants, the sweet shop, Sonia's house. It is not long before Edmund turns the horses down a quiet lane hidden behind the clean and bustling streets.

The lane is dark, shaded on all sides by the tenement buildings that house the less fortunate. Through the window of the carriage, I see laundry swinging on clotheslines strung above the litter-strewn lane. The ride becomes bumpier, the ground further parched, as if even the water does not want to stay long here. I am beginning to feel green about the edges when Edmund finally pulls the horses to a stop with a soft, "Whoa, boys."

Looking out the window, I cannot fathom a reason why Sonia should ask me to meet her at such a place, but Edmund is at the door, opening it wide before I can think further about the wisdom in coming.

"Are you certain you'd like to stop here, Miss?"

I step from the carriage, determined to see my journey through. Ours is not a quest for cowards. "Yes. Most certain, Edmund."

Edmund holds his hat while we wait for Sonia. Two small boys kick a large rock down the lane. They make a racket, but their playful laugh is a welcome distraction from the silence of the deserted street.

"Which one is it?" I ask Edmund.

He nods toward a narrow doorway a few feet from the carriage. "That one there."

I am beginning to wonder if I've made a mistake when Sonia rushes around the corner, breathless and pink at the cheeks. "Oh goodness! I'm sorry to be late! It's ever so hard to escape Mrs. Millburn's eye! She books me for so many sittings, I barely have time to breathe!"

"It's quite all right, Sonia, but . . . whatever are we doing here?"

She stands for a moment, her hand on her chest as she attempts to catch her breath. "I asked around, carefully, mind you, and found someone who might have some answers to . . ." She eyes Edmund cautiously. "Well, to the things we've been discussing."

Edmund does not look amused.

I nod. "All right."

Sonia takes my hand, leading me to the dark doorway ahead. "I've thought and thought about the prophecy, but it makes no more sense to me now than it did when you first showed me the book. I thought we could do with some help.

It was not easy to find such a person. But if anyone will assist us in finding answers, it will be Madame Berrier."

The name itself is mysterious, but I follow Sonia to a nondescript door. She raises her hand and knocks, and the door is opened a moment later by a svelte, fashionable woman.

"Good afternoon. Please do come in." The woman is obviously French but with the hint of a more exotic accent that I cannot quite place. She ushers us into a cramped foyer. Her eyes focus on something over my shoulder, and it is only when I follow her gaze that I realize Edmund has not stayed at the carriage. She looks at him appraisingly, her eyes flickering with interest over his strong face.

I turn to him. "Edmund, would you mind waiting here while we speak in private?"

He considers this thoughtfully, rubbing the coarse stubble along his jaw.

"We shall be right here in this very apartment."

His nod is small, but he folds his large frame onto a small bench set against one wall.

"Follow me." Madame Berrier leads us down a narrow hallway with doors on either side.

"Thank you, Madame, for seeing us on such short notice. I know how very busy you are." Sonia's voice echoes through the shadows of the dimly lit hallway. She turns to me as we walk. "Madame Berrier is one of the most sought-after spiritualists in New York. Some of her customers come from hundreds of miles to get a reading."

I smile as if I have always had a friend who is a spiritualist,

as if I am accustomed to meeting in the back lanes of town those with dark and questionable powers.

Madame Berrier's voice is muted as she speaks ahead of us. "You are most welcome. You have powerful gifts of your own, my dear. It is only right that we should help one another, yes? Besides, it is not often I have the opportunity to speak of the Prophecy of the Sisters."

"The Prophecy of the Sisters?" I mouth the words back to Sonia as Madame Berrier ushers us through an elegant apartment that belies its decrepit-looking exterior.

Sonia shrugs, following the older woman into a well-appointed parlor.

"Please sit down." Madame Berrier waves us toward a red velvet settee as she sits in a carved chair opposite. Between us is a small wooden table that glows with the warmth of a well-polished apple. It is set with a silver pot, delicate porcelain cups and saucers, and a small plate of cookies. "Would you like some coffee? Or do you take tea in the tradition of the British?"

"Coffee, please." My voice emerges firmer than I expect under the circumstances.

She nods, reaching for the pot on the table with a smile something like approval. "And for you?" she asks Sonia.

"Oh no. Nothing for me, thank you. It sometimes interferes with my sittings."

Madame Berrier nods, placing the pot back on the silver tray. "Yes, the coffee and tea did the same for me when I was younger and more sensitive to external stimuli. I would wager

these things will bother you less and less as you grow more sure in your powers, dear."

Sonia nods, and I see her struggling against the words she wants to say.

Madame Berrier saves her the trouble. "Sonia tells me that you find yourself in an . . . unusual situation, Miss Milthorpe."

I don't answer right away, feeling unsure confessing to a stranger the things I have worked so mightily to keep secret. But in the end, I nod, for what purpose is there in trying to find answers if I'll not speak to those who might give them?

"May I see your hand?" She holds her own across the table with such authority that hesitating does not seem an option.

I proffer my hand over the coffee and sugar.

Pulling up the sleeve of my gown, she eyes the mark coolly before releasing my hand. "Hmmm . . . Quite interesting. Quite interesting indeed. I have seen it before, of course. In the tales of the prophecy, and on the chosen few who play a part. But never one quite like this. It is most unusual." She nods. "But of course, it is to be expected."

Her last words take me by surprise. "Why . . . Why is it to be expected?"

She places her cup back into the saucer with a *clink*. "Because the prophecy dictates it, my dear! The prophecy *promises* it!"

I shake my head, feeling dimmer than ever. "I'm most sorry, Madame. I'm afraid I don't understand."

She tilts her head, as if trying to gauge my ignorance as crafty deception or the more simple variety of stupidity. At last she leans in, speaking in a low and urgent voice. "The

Souls are helpless without Samael. They have been amassing an army for centuries, but the prophecy dictates that they can do nothing to bring about the Doom of Gods without the leadership of Samael, the Beast. And there is only one who can summon him. Only one who will carry the singular mark of that authority." She pauses, meeting my eyes with both reverence and perhaps the smallest slice of fear. "Clearly that one is you. You, my dear, are the Angel. The Angel of Chaos."

Through the haze of shock, the realization is a primordial chant, a drumbeat that begins as a flutter in my bones before spreading its wings through my body. I cannot speak around it, around the dawning apprehension. It has been difficult enough to accept my role as Gate. What can this new assignation mean for my place in the prophecy?

"But . . . I thought Lia was the Guardian? She is, is she not?" Sonia's voice comes as if through a tunnel, and I remember that there has not been time to tell her of my discovery that I am the Gate.

Surprise shades Madame Berrier's eyes. "*Mais, non!* There is no other with this mark, not one such as this! It names your friend as the Gate, and not just any Gate, but the Angel, the one Gate with the power to summon Samael. The one Gate with the choice to bring him forth or destroy him forever."

"But . . . Lia?" Sonia turns to me, pleading for a truth that I wish I did not have to give her. "Is this true?"

I inspect my hands in my lap as if they somehow hold the answer to Sonia's question. But only I hold the answer she must hear, and I raise my eyes to hers, nodding.

"Yes." It is a whisper. "I haven't had the time to tell you. I just found out last night, and I didn't know I was the Angel until this very moment."

Madame Berrier is aghast, and when she turns her eyes to me I see that they are so black as to be nearly without color. "You did not *realize* your place? Your mother does not teach you the ways of the prophecy, of your place in it? Did she not once hold a role of her own?"

Sonia murmurs next to me as if thinking aloud, her voice soft and without emotion. "Her mother passed, Madame, when she was but a child. And her father, too, more recently."

The older woman's eyes widen, her gaze not without pity. "Ah, that would explain it, then, for it is left to the older and wiser sisters of the prophecy to ensure their daughters' education in its ways. And your father passed recently as well?" Her voice is a low purr, the question asked more to herself than to me. "Well. There you are, then. You have lost your protection. You have lost the veil."

The words in the book come back to me, twisting softly through my memory like smoke. *Guarded only by the gossamer veil of protection.*

"The veil?" My voice cracks with the words.

She finally loses her patience, throwing her hands into the air as if in surrender. "Do you face the prophecy with no knowledge at all? How are you to do battle if you do not know your enemy? If you do not know the weapons at your disposal?" She sighs deeply. "It is foretold that the Angel will be given a protector. An earthly protector, but a protector nonetheless. Otherwise, the Angel would be helpless, and Samael would find his way through her before she was old enough to harness her power. Before she was old enough to make a choice. And everyone has a choice, my dear, as was dictated at the beginning of time. It is through the protection of the veil that the Gate may grow old enough to make her choice. As long as that protector is alive, the Beast cannot come for you. When did your father pass, dear girl?"

"A-About two weeks ago."

"And were the circumstances of his death . . . *unusual?*"

"Yes." It is a whisper.

She dabs at the corners of her mouth with her napkin. "I am most sorry. The prophecy is a burden for the most educated and prepared in the Sisterhood. For one so adrift as you . . . for one with your role . . . well, it must be quite overwhelming. I shall fill in as much as possible. Let us begin with your father. With his death."

My throat closes at the mention of my father. "What does that have to do with the prophecy?"

"Everything," she says simply. "The Souls have been waiting for centuries to return to our world. You are their Angel, the one with the power to make it so or banish them forever. Make no mistake, they will stop at nothing to get to you."

I want to laugh at the absurdity of the implication. But then I think of Father's face in death. The open eyes. The unfamiliar grimace on a face that was too horrified to be his. I think of these things and am filled with an all-consuming sadness that grows to something more like anger and a disbelief that is not altogether disbelieving.

When I look up at Madame Berrier, my words are no longer a question, but a truth. "He was killed by the Souls. He was killed because of me."

She shakes her head sadly. "You needn't feel responsible for your father's death, Miss Milthorpe. No protector acts as the veil unwillingly. To accept such a role, he must have loved you very much, dear. He, too, made choices." Madame Berrier's voice is as soothing as a mother's. "It is a wonder they did not take him sooner. To resist them for so long . . . well, he must have been a very strong man and quite determined to protect you."

I shake my head, trying to get my mind around the truth of my father's death. "But he didn't travel the Plane. He never spoke of it to me, and he would have, if he had known."

Madame Berrier considers this for a moment, nodding curtly. "Perhaps. But the Souls are crafty, child, and Samael immeasurably more so. It is possible that the Souls enticed him just that once with something of great significance. Something he dearly loved."

With those words, the Dark Room flashes in my mind.

And now I know. I know how they enticed him to travel. "My mother."

15

When she speaks, her voice holds no surprise, the questions not really questions at all.

"Would he not have succumbed to the call of seeing her face, to the possibility of hearing her voice? Especially if he were worried about his daughter, about her role in the prophecy of which few men have heard and even fewer believe?"

I see the door of the Dark Room the day of my father's death, cold air leaking from the abandoned chambers in the thin light of morning.

The Dark Room. My mother's room.

I remember my effortless travels, how easily I slipped into them, unaware that they were something more than simple dreams.

"He didn't know." I murmur. "He didn't know he was

traveling. He didn't know that he would be vulnerable to the spirits in the Otherworlds."

She nods. "It is easy enough to answer the call of the spirits under guise of a pleasant dream, and the Souls had every reason to detain your Father's soul, to set him adrift in the Otherworlds."

The tide of anguish that rises on my next thought threatens to push me under. "Are you . . . are you saying his soul is in the Void?"

She lifts her chin, studying the ceiling as if the words she needs can be found on the plaster overhead. "Miss Sorrensen mentioned receiving a message from your father at one of her sittings."

The memory of that first mystifying altercation with Sonia makes me shift uncomfortably in the settee. "Yes. That is, I think so," I tell her. "I didn't hear it, actually. It was passed to me by Sonia."

Madame Berrier smiles her encouragement. "Miss Sorrensen has a formidable gift. If she says the message was from him, it likely was. And if it was, it means that he somehow managed to escape the Void." She shrugs. "It is possible. There are those in the Otherworlds with power enough to aid one in escaping the Void, though they would put themselves in danger to do so. Your mother perhaps?"

Something Aunt Virginia said drifts like smoke into my mind. "My aunt said my mother was a . . . a Spellcaster?"

Madame Berrier nods. "Ah. Then she may well have intervened on his behalf. There are very few true Spellcasters. A

Spellcaster would almost certainly be powerful enough to stage an intervention. His soul would still be stranded in the Otherworlds, but he would be free to wander there or cross if he chose."

As painful as it is to imagine my father's soul adrift in the Otherworlds, I am grateful for any intervention that allowed him to escape the Void, especially if it reunited him with my mother.

It is Sonia, looking at Madame Berrier with a small measure of hope, who asks the question I should have been asking all along. "You said there is a choice, Madame, that Lia has a choice."

"But of course. Miss Milthorpe has choices to make just as the rest of us do, though they are undoubtedly quite a bit more complicated and dangerous. She may choose to open the Gate to the Beast or she may choose to close it forever, as is her right as the Angel." She leans closer, her smile hidden behind a trace of irony. "I, for one, sincerely hope she chooses the latter."

I shake my head. It is difficult to imagine that anyone would choose to allow entry to the Beast. "Well, there is no question at all! I choose to close it, of course! But I know nothing of the prophecy save what we have read."

Sonia clears her throat. "It is for this reason we have come, Madame. We have heard there is a way to end the prophecy. A way to close the Gate forever. There is a reference to keys, you see. We think they may be the way to an end, but we aren't sure where to find them or even where to begin looking."

Madame Berrier considers Sonia's words. "Well, there *is* rumor of a way for the Angel to close the Gate forever, but I've never been privy to the prophecy itself. Very few have ever laid eyes on the ancient text, and those that have are most assuredly connected to it in some way."

Sonia raises her eyebrows. "Well, we have, Madame. And in it is the mention of keys, together with something else, something that rings familiar but which I cannot place. Something called Samhain."

Madame Berrier purses her lips. I can see the wheels turning in her mind, and when she speaks it is not with an answer but a question. "In what context is Samhain mentioned in relation to the keys?"

Sonia licks her lips, trying to remember. "Something about the first breath . . . the —"

" 'Formed in the first breath of Samhain.' " I meet Madame Berrier's gaze. "That is what it says. 'Four marks, Four keys, Circle of Fire, Formed in the first breath of Samhain.' "

She taps her fingers on the table, considering her words. "Let us take a stroll, hmm? I believe I know where to find some of the answer you seek."

❦

The streets are crowded, bustling with people. Horses clop past, the carriages they pull rattling on the dusty road. Edmund, ever vigilant, follows us without a word.

We walk for some time, and I wonder at Madame Berrier's strange authority that we follow her so willingly, without a single question about our destination. She is so sure-footed, so purposeful in her stride that it seems almost insulting to inquire, and so we follow along, trotting to keep up with her swift pace.

It is only after we have passed the tailor, the milliner, the sweet shop, and a number of taverns that Madame Berrier turns a corner, leading us down a quieter back lane. Narrow houses stand on either side of the street like somber watchmen. They are not as grand as the homes on Main Street but simple and well-kept, much like Madame Berrier herself. We approach a house that looks like all the others, but I see from a plaque on its front that it is the town library.

"The word you mentioned rings familiar, my dear," Madame Berrier says, looking over at Sonia. "But with so many translations and pronunciations, it is best to be sure, especially with something so important, is it not?" She doesn't wait for an answer, but continues her steady march up the front steps, opening the door with a flourish.

Stepping into the cavernous main hall, I find the library is more than quiet, it is deserted. Indeed, I don't see a single person as we make our way across the scuffed marble floor. Its emptiness is more than the lack of living, breathing beings. It is the unread pages of the many books that reside on the shelves throughout the room. I should not have thought one could tell when books have gone unread, but after the company of Birchwood's well-loved library it is as if I can hear these books whispering, their pages grasping and reaching for an audience.

Madame Berrier stops at a large desk in the center of the main room, casting a meaningful glance at Edmund before turning to me, eyebrows raised in question.

I breathe deeply. "Edmund, would you mind looking around or waiting here, or . . . something?"

I feel badly asking him to occupy himself yet again, but it is clear from Madame Berrier's demeanor that she means our visit to the library to be a private one. Edmund does not seem to mind. He nods, wandering to one of the many tall shelves and disappearing around its corner.

We scan the library for any sign of life. There are smaller rooms visible on both sides of the main hall and a narrow staircase that winds to the floor above.

"Perhaps we should —" I am interrupted by the heavy click of shoes approaching from one of the rooms at the back.

The woman who approaches carries a smile of welcome. But only for a moment. The minute her eyes light on Madame Berrier, her round face tightens, her mouth setting into a grim line.

Madame Berrier's smile is dazzling. "Bonjour, Mrs. Harding! And how are you this fine afternoon?"

Surely Madame Berrier can see the distaste with which the town librarian views her, but there is nothing in her manner to acknowledge such a truth. Instead, she greets the other woman as if they are long-lost friends.

The woman called Mrs. Harding nods her head in a minute gesture of acknowledgment. "How may I help you?" She asks

as if she has never seen Madame Berrier before this day, though it is clear they have had some dealings in the past.

"Now, Mrs. Harding," Madame Berrier teases, leaning her head to one side, a playful smile touching her painted lips as she holds out an open palm, "I'm quite certain you know why I have come."

Mrs. Harding's face sets even further. She reaches into her pocket, withdrawing something from it and dropping it into Madame Berrier's hand. The Madame's fingers close quickly around it, but not before I see a glint of silver and realize it is a key.

"Merci, Mrs. Harding. I shall return it when I am finished, as always!" Madame Berrier calls over her shoulder, already making her way to the back of the library.

Sonia and I are spurred from our reverie by a scowl from the librarian directed, this time, at us. We rush forward to catch up to Madame Berrier, already halfway down the hall leading toward the back of the building. When we finally reach her, she has opened the back door of the library and is standing outside on a small porch.

Sonia shakes her head in confusion. "Where are we going?"

Madame Berrier waves to the well-groomed garden behind the library. "The answer you seek, my dear, lies not in the carefully catalogued books within the library but in those cast aside, hidden in shame behind it."

There is no time for further questions. Madame Berrier steps off the porch, and we scramble to follow as she leads us through the manicured garden, beautiful even with the approaching winter. I think we have come to the end of the property when we step around a potting shed that, for all its diminutive size, is still better kept than the decrepit building to which Madame Berrier crosses.

She takes the key given her by Mrs. Harding and inserts it into the lock hanging from the door. It catches with a click, and Madame Berrier pulls open the doors with a great heave and creak. We follow her in, our eyes drawn upward.

"Oh! It is . . . it is unbelievable!" I cannot keep the amazement from my voice, but there is sadness, too. Father would have wept to see the books piled high in every direction with so little thought to their care. "What is this place?"

The ceiling soars three stories above us. Even from the ground, I see small holes in the roof. It is clear from the damp smell permeating the building that no one minds the rain leaking onto the books within these walls.

Madame Berrier's neck is stretched, taut and white as a swan, as she surveys the room with equal awe, as if, even knowing what it holds, she cannot help but be impressed. "It is an old carriage house. It was used when the library was still a home."

"Yes, but . . . all these books! Why aren't they catalogued and kept with the others?" It is a question my father would have asked, though with a good deal more anger, I'm sure.

She smiles sadly at us. "These are the books the town does not want sitting in full view beside the more . . . traditional offerings. They cannot destroy them altogether, you see. That would not be good for appearances. But they can, and as you see, do, keep them separate from the others."

Sonia's eyes shine in the dim light of the carriage house. "But why?"

Madame Berrier sighs. "Because these are the books about things people do not understand, things you and I know are as real as the world in which we stand this very minute. Books on the spirit world, on witchcraft and the history of it, sorcery . . . anything that does not fit into a neat and tidy box, I should say." She walks farther into the room, startling a bird that rises toward the ceiling, disappearing in a flutter of wings somewhere above us.

The sudden movement shakes loose my awe. "I don't understand what this place has to do with the keys, Madame, though I must confess to being quite astonished at the sight. My father would have had a conniption!"

She meets my eyes, smiling. "Then I'm quite sure I would have been very fond of your father, dear girl." She gestures for us to follow. "As to your question, I think there may be a reference to Samhain in an old Druid text I have seen lying about. As far as I know, I am the only one who comes here. I'm quite sure it will be just where I remember it."

Sonia and I follow her farther into the building, past stacks of books streaked with bird droppings and mildew. We step carefully over anything we cannot identify and almost bump into Madame Berrier when she stops at one of the warped and leaning bookcases.

"Let me see . . . I think it was near here. This may be it. . . ."

No. Not that one. Perhaps it was over here." She mutters to herself as if we are not present, crossing to different shelves several times as we look helplessly on. "Ah! Here it is. Let me have a look."

Balancing the book in one hand, she turns the pages with the other. It is an incongruous site — the elegant Madame looking entirely at home surrounded by such filth and disrepair. I flash Sonia a nervous smile, afraid to interrupt whatever thought process seems to go along with the Madame's muttering.

"Ah! Yes, yes! I knew it! Here it is! Come closer, girls, and we shall see if this might be of help." We shuffle closer, stopping as she begins to read. "Since twenty-three hundred B.C. the Beltain Fires have signified the beginning of Light, that joyful season when the days shall be full of plenty and the nights full of passion and new life. The Season of Light, or Beltain, begins on May first and lasts for six months until Samhain, the Season of Darkness. Following the harvest and Celebration of Light comes a time of Darkness, that sorrowful season when night reigns and darkness rules the land, and when the veil between the physical world and the Otherworld is thinnest and most transparent. Samhain and the time of Darkness begin each November first." Her words echo through the carriage house. They inspire a kind of reverence, and we stand silently for a moment, side by side, before Madame Berrier lifts her eyes from the book and speaks. "Does it mean anything to you? Could it be a clue to the keys you seek?"

I shake my head. "I don't think so. It means nothing to me. Nothing at all. I —"

"It's my birthday." Sonia's voice is a whisper. "At least, that is what Mrs. Millburn tells me."

Her words do nothing to clarify my thinking. "What do you mean? Your birthday is November first?"

She nods. "November first, eighteen seventy-four."

Madame Berrier looks as puzzled as I feel. "Might it be a coincidence?"

Chewing my lip, I wonder if she is right. I drop onto a be-draggled stool, ignoring the plume of dust that rises from its seat as I try to push down a tide of anguish. All of this and we have found next to nothing.

"Do not despair, Lia. We shall figure this out, you'll see." Sonia's voice is calm and reassuring, and I wonder how she can always be optimistic when I should like to throw something at the walls and scream.

I look up at her. "But we still don't know where to find the keys. The date . . . Well, that November first is your birthday is interesting, but it doesn't tell us a single thing about the keys. I had hoped . . ."

"What, dear girl?" Madame Berrier is still holding the book, looking down at me with sympathy.

"I don't know. I suppose I had hoped Samhain was a land-mark of some kind, a city or town or something. I hoped it would lead us clearly to the keys."

I am ashamed to feel tears burn the backs of my eyelids.

They are not tears of sadness, but of frustration, and I blink rapidly, inhaling the dusty air and trying to compose myself.

"All right," Sonia says, "we shall simply file this bit away for now, that's all. The reference to Samhain clearly refers to a date. Perhaps that will be important later. There's still the next bit, is there not?"

I nod, pulling James's notes from my bag and peering at them in the dim light of the old building. "Yes. All right, then. Let me see . . . here it is: *'Birthed in the first breath of Samhain, In the shadow of the Mystic Stone Serpent of Aubur.'*" I look up at Madame Berrier.

She holds out a hand. "May I?"

I hesitate. My shock at realizing first I was the Gate and now the Angel has made me feel that no one is what they seem. Certainly not Alice or I. And not Father, either, working all those years to protect me while I remained ignorant. Even still, Madame Berrier has tried to help us, and it is obvious we must widen our circle if we are to have a chance of finding the keys.

I hand over the notes. "Perhaps it will make sense to you."

She lowers her head, the proximity with which she holds the paper to her face making me wonder if she is nearsighted. She reads for a moment, eyebrows knitted together in concentration, before handing the notes back to me across the darkness.

"I am most sorry, but . . . I'm not sure. That is, it sounds rather familiar, but only in the sound of the word itself, not with any sort of recognition."

Sonia shakes her head. "What do you mean?"

Madame Berrier sighs. "'Aubur' sounds English, or . . . perhaps Celtic. But I don't recognize it as the name of a town or place." She brings her other hand to her mouth, tapping there as if this will bring to mind the answers we seek. "Let me ponder it a bit." She moves past us toward the door. "And let us leave this place. We have been thinking too long and hard on the prophecy. I should like to get back into the sunlight, away from the shadows of the past and the things yet to come."

❧

We stop in front of Madame Berrier's building before leaving. A biting wind lifts her hat, and she places a hand on top of it to keep it in place, glancing at Edmund a few feet away before speaking.

"There is one thing I feel I should say. . . ."

I swallow the apprehension that rises in my throat. "What is it?"

"If what I have heard is true, the simplest thing you can do to protect yourself from the Souls is to guard against wearing the amulet." Her words are said with such nonchalance that they take me off guard.

"The amulet?"

Madame Berrier gestures with one hand, as if it is obvious to what she is referring. "The amulet. The bracelet. The medallion. The one with the mark."

My gaze slides to Sonia. I have not made a point of telling

her about the medallion because I knew not its place in the prophecy.

"The medallion?" I try not to betray any emotion. "What of it?"

"What of it indeed!" Madame Berrier is aghast. "My dear, it is said that every Gate comes into possession of a medallion, a medallion that matches perfectly the mark on her wrist. The Souls can make their way back only when the mark on the medallion is aligned with the mark on the Gate. But for you . . . well, for you the medallion is even more dangerous. You are the conduit for Samael himself. The small protection you have is to shun the medallion, avoid wearing it, though even this may not be enough."

Her words are not the surprise they should be. I knew instinctively that the medallion was in some way connected to the pathway back for Samael. Still, this new proof brings forth a question that has teased the darkest parts of my mind. One I have not dared speak aloud until now.

"There is something I don't understand, Madame. Even if I were to wear the medallion, how might Samael pass into our world? He is but a spirit thing, is he not? An empty soul. How would he move in our world without a body?"

"That, my dear girl, is rather simple." Madame Berrier presses her lips into a grim line before continuing. "He will use yours."

16

I cannot keep the disbelief from my voice . . . "What you say is mad! What havoc might a thing wreak in the body of a young girl?"

Madame Berrier eyes me solemnly.

"Once here the Beast and his Army may change into any form they desire. It might be a man, a demon, an animal, even a simple shadow. But you . . . well, once your body has been occupied by the spirit of the Beast, the astral chord will be severed. And your body lost to you forever."

☙

"I'm sorry, Sonia. I didn't . . . I truly didn't know until just last evening."

Sonia does not answer as Edmund navigates the street toward her residence. Her silence plants seeds of fear in my belly. Fear that she will no longer be my ally, my friend, for who would align themselves with someone like me?

"If you and Luisa wish to work together, I shall understand."

She turns to me. "Do you feel yourself the Gate? Do you feel anything . . . untoward?"

My face feels warm, and I am glad she cannot see me clearly in the darkening carriage lest she should take my blushing cheeks as a sign of guilt. "In truth, I feel like myself most of the time, though a good deal more confused and uncertain."

But Sonia is trained to listen for the nuances of a thing, and my words are not lost to her ears. "Most of the time?" she prods gently.

"There are times . . . not many, but some, when I feel the pull of . . . something. Oh, it's so difficult to explain! It isn't that I find myself on the verge of committing some terrible act, it is only . . . well, it is only that I sometimes feel a connection to the medallion. I sometimes feel the call of it. Of wanting to wear it. Of wanting to fall into sleep and the travel I know it will bring. And then . . ."

"And then?"

"Then I come to my senses, quickly, and remember that it is my call to fight it."

"And you remember this even now? Now that you know it is *not* your call? That you are not the Guardian but the Gate?"

"Now more than ever." I find comfort in the certainty of my belief.

She nods before turning her face to the window for the rest of the ride.

When we come to the house of Mrs. Millburn, I step out of the carriage and stand next to Sonia on the walk while Edmund anxiously looks on, tapping his foot in a not-so-subtle reference to the passing time. The people streaming past us seem strangely ominous, perhaps even dangerous, and I hear Madame Berrier's words in my mind; *the Beast and his Army may change into any form they desire . . . a simple man, a demon, an animal, perhaps even a simple shadow.* There are likely thousands of Souls already in our world from previous Gates. And they could be anywhere. Everywhere. All waiting for one moment of weakness from me.

Sonia takes my hands in hers. "There is a reason you were chosen to be the Angel, Lia. If the power of the prophecy deems you fit to make such a decision, why shouldn't I feel the same?" Her smile is small but true. "We shall stick together. It is our best hope of finding the answers we need. Luisa shall have to speak for herself, but I am with you."

"Thank you, Sonia. I will not disappoint you. I promise." I reach over and embrace her, overcome with gratitude at the show of her friendship.

She shivers, wrapping her arms around her shoulders as the cold of evening approaches ever faster.

I think about the children, the ones that Father brought from England and Italy and the others not yet found. "Oh, there are so very many things to discuss! And no time! No time at all, with Luisa at Wycliffe and you here with Mrs.

Millburn and me at Birchwood and the coming..." My thought hangs, unfinished, as an idea begins to take shape.

"The coming what? Goodness, Lia! I shall freeze if we do not say goodbye soon!"

I nod, coming to a decision. "The three of us must have more time together. That is what it comes to, isn't it? Leave it to me. I shall take care of everything."

❦

Sonia and I have said our goodbyes, and I am halfway back to the carriage when I feel a hand on my arm. "Oh, pardon me, but do please —" The rest of the words escape me when I turn to shake myself loose and find myself looking straight into James's face.

"Lia," he says, his eyes colored with something I have never seen before. Something too close to anger to be called anything else.

"James! What are you . . . ?" I look around the street, stalling for an explanation for my presence in town. "What are you doing here?"

"I happen to live in town. In fact, it's quite unusual for a day to pass when I do *not* have to stroll the streets for one reason or another." His eyes flash. "You, on the other hand, live some distance."

His words set a quiet fury boiling in my veins, and I feel anew the pressure of his fingers, still on my wrist. Pulling my arm away takes effort, but I do it. I pull it away and step back, feeling the anger burn hot on my cheeks.

"Shall I stay home like a proper girl, then? Is that what you'd like? Shall I take up the needle and worry over taking too much sun? Oh, you are just . . . just . . . Ugh!"

Anger matching my own flashes in his eyes. But it is only a moment before he shakes his head and lowers his eyes to the walk under our feet. "Of course not, Lia. Of course not."

He is quiet for a moment, and my eyes drift to Edmund. Were my public altercation with anyone other than James, Edmund would have seen me to the carriage long ago. But now when our eyes meet, he drops his to the ground in embarrassment. James's voice, softer now, pulls my thoughts away from Edmund.

"Can't you understand my concern? You remain . . . distant after your father's death. I know it is a blow, but I cannot help but feel something else lies between us. And now . . . well, now you are wandering around town, unchaperoned, with people I don't know, and —"

My mouth falls open in shock. "You've been following me? You've followed me through the streets of town?"

He shakes his head. "It isn't like that. I was in the library myself when I saw you leaving. I've never seen the woman and girl whom you were with. You've mentioned no such new acquaintances to me. I didn't think, all right? I simply started to follow you, carried along by own curiosity and . . . well, I suppose my own worry over your strange behavior of late. Can you not understand why I might feel compelled to do so?"

I am stung by his words. I hear the pain in them and cannot

refute the things he says. I have held him at bay, kept him outside the prophecy even as I have been pulled deeper and deeper into its depths. Would I not feel the same worry? Would I not want to find out everything possible to explain such behavior on the part of my beloved?

I take a deep breath, and all the anger leaves me. I wish it would not, for I prefer the blood-pounding fury to this new emotion. This hopelessness that only seems to grow in its insistency that I will never find a way to reconcile my place in the prophecy, my duty to it, with my love for James.

I take his hand and look into his eyes. "You're right, of course. I'm sorry, James."

He shakes his head in frustration. It is not my apology he seeks. "Why won't you talk to me? Don't you still care for me?"

"Of course, James. That will never change. This . . ." I wave a hand at the street. "This outing has nothing whatsoever to do with you or with my love for you." I try a smile. It feels strange on my face, as if I am wearing it and it does not quite fit, but it is the best I can do. I make a quick decision to stick as closely to the truth as possible. "I simply snuck out with a friend of mine from Wycliffe, that is all. She is acquainted with a woman well versed in matters of witchcraft, and —"

"Witchcraft?" He raises his eyebrows.

"Oh, it's nothing!" I dismiss his curiosity with a shake of my head. "Won't you believe me? I was simply curious and Sonia's

friend offered to show us some books on the matter, that is all." I look back at Edmund, who flips open his pocket watch while looking pointedly at me. "And now I *must* go or Aunt Virginia shall discover I've been gone and then a short trip to town that was meant to be a bit of fun shall turn into a heap of trouble."

He stares into my eyes, and I know he is trying to see whether or not there is truth to my story. I hold his gaze until he nods slowly as if in acceptance. But as we say our goodbyes and I make my way to the carriage, I know it is not understanding but defeat that I saw in the blue of his eyes.

❧

I sit in the parlor, reading next to Henry, when Margaret's voice comes to me from the doorway. "Something has arrived for you, Miss."

I rise to meet her. "For me?"

She nods, holding out a creamy envelope. "It came by messenger just a moment ago."

I take it from her, waiting until the sound of her footsteps fade down the hall. "What is it, Lia?" Henry looks up at me from his book.

Shaking my head, I return to my chair by the fire and open the envelope. "I don't know."

I withdraw the stiff paper from inside, noting the handwriting, practiced and elegant, that slants across its pristine surface.

Dear Miss Milthorpe,

I believe I know someone who may be of help to you.

Alastair Wigan
Lerwick Farm

You may trust him as you trust me.
He will be expecting you.

Mme. Berrier

"Whom is it from?"

Henry is excited beside me, and I am both heartened and saddened that his days are so staid that even the arrival of a simple letter can elicit such enthusiasm.

I look up and smile. "It's from Sonia, saying that she has been granted permission for a holiday visit." I push aside a twinge of guilt at the newest lie I tell. It is only a partial untruth. I have already spoken to Aunt Virginia about inviting Sonia and Luisa for the holiday.

He beams. "Well, that *is* grand, isn't it?"

I fold the paper, putting it back into the envelope, feeling a corner of my heart lift with hope.

"Yes, it is, Henry. It is grand indeed."

17

"Are you very excited, Lia?" Henry's voice is behind me as I look from the parlor window for the carriage.

I turn to him. "Goodness! For the last time, yes! Though I would wager you are more excited than I, from all the times you've inquired!"

He blushes but does not try to hide the smile that starts at his mouth and spreads all the way to his eyes. Sheltered as he is, it is easy to forget that Henry is a boy of ten, but I saw the way he looked at Sonia when she came to tea and know he fancies another chance to see her.

When I turn back to the window, the carriage emerges from the tree-lined drive. For a moment, I forget that I am sixteen and not as prone to excitement as Henry.

"They've come!" I rush to the front door, flinging it open

and waiting impatiently while Edmund helps Luisa and Sonia from the carriage.

I will greet my guests alone. Aunt Virginia is busy with Margaret, and Alice, even more sullen since learning of my plans to include Sonia and Luisa in our holiday, will likely be sulking on one of her long walks.

Luisa bounds up the steps like a puppy, all enthusiasm and no decorum, making me laugh into my gloved hand.

"I cannot believe Miss Gray let me come! I thought I should have to spend another Thanksgiving eating in the grim dining room at Wycliffe. You've saved me!"

Her laugh is catching, and I feel my own bubble forth from my throat. "Nonsense! I'm so happy to have you both here." I reach over and kiss her cool cheek, doing the same to Sonia as she reaches the top of the stone terrace. "Ready for our holiday to begin?"

Sonia smiles, the radiance behind it glowing from within even on this gray day. "Oh yes! I've been beside myself for days! I thought I should drive Mrs. Milburn mad!"

I lead them into the house, the prospect of their companionship for the next three days as warming to me as the hope that together we might find the keys. We share a laughter-filled lunch, retiring to the parlor satiated and happy. Aunt Virginia kindly keeps Henry out of the room so that we might have privacy. He peeks around the corner from time to time, gazing wistfully at Sonia, but we pretend not to notice. We talk and laugh, and for a time, I believe that we are ordinary. That we care for nothing but gowns and books and eligible young men. It is only when Luisa lifts her face to the wall near the firebox that I remember why we have come together.

"That gentleman" — she points to a portrait on the wall — "he looks familiar. Who is he?"

I swallow, feeling the rope that binds us coil and tighten. "My father."

She nods slowly. "Perhaps I have seen him at Wycliffe. Before . . ."

I nod. "Perhaps." It seems we are not so ordinary after all, and I wonder how to tell Sonia and Luisa the one thing that still stands between us.

Sonia tips her head, bewilderment crossing her serene face. "What is it, Lia? You've gone so quiet!"

I glance at the empty doorway to the parlor. Alice is noticeably absent, and Henry's blushing face has not been seen in some time. Even still, it would not be wise to be careless.

"I think I'd like some fresh air. Do you ride?"

"I don't like this! I don't like this at all!" Sonia's voice trembles and shakes as she bounces atop Moon Shadow, the gentlest mare in the stable.

"Nonsense! You shall be fine. You're hardly moving, and Moon Shadow would not harm a fly. You're quite safe. I'll ride behind you, and Moon Shadow will do the rest."

"Well! That's easy for you to say. You do this all the time," Sonia mutters.

Luisa is already a few paces ahead, clearly a competent

horsewoman, though I'm sure she has not had occasion to ride often at Wycliffe. Taking out the horses seemed a fine way to escape the house, and it was an easy matter to locate some riding breeches and habits for my two friends. But as I watch Sonia bounce stiffly atop Moon Shadow's back, I cannot help wondering if I made an error in judgment. I ride behind her in silence, coming up alongside only when her shoulders have relaxed the smallest bit and her jarring bounce seems to flow more smoothly with the horse.

"Feeling better?" I grin.

She makes a sound like "Hmph!" and keeps her eyes determinedly forward.

Up ahead, Luisa slows her pace, turning Eagle's Run around in a smooth motion that belies the sleek horse's usual spirit. They trot back toward us, taking up a position on the other side of Sonia.

Luisa's cheeks are bright from wind and excitement. "Oh, this is such fun, Lia! Thank you ever so much. It's been far too long since I've ridden."

I return her smile, absorbing some of her happiness until I remember the reason for our ride. "Actually, I suggested riding because I wanted to speak to you in private." I glance at Sonia, the panic still evident on her face. "Though I wonder if a walk to the river might not have been kinder."

Luisa laughs. "I daresay she cannot hear us at all, so great is her fright!"

"I hear you quite well, actually." Sonia's voice comes from

between clenched lips, her face tight as she stares straight ahead.

I press my lips together to keep from laughing.

Luisa glances over at me with curiosity. "So? What is it, Lia? What did you want to talk about? Besides the usual; the prophecy, the end of the world, trifling things such as those!"

Even Luisa's attempt at finding humor in our strange situation cannot bring a smile to my face, for what if she and Sonia blame me for the circumstances in which they find themselves? And yet there is no way to know for certain except to say it. "I believe I understand why my father's face is familiar to you."

Luisa furrows her brow. "Well, it's certainly possible I came across him at Wycliffe, or —"

"I don't think that is why." I interrupt her. "Shall we dismount?"

We have come to the small pond where Alice and I used to feed the ducks when we were small. After our mother's death, it seemed a safer haven than the lake, its tree-lined shore a gentle dip to the water that provides plenty of shade even in summer.

Luisa and I are tying our horses to a couple of small trees when we notice Sonia, still perched atop Moon Shadow.

"Are you coming down?" I ask her. It takes her a moment to look my way, but when she does I feel a surge of sympathy at the sheer terror still displayed on her face.

"Down? Now that I'm up here you want me to get *down?*" Her voice borders on hysterical.

"It will be fine, Sonia. Trust me. I'll help you."

It is only after I have given her detailed instructions and helped her down from Moon Shadow that Sonia's face relaxes into something of its normal calm. She sits on the grass with a groan. "I'll never be able to sit properly again!"

Sitting next to her, I let the silence settle between us as I work up the courage to say what I must say. I look over at Luisa, leaning against a tree near the water with her eyes closed, her lips hinting at a faint smile of contentment.

"Luisa? How did you come to be at Wycliffe all the way from Italy? It seems an odd thing, really, for you to be at school so far from home."

She opens her eyes, laughing harshly and bending over to feel along the grass until she rises with a few small rocks in her hand. "Odd indeed! My father had planned to send me to school in London, but a business acquaintance convinced him America was the best place to get a modern-day education. 'The best schooling money can buy,' my father said. No doubt the same words used to convince him to send me halfway around the world to Wycliffe." She throws one of the rocks angrily into the water. It lands with a *plunk* a good deal farther than I can throw even on my best day.

"I believe that was my father."

She drops her hands to her side. "What do you mean? What was your father?"

"I believe *my* father is the business acquaintance who recommended *your* father send you to Wycliffe."

Luisa makes her way toward me, sinking onto the grass as confusion flickers across her face. "But . . . how would your father be acquainted with mine, and perchance that he was, why would he concern himself with my schooling?"

"I don't know, but we all have the mark. Even though mine is different, it is close enough to be strange in the extreme. The fact that we are all in the same town, in the same place, is even stranger, don't you agree?"

Sonia does not nod or show any sign of agreeing at all, except to start speaking. "My parents were English. They . . . well, they were quite poor, actually." Her laugh is wry, a whisper of her normal laugh. "In any case, they didn't need an excuse to find me other accommodations. When I started showing signs of . . . well, you know, all the strange things I'm able to see and do, they thought I might be happier surrounded by others of my kind. Or so Mrs. Millburn tells me. More likely *they* were happier to have one less mouth to feed."

I offer her a smile. "Well, I'm glad you're here, Sonia. I could not have managed without your friendship these last weeks!" She returns my smile with a shy one of her own, and I continue. "But it cannot be a coincidence that we have all come to be in the same place. That we all carry the mark. My aunt informed me that my father was seeking out children, children with the mark, from all over the world. She told me . . ." I stop. Will they be angry? Will they blame me for everything?

"What, Lia? What did she tell you?" Sonia's voice is soft.

"She told me that he started bringing them here . . . the children. That he arranged for them to come to America. Only two of them before he died. One from England, one from Italy, she said."

Luisa blinks in the fading sunlight. "But . . . why would your father want us here? And in any case, how would he have found us? How would he have known we had the mark?"

"I've been thinking about that; you and Sonia have had the mark since birth. I imagine that, with the right resources, it would not be very difficult to find children with the mark. My father was a determined and influential man. Even if your marks were kept a secret, there are those who might see it, are there not? Doctors, teachers, nannies, relatives . . ." I sigh, not sure any of it makes sense now that I've said it aloud. "I'm sorry. I don't know for certain, all right? I've been asking myself the same question for weeks. It's part of the riddle, I think. It must be."

Luisa suddenly jumps to her feet, pacing the bank in front of us with the taut energy of a caged animal. "Perhaps we should just leave all of this alone! After all, what is the worst that will happen if we simply let it be? Is it not better than digging into this thing that we don't understand?"

"We cannot do nothing, Luisa." Sonia's words surprise me.

Luisa opens her palms, a breeze off the water lifting a small lock of her raven hair. "Why ever not? Why can we not?"

Sonia sighs, dusting herself off and rising stiffly to walk toward Luisa. "Because the visions are coming to me more frequently since we have found each other. The spirits are more insistent. They are trying to tell me something, to pull me into their world, and they will not stop until I address them." She takes Luisa's hands. "And tell me, haven't the spirits given chase to you as well? Haven't you found yourself falling more and more often into swift and strange dreams? Into the travel that only leads you to places both dark and frightening?"

Surprise courses through my body. Sonia knows something I do not.

Luisa's face is a mask of conflict before she crumples, burying her face in her hands. "Yes! Yes, all right?" She looks up at us with naked fear. "But that does not mean we should give chase in return. Perhaps the Souls are only angry that we have been so persistent. Perhaps if we ignore it . . . if we stop trying to find the answers, they will leave us all alone."

But this will not happen. I am certain of it. The thing that stands in the shadows of our dreams, my dreams, is waiting. And it will not be ignored.

Sonia wraps an arm around Luisa. "I'm sorry, but I don't think that is how the Souls work. They want something of us, something of Lia, and now . . . well, now they shan't rest until we give it to them."

18

We pass Thanksgiving Day in pleasant forgetfulness. James and his father join us, and sumptuous smells waft to us from the kitchen as we play parlor games. Henry's face lights like a shooting star when Sonia agrees to play a game of chess. He does not seem to mind when she beats him soundly, favoring him with a gracious smile while putting him into checkmate.

Alice is wary. Like an animal that smells danger, she watches from a distance as we laugh by the light of the fire. When we adjourn to the dining room, I take my seat to the right of James. Alice surprises me by claiming the seat to his left. Her presence unnerves me, though she is mostly blocked from my view. I push aside my unease. The feast is delicious, filled with wine and conversation that goes on for two lovely hours.

We retire to the parlor once again after eating in proportions that would surely cause Miss Gray upset over our gluttony.

After much prodding, Aunt Virginia sits at the piano. We gather around to sing, laughing and poking each other with elbows when we forget the words. Even Alice joins us in song, though she keeps her distance from Sonia and Luisa, and the room grows quiet as the final refrain of our last ballad rings through the parlor. The fire burns low in the grate, and Aunt Virginia, who never displays weariness of any sort, covers her yawn with a tired hand. Henry sleeps in his chair by the firebox, thick hair falling over his closed eyes.

"Well, I don't want to break up the celebration, but I think *someone* needs to be brought to bed." James looks over my shoulder as he says it, and my eyes drift to Henry.

But when I follow the sparkle in James's eyes, it is Mr. Douglas I see, hunched and sleeping on the sofa. I smother a laugh, trying not to wake either one of them.

"Yes, well . . . it *is* rather late. Shall I ask Edmund to help you to the carriage?" I tip my head to Mr. Douglas.

"No, thank you. I'll manage."

There is a sleepy stumble to the waiting carriage as James settles his father and then a flurry of gay goodbyes. Aunt Virginia has disappeared to supervise cleanup in the kitchen, and Luisa and Sonia have gone to dress for bed. I look around to be sure no one is about before slipping from the warmth of the house to the terrace with James.

He wastes no time pulling me into his arms, twirling a piece of my loose hair around one fingertip. And then his lips are on mine, opening my mouth like the bud of a flower, blossoming until the petals are lush and swollen. These are the times when

I feel like another Lia altogether — one who doesn't care about Miss Gray and her books and books full of rules. One who doesn't care what is expected of me. These are the times when I think that it is not possible for something to be wrong that is felt so fully, filling me up from the inside out.

It is James who pulls away. It is always James who pulls away, though he is the one who pulls me close as well. "Lia, Lia. I am so happy when I'm with you. You know that, don't you?" His voice is brusque.

I smile, teasing. "Yes, of course, when I'm not driving you mad with arguments and curiosity!"

"You drive me mad with something else." He grins before becoming more serious. "It's true that we've not talked about it in any serious way. And I cannot offer you the life to which you are accustomed. But I want you to be mine, someday, when the time is right."

My nod comes slower than I intend. "Only . . ."

"Only what?" Naked worry shades his eyes. We have laughed and enjoyed the evening, attempting to forget the small distance that has grown between us. It is a distance borne only by my own secrets and uncertainty, but that does not make the divide any simpler to cross.

I shake my head. "It's nothing. I am only sad to be without Father for the holiday. Christmas shan't be the same." My voice rings with the truth of it, and for a moment I am able to convince myself that my grief is the only thing between James and me.

"Is that all, then? The only thing that has made you brooding

and quiet these last weeks? Because I can't help feeling there is more to it."

Tell him. Tell him now before it is too late, before you push him away altogether. But the voice is not insistent enough. I nod, smiling up at him with as much reassurance as I can manage. "I'm sorry if I've caused you worry. I shall be all right with time."

I want to believe I am protecting him, but instead it is shame that keeps me quiet. Deep down, I cannot deny that I am anxious James will not have me when he realizes the wicked, ageless story of which I am a part.

"Miss Gray would not approve." Alice's voice greets me as I close the door, but it is not the new, hard Alice I have come to watch with guarded eyes. Her voice is playful, her figure a dim outline on the stairs. She sits carelessly on the steps, leaning her body back to rest on her elbows.

I make my way to the staircase, dropping next to her on the step. "Yes, well, I would venture a guess she would not approve of your posture at the moment, either."

Her teeth flash in the dark, our smiles finding each other across the mystery of the quiet house. "Will you marry him?"

"I don't know. I once thought so. I was once more sure of it than anything in the world."

"And now?"

I shrug. "And now things are not so simple."

It takes her a moment to answer. "No, I suppose not. But

perhaps there is a way. A way for us both to have the thing we most desire."

I hear the unspoken promise of the subject around which she dances. But I am not ready to give away my hard-found knowledge. Not until I hear what she means to say. "I'm sure I don't know what you mean."

She lowers her voice further. "And I'm sure you *do*, Lia. You wish to marry and have children, to live a quiet life with James. You must realize how impossible such a dream is with . . . the way things are now. With your fighting the Souls as you are."

The frankness of her words surprises me. All at once, the mask has been lowered. She knows as much as I do, perhaps even more. It is quite obvious now, and I wonder why I thought her even a little bit oblivious to the prophecy and its workings.

In the absence of my denial, Alice continues. "If you will only fulfill your duty to Samael, you will find peace. He will leave you alone to the life that you desire. Will that not be easier for all concerned? Is there not a small part of you, the part that was born to be the Gate, that wishes it so?"

I should like to say her words are to no avail, that I am unmoved by the black promises. But it would be a lie, for part of me thrills with anticipation as she speaks of fulfilling the prophecy's ancient promise. I want to believe it is only the part that desires to live my life with James as any girl would, but somewhere in the halls of my conscience I know it is more. It is the siren's song of my intended role in the prophecy. It is the deepest part of me, the part I try to pretend is not there at all, the part that must fight the temptation to do just as Alice wants.

I shake my head, denying it, not wanting to betray any weakness. "No. It . . . it isn't as you say." I soften my voice, appealing to the Alice of my childhood, the Alice I love. "It is true that I want my life with James, but I will not have that life in the darkness of a world ruled by the Souls. Surely you understand this, Alice. We agree on one thing: that we should work to a common purpose, a purpose that is an easy matter to decide. You are the Guardian. It is your duty to protect the world from the Souls. And I . . . Well, I have a choice as well. And I'll not aid them. I'll not do a single thing to aid them in destroying the things, the *people*, I love. And is *that* not our common purpose? To protect Henry and Aunt Virginia, the only family we have left?"

Her face is half hidden in the shadows, but I see her hesitation at the mention of Henry and Aunt Virginia. It takes a moment for her to speak, and in that moment a lifetime of expression passes over her features. In a heartbeat, childish uncertainty gives way to resignation.

"I was not meant to be the Guardian, Lia. We both know it. It's why I feel the way I do. Why I have known since I was a child that my duty lies with the Souls, whatever name the prophecy gives me. I . . . I cannot help the way I feel. The way I *am*."

I shake my head, not wanting to hear her speak this way. It is harder to have this Alice speak of these things. Were it the Alice of recent days, the cold-eyed, hard-faced Alice . . . well, then it might be easier to discount her words.

She licks her lips, and they shine in the dark. "If we work in concert, we shall be protected, Lia. We and those we love. I can guarantee your safety. And the safety of James and Henry and Aunt Virginia. Those are the things that make the world worth living in, are they not? As long as those things remain, what does it matter who is in charge? Isn't it worth the small sacrifice of conscience to live your life in peace?"

Something desperate has crept into her words, waking me from the silken spell of her voice. I shake my head with force, as if to push away the whispered promise that pulls me close even as I want to push it away.

"I cannot . . . I cannot do such a thing, Alice. I simply cannot. I cannot help the way *I* feel either. *This* is the way *I* am."

I think she might be angry, but her voice is filled only with sadness. "Yes. I thought as much. I'm sorry, Lia."

Her hand finds mine across the step, and she takes it the way she used to when we were small. It is not any bigger than mine, not really, and yet there was a time when I always felt safe with my hand in Alice's. I don't know why she says she is sorry, but I fear I will soon find out.

And my hand will not be safe in hers again.

19

"Lia!" Sonia waves me into the guest room as I creep toward my own, the conversation with Alice ringing in my ears.

I step into the room. "I thought you would be asleep after such a long day."

"We had a wonderful day, Lia. But there is still work to do, is there not?" Sonia's eyes drift to Luisa, sitting on one of the beds.

I hesitate before nodding. I can only hope that Luisa is as understanding as Sonia.

Luisa lifts her eyebrows. "What is it, Lia? Is something wrong?"

I sit on the end of the bed, shaking my head. "Not wrong, exactly. But there is something that I haven't had the chance to tell you. Something I found out just after you and Sonia came to tea."

"What is it?"

I run a hand along my brow, trying to calm my nerves before making the revelation that may sever a friendship I have come to treasure. There is no easy way to say it, and so I say it as simply and quickly as possible. I tell her the reason my mark is different, resisting the urge to soften the information with reassurance or rationalization. If we are to work together truly, Luisa must understand exactly what I am.

She does not say anything right away. Absent are the protestations and anger that I expect. She looks into my eyes, as if the answers to all her questions lie there. At last she reaches over and takes my hand, the hand Alice has just let go for good. When Luisa speaks, her words are simple, but they give me room to hope.

"Tell me everything."

And so I do. I tell her about the prophecy, my role in it, the medallion. She meets my revelation with stoic calm, the realization that I am the Angel, the Gate, no more than a hiccup in her resolve. I come to the end of my tale, knowing that the rest of the story will be written by us all.

"And so, we are back to the keys," I say. "But not with so little as we had before."

Luisa nods, the curls bouncing at the nape of her neck. "And this is where the mysterious Madame comes in, is it not?"

I look at Sonia, raising my eyes in surprise.

She tips her head with a smile. "I told her about our visit to Madame Berrier's."

"Good. Then you are all up to date."

"Yes," Luisa says, "only . . ."

"Only what?"

"Well, why didn't you invite me along? I should have liked to learn more about the prophecy. . . ." I hear the pout in her voice and feel a pang of guilt, but Sonia answers for it before I'm able.

"It was my doing, Luisa. The maid at Mrs. Millburn's is acquainted with one of Lia's maids. I was afraid to try and slip you a note at Wycliffe. I didn't want you to get in trouble, and I knew there would be no stopping you if you knew of our meeting, no matter the consequences."

Luisa's silence makes me fear we have hurt her feelings, but her grudging admission follows. "I suppose you're right. I *can* be ever so stubborn!" She laughs in response to her own criticism. "So? What did she say, this mysterious woman?"

"She told us that Samhain is an ancient Druid holiday marking a period of Darkness." I sit up, pulling the pins from my hair. "Apparently, it falls on November first, though we cannot figure what that has to do with the keys. The only thing even a little bit interesting is that it is also Sonia's birthday."

Luisa sits up straighter. "What did you say?"

Her expression makes me stop, and I lower my hands as my hair falls to my shoulders.

Sonia breaks in from the other bed where she sits, her head tipped back against the headboard. "She said my birthday happens to fall on the day of Samhain, November first."

Luisa's face has grown pale. "Luisa? What is the matter?" I ask her.

"Just that . . . well, it's ever so strange. . . ." She gazes into the fire, speaking softly as if to herself.

"What is?" Sonia slides to the edge of the other bed.

Luisa meets Sonia's eyes. "That November first is your birthday. It's strange because it is mine as well."

Sonia stands, making her way to the fire before turning to face us. "But that's . . . Of what year?" Her voice shakes as she asks the question.

"Eighteen seventy-four." It is a whisper that seems to crawl into the shadowed corners of the room.

"Yes." Sonia nods, slowly. "Yes. Me, too."

Pacing in front of them both, I try to wrap my mind around the many disparate pieces of the riddle. "It doesn't make sense. My birthday is *not* November first, so this is nothing to do with us all, but only the two of you." I mutter out loud but to no one in particular. "How are we supposed to figure out something so . . . so . . ."

"Mad?" Luisa offers from the bed.

I turn to look at her. "Yes. It *is* mad, isn't it?"

Sonia drops onto the settee by the fire. "Now what are we to do? The fact that we share the same birthday is odd, but it doesn't bring us any closer to finding the keys."

I remember the letter. "Actually, that's what I was trying to tell you. We may be closer yet."

Sonia looks up. "What do you mean?"

Withdrawing the envelope from my pocket, I hold it out to her. "Madame Berrier sent this to me after our meeting."

Sonia rises to take the envelope, opening it and passing it to Luisa when she has finished reading it.

"Who is he?" Luisa asks. "This Alastair Wigan?"

I shake my head. "I don't know. But tomorrow, we shall find out."

❦

The next morning, we make our way down the stairs, taking our cloaks from the entry and stepping into the cold sunshine. I have already arranged our outing with Aunt Virginia. I know she saw the lie in my excuse to go to town for a proper tea, but whatever happens to me, she is the one tasked with caring for Henry. I only seek to protect her. To protect them both.

Since my conversation with Alice on the stairs, I feel as if we have crossed an invisible barrier, a point beyond which can only lay sadness and loss. Our race to end the prophecy in the way we each desire will be dangerous, even deadly. Yet, there is nothing to do but go forward unless I should like to live in the shadow of it all my life through.

And that is simply not an option.

20

Sonia, Luisa, and I cross the lawn in a flurry of excited conversation, willing for the moment to allow ourselves to be happy about the day's outing, however dark its purpose.

We make our way up the stairs of the carriage house to the rooms Edmund has occupied for as long as I can remember. He comes quickly to the door in response to my knock, his eyes registering Sonia, Luisa, and me on the threshold.

Before we can say a word, he reaches for his coat, turning back to us. "So? Where are we going today, Miss?"

❧

We are jostled to and fro on the roads leading farther and farther away from Birchwood. I knew from the address that we would not be going to town, but I had not imagined it so far away or in a place quite so remote.

And remote it must be, for we travel so long our excitement dwindles to nothing but tired sighs and long glances out the carriage windows. I am grateful for the silence. My mind is full of hope that Mr. Wigan might help us find the keys.

Edmund turns off the main road, entering a wooded pathway that causes the carriage to grow dark with the shelter of trees above and around us. We sigh aloud when, all at once, everything lightens, and Edmund stops the horses.

"Thank goodness!" Luisa says, holding a hand to her forehead. "I thought I was going to be sick!"

She flings open the door, stumbling from the carriage without waiting for Edmund. I fervently hope that she will not, in fact, be sick. I don't know how happy Mr. Wigan will be to see three girls appear on his doorstep, but I imagine it will be immeasurably less so if one of them is losing her breakfast in his shrubbery.

But Luisa composes herself, wiping her brow with a handkerchief, and we step toward the door of the ramshackle cottage situated in the center of the small clearing. There is a small garden off to the side and a goat surveying us lazily from the yard. A few chickens peck their way through some stray seed, but other than these few animals, Lerwick Farm is a rather big name for such an unassuming place.

Edmund stands behind us as I knock on the door, peeling white paint drifting to the ground under the small pressure of my fist. No one comes, and we stand in the silence of the clucking chickens, wondering what to do next. Luisa is raising her hand with authority when we hear a voice behind us.

"Well, hello, there! You must be the young ladies Sylvia told me about!"

We turn as one to face a small man in tweed trousers and a half-unbuttoned shirt, his bald head gleaming in the sun. I cannot place the brogue in his voice, but I think it must be the remnant of a Scots or Irish accent long since dulled by blunt American speech.

"What's the matter? Cat got your tongue, eh?" He comes toward us. "Alastair Wigan, at your service. Sylvia said ye'd be coming." He seems happy to see us, as if we are long-lost friends, and it takes me a moment to realize that I don't have the faintest idea to whom he is referring.

"Good afternoon, Mr. Wigan. I'm Lia Milthorpe, and these are my friends Sonia Sorrensen and Luisa Torelli, and our driver Edmund." There is hand-shaking all around and a muttering of greetings. "But I'm afraid we don't know a Sylvia. . . ."

His face lifts in a smile, his eyes growing devilish. "Why, sure you do! Sylvia Berrier, that luscious lovely from town."

His language makes Sonia blush. I fight a smile as Luisa coughs, a runaway giggle escaping her throat.

"Well, now I'm even sorrier that I didn't get to meet the Madame myself," Luisa says with a grin. "She sounds quite fascinating!"

"Fascinating, indeed!" Mr. Wigan nods knowingly, his eyes taking on a far-off expression. He claps suddenly, as if remembering us. "Well! I can't have you standing on the stoop like strangers! Not when you're friends of Sylvia Berrier!"

He moves slowly toward the porch. "Come along, then. I'll

make us some tea. I've been experimenting with a new brew from the garden, you see, and it isn't often I have the chance to try it out on anyone other then Algernon."

I look around. "Algernon?"

Mr. Wigan waves toward the yard. "Yes, yes." He holds open the door as we pass through it, one by one.

I take one last look at the yard on my way into the house. There is no one there, only chickens and a goat. Oh my.

"Is . . . is Algernon the goat, then?" I ask.

"Why, yes, of course!" Mr. Wigan is heading toward another room, his voice growing fainter as he traverses the small house.

Luisa meets my gaze, humor lighting her eyes. It is clear she finds the situation entrancing. My eyes adjust to the dim light of the tiny house. I am quite awestruck by the oddities lying on every surface.

Bits of stone and feather dot the bookshelves, dusty and stuffed to the brim. Relics carved in wood sit beside eerie dolls while any number of strange skeletons stare at us, some with firelight flickering from behind sightless eyes. I think I recognize the tiny, walnut-sized head of a squirrel and perhaps even a cracked human skull resting as a bookend on the mantel. I shiver though the room is quite warm.

Edmund leans against the wall near the door. He takes in the room methodically, as if storing it away for future reference. The stubborn set of his jaw tells me that he has no intention of leaving us alone in the strange house, and in truth, his presence is a reassurance I need. It is undoubtedly selfish, but I am most glad he is here.

"Here we are, then!" Mr. Wigan returns bearing a tin tray. He looks around the cluttered room for a spot on which to set it. "Oh dear."

Sonia jumps to attention. "Shall I clear the books from this table here?" She gestures to a towering stack of volumes under which I suppose is a table, though I cannot see a bit of it from where I stand.

"Oh yes. Yes, indeed!" Mr. Wigan says.

I move to help Sonia and together we set the books on the floor amid a cloud of dust that makes us both cough. I try to ignore the dirty table when we are finished, for Mr. Wigan seems not to notice and places the tea tray there without any thought to cleaning it.

"There, now! Sylvia tells me ye have a bit of a mystery on yer hands." He pours tea into mismatched cups, handing them to each of us in turn, including Edmund, who steps forward with surprise, nodding gratefully. "She told me all about the prophecy, though I'd heard it myself, you know, from my wicked heathen mother." His eyes twinkle merrily, making it clear he thinks no such thing of his mother. "Quite wondrous to hear talk of it here of all places."

"What do you . . . ? Oh!" The tea on my tongue is a surprise. It tastes of orange and, I think, perhaps licorice. "This is quite good!"

Mr. Wigan leans forward, pleasure further creasing his already wrinkled face. "Do you think so? Not too strong, is it?"

I shake my head. "Not at all! It's wonderful!" I take another

sip before setting the cup down. "Why are you surprised to hear talk of the prophecy *here* of . . . of all places?"

"Why, because it's a Celtic myth, really. Oh, sure it is the Watchers are in the Bible, but the myth of the sisters came from the Celts, from Brittany, I believe."

I nod. "I see. Well, I'm not sure I understand why Madame Berrier, er, Sylvia, thought you might be of help —"

"I know well enough. I'm a bit of an expert you see, on things of the past. Not regular things. Not the things other people know. Sure enough, not anything most people think *worthy* of knowing. But nevertheless," he sighs. "I do know quite a bit about Celtic myth, biblical myth, the Druids. . . ." He waves a sun-spotted hand in the air. "'Tis all the same, whatever you might call it."

"I see. Well, then perhaps you *will* be able to help, Mr. Wigan." I pull the translated notes from my bag, handing them to him. "There is one piece of the prophecy we still cannot solve. Madame Berrier told us about Samhain, but she couldn't place the reference to the stone serpent. She thought the word *Aubur* sounded like something within your, er, area of expertise."

He nods, pursing his lips. "Mighty interesting, this is. Mighty interesting, indeed." He lowers the paper to his lap, taking a drink of tea and looking for all the world like he does not intend to speak again.

I clear my throat, "Yes, well —"

"What we need to know, Mr. Wigan," Luisa breaks, "is whether or not you can place the reference."

He looks surprised, as if it were never in question. Rising, he moves to one of the staggering bookcases, eyeing the volumes shelved there as if he knows each and every one, despite their rather haphazard organization. It takes him less than ten seconds to pull a fabric-bound book from the shelf. He turns back to us, reclaiming his seat by the fire and sipping his tea as he turns pages in the book.

Luisa leans so far forward that I fear she will fall off her seat altogether. Her mouth is set in a tight line, and I can only imagine the determination she must be exercising to keep from grabbing the book from Mr. Wigan and searching through it herself. But Mr. Wigan doesn't mutter or speak. He simply turns the pages slowly and carefully before stopping, finally, near the end.

He hands the book to me as he explains. "'Tisn't known as Aubur anymore, you see. That's probably why Sylvia had some trouble. Aubur is its old name. Now we call it *Avebury*."

I lower my eyes to the book. In it is an artist's drawing of small landmarks forming a circle with a line running through it. It doesn't mean a thing to me.

"I don't understand. What is it?" I pass the book to Luisa for fear she shall have a fit if she is not given something to do besides wait and listen to Mr. Wigan.

"Why, 'tis a stone circle! A lesser known one, but a stone circle nonetheless."

His description jars something loose in my memory. "A stone circle? You mean like the large one in England? Stonehenge?"

He nods knowingly. "Ah yes. Stonehenge. 'Tis the one everyone seems to know, but there are many others, scattered throughout the British Isles mostly."

Sonia has the book in her lap. She looks up at Mr. Wigan. "And this . . . Avebury is one of them? One of the stone circles?"

"Aye. 'Tis." He does not seem to have any more to say on the subject.

Luisa looks anxiously toward me before continuing. "What of the stone serpent? Why does the prophecy call Avebury such a strange thing?"

"Well, that is the odd thing. Not many people know of the connection between Avebury and the serpent, but if one were to trace the lines of it, one would find that it is laid in the shape of a snake, ye see. A snake that passes through a circle."

The look of alarm on Sonia's and Luisa's faces must be a mirror to my own, for the snake passing through a circle is very close to the snake winding *around* the circle on the medallion and on the marks we all bear.

"But what does a stone circle all the way in England have to do with us? With the prophecy?" Luisa asks.

I pick up the prophecy translation from the table, reading aloud. "*'Birthed in the first breath of Samhain near the Mystic Stone Serpent of Aubur.'*" I shake my head, looking at Mr. Wigan. "The keys. Something about the keys being shaped near Avebury . . . What of the towns nearby? Perhaps there is a town near Avebury, a town where the keys might be hidden or were made? A town known for smith work perhaps?"

Mr. Wigan scratches his head, his forehead wrinkled in thought. "Well, most of the stone circles are in out-of-the-way places, it seems. . . . But I might have something that will be of help."

He rises from the chair, crossing to a large desk pushed against one wall and covered with all manner of papers and books. Opening the deep lower drawer, he digs around before emerging with a roll of paper. He waves it in the air.

"Here. Come and take a look."

He does not bother clearing the desk, but lays the roll of paper on top of the mess, unrolling it bit by bit until it becomes clear that it is a map. Luisa places a rock, two books, and glass jar on the corners to keep the map from snapping back as we read.

Mr. Wigan puts his glasses on, and we lean over the map, Edmund included. I meet his eyes, seeing something there that makes me trust his knowledge of our secret. He was my Father's oldest employee. His oldest friend. If I cannot trust him, whom shall I trust?

"All right, then. Avebury. Here." Mr. Wigan points a gnarled finger at a place near the center of the map.

I can only faintly make out the letters *A-U-B* in the shadowed room.

"Yes, but I don't suppose the keys will be there, exactly," Luisa breaks in, studying the map as she chews her thumbnail. "The prophecy says *near* the stone serpent, does it not?"

"Aye." Mr. Wigan nods. "I see what you're gettin' at. Let's see, then. . . ." He slides his fingers outward from the center of

the map. "We have the village of Newbury. Here." He taps the map not far from the place where he marked Avebury. I cannot see any words identifying it as Newbury, but he seems to know his way around the map, so I listen as he continues. "And then we have the village of Swindon, here." His tap sends another small thump into the room. "From there we have the village of Bath, very well known. Very well known, indeed. Perhaps —"

But Sonia breaks in before he can continue. "Bath? Bath, England? But . . ."

Luisa looks up, her eyes shining in the light of the fire. "What?"

Sonia meets Luisa's eyes before turning to mine. "First the date, and now . . ."

"And now what?" My stomach has curled into a knot. I don't know what she will say, but I feel the turn of destiny's wheel.

"And now Bath," she says. "It's where I was born. That is what Mrs. Millburn told me when I asked — that I was born in Bath."

Something clicks into place with her words. I look at Luisa. "You were not born in Italy, were you, Luisa?"

Her words are a fearful whisper into the room. "No."

"But you said you were born in Italy." Beads of panic seem to spill from Sonia's voice, shattering like glass.

Luisa shakes her head. "No. I didn't. I said I was *from* Italy. And I am. But my mother was English. I was born in England and taken to Italy when I was a babe."

I look at Mr. Wigan. "What are the other towns, Mr. Wigan? The other towns near the stone serpent of Avebury?"

Even he looks flustered as he lowers his eyes back to the map, sliding his finger to and fro over the paper until he finds his place. "Let's see . . . we had Newbury, Swindon, Bath." He looks up briefly at Sonia before giving the map his attention once again. "Following that line in a circle, more or less, we have Stroud, Trowbridge, Salisbury, and . . . Andover. Any of these ring a bell, my dear?" He looks at Luisa expectantly.

At first I think I am wrong. I think I *must* have it wrong, for Luisa stands stock still as if nothing Mr. Wigan has said has made any sort of impression on her. He sighs heavily, gazing back at the map as if preparing to look for other towns, other villages, when Luisa finally breaks the silence.

"Salisbury," she mumbles. "I was born in Salisbury."

Four marks, four keys, circle of fire. Birthed in the first breath of Samhain near the mystic stone serpent of Aubur. The words of the prophecy whisper in my ear, and suddenly, I know. "Sonia? What time were you born?"

She shakes her head. "I have no idea."

I look to Luisa. "Luisa?"

"A-About midnight, I'm told."

And now I am certain, as I think they must be as well.

I look up at Sonia and Luisa in wonder. "It is you. You and others who carry your mark. You are the keys."

21

We are tired from the journey to Mr. Wigan's, and the celebra-
tory air of the holiday is all but gone as we pass a tension-filled
dinner with Aunt Virginia, Alice, and Henry. It is with mu-
tual relief, I think, that we retreat to our chambers after des-
sert. I have put on my nightdress and am preparing for sleep
when a knock makes me look up from the lamp.

When I open the door, Luisa and Sonia stand in dressing
gowns and slippers on the threshold to my chamber.

"You're still awake? I thought you would be well on your
way to sleep by now."

Sonia shakes her head. "I'm afraid sleep is still a long way
off, Lia."

I step back, holding the door open. "Come. Come in."

Luisa enters the room, leaning against the wall while Sonia
perches on the edge of the bed.

I sit next to her, peering at her pale face by the light of the fire. "What is it?"

"Luisa and I have been discussing things. And we are in agreement. If we *are* the keys, the sooner we find an end to the prophecy the better."

I nod, breathing deeply. "Good. But . . . are you all right?"

Sonia reaches out and takes my hand. "It was just so . . . so . . . surprising. I hardly thought I could breathe for a while. Of course, I knew we were a part of the prophecy somehow. Why else would Luisa and I have the mark? Even still, it suddenly seems very frightening, I suppose, to be in such a situation."

I smile into her eyes. "I understand. But working together is better than going it alone, is it not?" She nods, returning my smile, and I cross to the fire and turn to face them. "All right, then, it's time to make our next move. Time to find the other keys."

Sonia shakes her head. "But how? There will be four of us, won't there? Two more in addition to Luisa and me?"

"That's right, but we won't have to start from the beginning if we can only find the list."

Luisa's confusion is evident on her face. "What list?"

"The list of names my father compiled. Remember? I told you before that Aunt Virginia said he was looking for children, that he had a list of names and places. It seemed so random before, his finding you, but it makes more sense now. If all of the keys were born near Avebury around midnight on November first of the same year, it would not be very difficult to find four girls with the mark. It can only be that you and Sonia were on that list, and if you were on that list, there were probably others as well. If we can find it before Alice, we can try to locate the other keys."

Sonia rises, holding her fingertips to her brow in frustration. "Even if we have all the keys, we do not know how to end the prophecy."

I meet Luisa's gaze across the room. We are accustomed to Sonia's calm demeanor. Neither of us knows what to say in the face of her unexpected despair.

I speak the only truth I can. "I know this is maddening. Really, I do. But it took my father nearly ten years to come as far as he did, and right now there might be a way to find the other keys without going back to the beginning. If there is, we must find the list, and soon, for surely it would be dangerous in Alice's hands. Perhaps the rest will reveal itself to us, or perhaps we will have to find a way to unearth it as we have the clues so far."

Sonia drops back onto the settee, resting her head in her hands without speaking.

"All right, Lia." Luisa speaks calmly from across the room. I am relieved to see the light has returned to her eyes. "Where shall we look? Where might the list be hidden?"

"I've been thinking of just this thing. There is only one person, one person who knows more about the prophecy than any of us. . . ."

Sonia looks up. "Who?"

"My father."

Luisa speaks from the other side of the room. "But, Lia . . . your father . . . what I mean to say is —"

"I know well that my father is dead, Luisa. But it so happens that Sonia can sometimes speak with the dead, can you not, Sonia?"

Her face, smooth as alabaster in the light of the fire, betrays no emotion. "Well, yes. Sometimes." She comes over to me, looking into my eyes. "But not always. I cannot control who will come and who will not. I cannot control the messages that are passed from one world to the next. It is not for show that I tell my customers that I work at the will of the spirits. It's quite true."

"Yes, but you could try, couldn't you? To . . . to summon him? To bring about his presence?"

Her answer comes more slowly and with less enthusiasm than I expect. "I suppose so. But what about Virginia? You said she was once the Guardian. Can't we simply ask her?"

"My father kept everything a secret. She knew there was a list, but not where it was hidden, and she only knows a portion of the prophecy. Only her part in it and the part of my mother. And surely Alice will not share anything with us." I shake my head. "No. We must speak to my father. It's the only way."

"But even if I managed to locate your father, the spirits cannot intervene in the world they have left behind, not really. They can speak to us of the Otherworlds and of things as they were before they passed, but they cannot see anything in our world beyond the moment when they departed it."

She pauses, pressing her lips together as she tries to find the words she needs. "Once a soul moves on to the next world, it's as if . . . as if a curtain drops between that soul and us. Sometimes it thins so that we may speak to the soul, but your father won't be able to tell you anything that has happened since his death."

It would be a lie to say that I am not disappointed. I had hoped for a quick and easy answer to the location of the list. Even still, that does not mean Father cannot be of any help at all. "So . . . he could tell us where he hid it *before* his death?"

She nods. "I think so."

A feather of hope drifts into my heart. "Perhaps it is still there . . . It is worth a try, isn't it? A place to begin?"

Sonia nods, meeting my eyes. "All right, then. Let us try."

We move to the floor without speaking further, settling into a small circle in front of the fire. Once there, we quickly join hands, as if this alone might offer protection against whatever waits on the other side of this world. I remember that first encounter in the sitting room at Mrs. Millburn's. How long ago it seems, and how impossible that we should find ourselves together at Birchwood, forming yet another circle, this time without Alice, and for something far more dangerous than a lark.

Sonia closes her eyes. I look to Luisa, her impossibly long, dark lashes casting a shadow on the fine upsweep of her cheek. There is nothing to do but join them. I close my eyes, waiting, listening to the soft sound of Sonia's breath. When nothing happens, I open my eyes to find Sonia looking at me.

"Is something wrong?" I ask.

She swallows so hard that her delicate throat ripples. "It is only . . . well," she laughs nervously. "I find I'm suddenly afraid. Will you keep watch over me? If something should

happen, something that does not seem right, you must break the circle and force me out of the spirit trance."

I know of what she speaks. I have felt the dark thing. I have heard the throbbing of the Souls, felt their fiery breath on my back. "We'll keep watch, Sonia. You have my word."

She nods, closing her eyes against her fear.

For a time, nothing happens. I slip into a state that is almost hypnotic, aided by the crackling of the fire and the silence in the room. I have stopped expecting something to happen when I smell him, as I did before. It is the faint reminder of Father's pipe, the wool of his favorite jacket smelling of cedar from the wardrobe.

Sonia's voice breaks the heavy silence in the room. "Is that Thomas Milthorpe? Father of Lia and Alice and Henry?" There is a pause before she continues, this time speaking more softly. "Yes, yes. We shall be quiet."

Her eyes open, an unusual sharpness burning within them. The blue of her eyes is brighter, the black circle on the outer edge of her pupil more clearly defined. A strange pulsing energy, almost heard, has filled the room. It makes me feel warm and overwhelmed at the same time, and I fight the urge to cover my ears as if this will somehow block out the presence that seems to spill into the room from some unseen place.

"Before Lia will speak to you, Spirit, you must tell her something only she will know. Something that will prove your identity."

I wonder at this question, at her reason for asking it, waiting for Sonia to pass my father's reply back into the room. A

prickly tingling begins where my palm meets Sonia's, one that spreads to include my fingers so that my whole hand feels alive with fire. And then I hear the voice, hoarse and coming from what seems a very long distance.

"Lia? Lia? Do you hear me, Daughter?"

I shake my head, disbelieving. It is my father's voice, of this I'm certain, but I do not know how I have come to hear it, to make contact with my dead father simply by holding Sonia's hand. My eyes drift to Luisa, whose hand has become hot in mine. Her eyes are open and startled as she stares in wonder at Sonia's face. She hears it as well.

The voice, coming from everywhere and nowhere all at once, forces me to attention. "Lia . . . Listen. There is much to discuss . . ." The voice is crackly, breaking in the middle of some of the words. "I shall offer you the proof the Spirit Talker demands, but we must be quick. They will soon come. . . ." His voice fades for a moment before returning. "Lia . . . Daughter . . . Do you remember when you tried to build the raft? Henry dropped . . . into the river and . . . remember? You were so small, but . . . sure you could catch up to it if . . . paddled swiftly enough. You were never very good . . . building things, Lia. Remember? But you tried anyway. You worked and worked, though surely . . . it could not be done. . . ."

Tears sting my eyelids as I remember working to build a makeshift raft to find Henry's toy boat, certain I could catch it though it traveled purposefully downstream. Alice stood by, saying over and over again it could not be done. I think even poor Henry knew that we would never catch the toy, though

the river's current was gentle after a long season without rain. But I hammered wood together anyway, all the while in my best pinafore, using tools and scrap that father's workmen had left lying about when they broke for lunch. I worked feverishly, though with no real skill. When I finally launched my haphazard rescue raft, it sank before I could get in as much as a toe. I think I was more distraught over my inability to save the toy boat than Henry was with losing it.

"I remember." My voice is a whisper.

For a moment all is silent, and I fear we have lost the fragile connection to the Otherworlds. But the voice returns, though quite a bit fainter.

"Good, Lia. Good. You must find the . . . keys. I tried . . . I tried to . . . over. I located . . . but only two . . . You must . . . list . . . to complete the circle. I left it in . . . behind the . . . It is the only way . . . an end to the prophecy. You are the . . . It is your . . . once and for all, but not without the four."

I feel him fading as much as I hear it in his broken voice. The energy that filled the room ever fuller now fades, growing slightly stronger for a few seconds before diminishing even further.

Sonia steps in, more authoritative in the spirit trance than in the real world. "Mr. Milthorpe, we must find the list of keys. Your presence is fading. . . . We didn't understand all that you said. Can you repeat it? Can you stay with us, Mr. Milthorpe?"

We wait in silence for his answer, at last hearing a whisper more urgent than before. "Shhh . . . He is coming. I . . . go. Lia . . . You must find the list . . . they are the keys. Look . . .

Henry is all that is left of the veil. We are . . . you, Daughter. We . . . you."

And then he is gone. I feel it in the absence of his presence. The room that before felt as normal as any other, now feels empty without the heat of my father's spirit. Sonia's head falls forward against her chest as if she has fallen fast asleep.

"Sonia? It is over, Sonia. You can —"

But I do not get any further. Her head suddenly snaps up, her blue eyes open, looking directly at me, the strange vibrancy even more clear. The voice that emerges is not hers, nor is it my father's.

"You play a dangerous game, Mistress."

A shiver drips like a drop of rain from the back of my neck all the way down my spine. Sonia's eyes are glassy, and I know that this is not really her.

I sit straighter, frantically considering our options while trying to maintain a look of calm. "You must go. You do not belong here."

"You are mistaken. Why do you not allow me passage? Why must you seek the keys when it is I who can provide all you desire? Summon me, Mistress, and let chaos reign."

I am entranced by the eyes, Sonia's eyes and *not* Sonia's eyes. It is both morbid and fascinating to hear the eerie voice coming from Sonia's delicate face.

"Be gone, Spirit. You are not welcome." I try to keep my voice steady, but the presence of evil, the knowledge that I am far too close to something I don't understand, causes me to shake.

"There will be no peace until you open the Gate." It is a chant,

the call of a thousand voices, soft and insidious. *"Open the Gate . . . Open the Gate . . . Open the —"*

I scoot back, breaking the circle as Luisa lunges across its center, grabbing Sonia by the shoulders and shaking . . . shaking "Sonia! Wake up, Sonia! You must come back!"

Her pleas become more panicked and insistent, and the words of the spirit being warp and garble as Luisa shakes and shakes. *"It is time . . . Time for chaos to reign."*

Sonia's body goes rigid, her face contorting in a look of sheer terror and pain before she slumps onto the floor. With her release I feel my own. I scramble over to her side, lifting her head from the hard floor onto my lap.

"Oh my goodness! Oh my goodness!" Luisa repeats the refrain over and over.

It takes me a moment to speak over the thudding of my heart. "Sonia! Wake up, Sonia. Come back!" I speak to her harshly, willing her back with the force of my fear.

I don't realize we have stopped being quiet. Everything worldly has fallen away in the strange seclusion of the room. It is only when the door opens, closing just as quickly, that I realize we have been too loud for the sleeping house.

The footsteps are fast but graceful across the floor. I hardly have time to register her presence when Aunt Virginia bends to the floor, her eyes taking in our broken circle, the panic on our faces, Sonia lying on the floor, eyes still closed, her face a deathly white.

She looks at me, her face filled with anguish. "What are you doing? Oh Lia! Whatever have you done?"

22

"I feel as if my head will split in two." Sonia lies on the bed nearest the window, her pale hair a shimmering web across the pillow.

I cannot think of a thing to say, for this is surely my fault. If I had not pressed Sonia to try and reach Father, she would not have fallen victim to the horrid spirit-thing.

"Are you . . . are you all right?" Luisa's voice is hesitant, and I know she is unsure how much to say in front of Aunt Virginia.

Sonia presses her head to her temples before answering. "Yes. Yes, I'm sure I'll be fine." She, too, steps carefully around the issue of what we were doing when Aunt Virginia happened upon us.

But my aunt does no such thing. She stands up, confident now that her charge is in good health or soon will be. "Whatever were you doing? Whatever were you thinking? Do you not know how dangerous the Otherworlds can be?"

There is nothing to do but take the responsibility I know is mine. "It was my fault. I . . . I wanted to speak to Father. I pressured Sonia to lead a sitting . . . to try to make contact with him."

There is no disbelief on her face, only a calm and fearful acceptance. "You, all of you, do not understand the thing with which you play." She makes eye contact with each of us, even Sonia, who shrinks from the glare of her eyes as if it is a ray of bright sun against her headache.

I move toward her, anger surging in my blood. "Surely I would understand more if only *you* or Father or Mother or *someone* had told me when they had the chance! Instead I've been forced to skulk about, looking for answers to questions I don't even understand. We have searched high and low to decipher the riddle of the prophecy. And do you know what? We found the answer! We did! But it is not so neat as that."

I am aware of a gathering madness, of being pushed so close to the edge of a great precipice that I would rather fling myself from it than continue fearing it. "The keys are the children, Aunt Virginia. Those Father sought and those for whom he was still searching when he died. Except it is only Luisa and Sonia who are here. We need the list to find the other keys, and I thought Father could tell us where he hid it, all right? That is why I asked Sonia to make contact with Father." I am breathless with fury, breathing heavy as if I have run a long way when I have done nothing but empty my soul of all the bitterness and blame that has hung like a noose around my neck.

Aunt Virginia drops onto the bed next to Sonia, her voice but a murmur. "It cannot be."

I sit next to her, my anger reduced to a slow boil. "It is. It *must* be. We saw someone today, Aunt Virginia. Someone who helped us find the answer."

I take one of her hands in mine as I tell her of our visit to Madame Berrier's and then to Mr. Wigan's, hoping she will be able to fill in the blanks and guide us to the list.

"Do you have any idea, any idea at all, where Father might have hid it?" I ask her when I am finished.

Aunt Virginia's eyes are still hazy with surprise. I recognize the expression as a kind of stupor, a kind of denial as her soul tries to refute the things her mind knows.

"I've no idea, Lia. I told you, he never showed it to me. He was most secretive about it, and now I see why. According to the prophecy, you must have all four keys to bind the Beast. If they are indeed people . . . if their identities should be revealed . . ." She looks up at Sonia and Luisa with fearful eyes. "They would be in grave danger."

I know she is thinking of Alice. The thought of Sonia and Luisa in danger from my sister fills me with dread. "Do you think we should get them away from Birchwood, Aunt Virginia? Should they leave now, before Alice discovers the things we ourselves have discovered?"

It is not my aunt who answers, but Luisa, folding her arms across her chest. "I don't know about Sonia, but I have no

intention of leaving. This battle is mine as well, and I intend to fight it. Besides, Alice may not yet know about the keys. Our leaving suddenly would only serve to draw undue attention to us."

Sonia steps forward, wincing and touching her head. "Luisa is right. It will cause a great fuss if we leave now when we're meant to stay until Sunday, and who knows when we will have such time together again to search for the other keys. Besides, there are more fearsome things to face in the Otherworlds. I'll not be frightened of a girl, even if that girl is Alice."

They do not know Alice, I think. They do not know of what she is capable.

But this I do not say aloud, for whatever else Alice may be, she is still my sister. And besides, we are all taking risks to see the prophecy brought to an end.

The magnitude of the task at hand, the danger in seeing it through, hits me with sudden force. How are we to find two more keys? Even with the list, Sonia and Luisa are proof that the other keys could be scattered the world over.

"What if we cannot find them, Aunt Virginia? What if we cannot do it?"

She presses her lips together, rising to the bureau between the two beds and removing something from its drawer. When she returns, it is with a small Bible in her hands. Her hands shake as she turns to the back, very near the end.

She reads without further pretext. " 'And I heard a great voice out of the temple saying to the seven angels, "Go your ways, and pour out the vials of the wrath of God upon the earth." And the first went, and poured out his vial upon the earth; and there fell a noisome and grievous sore upon the men which had the mark of the Beast, and upon them which worshipped his image. And the second angel poured out his vial upon the sea; and it became as the blood of a dead man: and every living soul died in the sea. And the third angel poured out his vial upon the rivers and fountains of waters; and they became blood. And I heard the angel of the waters say —' "

"The Seven Plagues." Luisa's voice is a whispered interruption.

Aunt Virginia closes the Bible, looking up at Luisa nodding. "That's right."

Luisa turns to me. "The Seven Plagues are a sign of the end in the Bible. A return to the fathomless chaos that existed before the beginning of time."

A noiseless remnant of the mysterious puzzle clicks into place, and I add my own piece to the rest. " 'Death, Famine, Blood, Fire, Darkness, Drought, Ruin.' " I have read the words of the prophecy so many times since finding the book that I shall never forget them.

"Yes," Aunt Virginia confirms. "The Bible presents the plagues as an end that precedes a new beginning, one in which the world will be ruled by God in light. But the Bible is a written history, and like all written histories that are translated into thousands of languages and passed down through thousands of years, it includes things which are perhaps less than true. And omits others that are perhaps even truer."

"So what *does* it mean, then?" I ask.

Aunt Virginia reaches over, taking my hand in hers. "The plagues are simply the sign of an end. An end to the world we know and the beginning of a world ruled by the Beast forevermore. If you cannot find the four keys and close the circle, Samael will find his way through you and it will be too late. The Seven Plagues will begin, causing great torment and destruction before an end that is nothing more than that. The end."

I shake my head furiously, thinking of Henry, of Luisa and Sonia and Aunt Virginia. "But I am the Angel. Everyone says so. I have a choice. If I refuse him passage, he cannot come." I sound a child, even to myself.

Virginia looks into my eyes. "I wish it were so, Lia. But Samael will exploit your weakness. He will lie in wait for you while you sleep. He will send his Army to find you, those that wait in the Otherworlds and those that have already crossed into ours. He will use those you most love against you.

"You may fight him for a time, but I fear you will not be able to do so for very long. The Army has been gathering for centuries waiting for their King. Waiting for the Gate that will bring him forward to begin their reign of terror. Waiting for you, Lia. They will not give up so easily. You *must* find the list. You must find the other keys. And you must do it quickly."

❧

I do not want to sleep. Finding the answers I wanted has not offered me the comfort I imagined, and I wonder if Sonia and Luisa are as fitful as I. There is much to do, but the hour is late, and we have resolved to search the library for the list tomorrow in the clear light of day. The book was in the library, and so, too, may be the list.

It is the only place I can think of to begin our search.

We did not discuss what we will do once we find it, how we will go about locating the two remaining keys. What has been left unsaid, but is understood nonetheless, is that we must take one small step at a time or else we shall all go mad.

I sit with my back against the tall wooden headboard, trying to remain alert. I have knotted ribbons around my wrist. Even if the medallion finds its way to my wrist, it will not be able to line up to the mark unless the ribbons are removed, though this may well be possible, for all I do and do not know. The medallion found its way to me in the most improbable way imaginable and, even more unlikely, found its way back from the depths of the river. What is there to do but accept that it is mine?

And try not to wear it, not to open the Gate.

23

The field in which I stand is barren. There is a vague familiarity in its rolling hills and shallow valleys, and I think I recognize it as one of the many fields bordering Birchwood Manor. But the tall grass and enormous oak trees at the edge are where any sense of comfort or recognition ends.

The sky is a forbidding gray, mirrored by the ashen fields that look nothing like the rich, golden grass that sways around Birchwood much of the year. The tree line at the edge of the field is so black it is almost purple. It is a wasteland, at once recognizable and foreign in its bleakness. The cold bites through the thin fabric of my nightgown, and my feet are wet with dew as I stand on the dead grass.

The ribbons are still wrapped around my wrists. The medallion is not there. The Beast will not come through me this night, but relief does not find me as it should. It is clear that I have been summoned. By whom and for what purpose I shall no doubt discover.

Turning in a circle, I peer into the distance, trying to get my bearings. I cannot know for certain, but something about the rise to my left is familiar. I am trying to decide what to do next, when something catches my eye. Something small and moving toward me. I squint into the distance, and as I watch, the thing becomes clearer, its slow and graceful gait marking it as a person.

A regular person heading my way.

There is no point standing and staring. Whoever it is will reach me soon enough. I begin walking, making my way toward the figure, now considerably closer. At first I think it is Sonia. She is the only recognizable person I have seen in my travels, unless one counts the Souls. But as the figure draws nearer, first close enough that I can make out her gown and then even nearer so that I can see her face, I realize it is Alice.

I stop walking, not eager to speed along whatever has brought us both to this dead place. She makes her way toward me until she stands directly in front of me. A smile plays at the corners of her mouth, and I have no doubt who is in charge, who has called me to this meeting place.

"Surprised?"

"Not really." I shrug. "Who else would I meet here?"

Her smiles spreads, and for a moment she looks just like the excited girl who used to clap her hands when Father brought

us presents from his many trips. "Why, it is possible to meet all kinds of people . . . all kinds of *things* here, Lia!"

"Why have you called me here, Alice?"

Her smile fades as she notices the ribbons on my wrist. Gone is the soft voice from the stairs. Her face takes on the stony edge to which I have become accustomed. "Why will you not use the medallion for its intended purpose, Lia? Why do you fight the will of the prophecy, the honored role that is meant to be yours?"

A slightly insane laugh escapes from my throat. "*Why?* Why, indeed, Alice? Shall I throw caution to the wind, then, and let whatever wants to come back with me, *through* me, come back?"

Her voice rises. "Why not? Why must you make everything so difficult? I've already told you that you shall be protected. Do you think the Souls will harm the champion of their King? What do you have to fear?"

"My fear is not for myself, Alice. What of the world that is left when the Beast reigns? What good is our safety if those we love are left to live in a world of darkness?"

"Samael has been stranded in the Otherworlds for centuries. He will richly reward the one that brings him forth at last. Anything you want will be yours. You will be treated as a queen. It is the purpose for which you were born." The pools of her eyes shimmer with the murky depth of the river.

"Perhaps you have it wrong, Alice. Perhaps it is your purpose to act as Guardian, as *you* were born to do. Perhaps it is our purpose to work in concert. Working together, we might secure a peaceful world. We might find an end to the prophecy once and for all. Wouldn't you rather be party to the good in it?"

By my words do not have the intended effect. Her face only hardens further as she continues. "Is that what you want, Lia? To be party to an ideal of good that no one shall ever even know? To risk your life for it? Do you think it is enough? Because it is not. It is *not* enough. Not for me. We can have authority no one in this world has ever had, not since Maari, the last sister who was wise enough to take her power when she had the chance."

I cannot hide my surprise.

"What? Didn't you think I knew? Didn't you think I knew the story that belongs to us, to our mother?"

"I wasn't sure *how* much you knew. The book . . ."

She laughs again, pacing in front of me, although her footsteps make no tracks through the long grass. "The book!" she mocks, stepping closer. "Do you think that is the only way of knowing the story? Because it is not, Lia. I have other ways of knowing things."

She walks around me so that her voice comes from behind. It is a ploy, a way to unnerve me. I remain facing forward, willing myself not to whirl and face her.

"Samael and his Souls summoned me long ago, Lia. They whispered to me in the cradle as they whisper to me still. It is not our mother's voice I first heard, nor even yours, my twin. It is the call of the Souls that I first remember. Perhaps they knew of your . . . weakness. Perhaps they anticipated the confused loyalty brought on by the mistake of our birth. Or perhaps they simply wanted to be certain, certain that one sister would work to their end." She has made her way back to my face, but she turns and faces the empty field in front of us, opening her arms as if to encompass it all. "They taught me everything, Lia. How to travel, how to summon others into travel . . ." She turns to face me once again, and I swear that it is love I hear in her voice. "Everything."

While I have been taught nothing, I think.

I remember Sonia's words, her assertion that those in the Otherworlds cannot intervene in ours. And then I realize that the Souls have not broken this ancient law. By teaching Alice how to use her gifts, the gifts with which she was born, her destiny has still been her own. The choice has still been hers. That she has made it, that she has chosen so easily the way of evil, can be blamed on no one but my sister.

Not even the Souls.

Alice takes advantage of my silence, trying to affect the soft and gentle voice of my sister. "You only make things more difficult for yourself, Lia. Samael will have his way in the end. He will have his way as you open your arms, or he will force his way through them, but you are no match for such power. Will you not take the easier road? It will all end the same, so what does it matter?"

What does it matter? The words echo through the fields of stiff, brown grass.

I see my mother, letting go of all that she loved to be free of the legacy that was hers. I see the sisters after us, my daughters

or Alice's. And then I see Aunt Virginia, raising Alice and me, watching all these years. Watching to see who would be the Guardian, who the Gate. These things come to me in a flash, until I am left with nothing but the lamenting wind.

"No." I can barely hear the words myself, they are uttered so softly, and Alice leans toward me, her faltering smile proof that she has heard me after all.

"What did you say, Lia?" She is giving me a chance, a chance to pretend I did not say it, to say something different.

I clear my throat to be sure there is no mistaking my answer. "I said no. The choice is mine to make, and I am making it. I will put an end to it for good."

She glares at me, unmoving, before the sneaky smile returns to her lips. "And how do you propose to do that, Lia? Even if you sacrifice yourself like our dear mother did, it will only continue, on and on, mother to daughter and sister to sister. No, the only way out for you is to give in to the Souls. They are quite patient, you know."

I hear Aunt Virginia's words once more — *He will find your weakness. He will lie in wait for you while you sleep. He will use those you love most against you.*

I shake my head. "I would rather die." And I am surprised at my conviction. Surprised to find I actually mean it.

Alice leans even closer, so close I can feel her breath, warm on my face. "There are worse things than death, Lia. I thought you understood that."

She leans back, staring me down. And then I hear them coming.

They beat a path across the sky, at first sounding like the distant crack of thunder but soon growing to the terrifying crescendo of a thousand hooves, all racing toward the place where Alice and I stand. When I look upward, the sky has blackened. The wind, before an eerie groan, is now a roaring monster, whipping our hair around our faces so that we have to pull the strands away in order to see.

"You see, Lia, you may be the Angel, but I can summon the Souls at will. They know the sister who remains loyal to the prophecy. They come to me because I am the rightful Gate." Her voice rises triumphant over the howling wind. "We will work together, the Souls and I, for as long as it takes. I wish it were not so, Lia. But you have made your choice, and now I must make mine."

Even as the Souls converge in the sky above, a faraway part of me thinks it is not possible, that I will be protected as I was the last time after my sea flight. But my helplessness cannot be denied. I am powerless to move. The strand connecting me to my body, so present during my other travels, feels as if it has been severed, leaving me adrift in the bleak Otherworld.

This is what it must feel like to be detained. To be separated from one's body. To be taken to the Void. The thought comes to me from a last remnant of my rational mind.

The sky darkens further over my head, swirling until I feel I will be sucked into its blackness. The last strands of strength seep from my body. I want to slump to the ground and sleep, only sleep, as I slip into beguiling apathy.

"Lia!" A voice calls to me from the fields in the distance. I lift my head, trying to place the familiar voice. "Li-a!"

In the distance, another figure flies toward us, calling my name. Alice looks as puzzled as I, staring at the approaching figure with curiosity and annoyance. Even the darkness above us seems to waver.

The figure approaches faster than would be possible in any other place, traveling the fields so quickly the face is a blur. It is only moments before she slams into me, shoving me with a force so tremendous that it knocks the breath out of me, that I see Aunt Virginia's face.

I do not have time to speak, to thank her or worry for her safety. I try to reach out, to grab her by the hand, to take her back with me, but it is no use. The moment she touches me there is a painful tug on the strand, and I am suddenly pulled, back and back. Alice and Aunt Virginia and the darkness above them become smaller and smaller as I return the way I came, over the dead landscape below.

24

"Lia?" The knock is soft. "Are you awake?"

I pull myself upright in bed, relieved to hear Aunt Virginia outside my door. Whatever happened in the Otherworlds, she has survived it.

"Yes, come in."

She steps hesitantly into the room, closing the door behind her and coming to sit on the edge of the bed. She doesn't say anything right away, choosing her words before finally speaking. "You must learn the ways of the Otherworlds before you travel, Lia."

I nod. "I know. I'm sorry. I . . . I didn't mean to go. Sometimes, no matter how hard I try, I find myself there through no will of my own."

"They summon you, Lia. They know they must get to you now, before you become surer, before you establish more control over your powers, before you find all the keys." Her face is grave. "In time, you shall have more control over the circumstance of your travel, though you may always be vulnerable to the will of the Souls."

I nod. Her face is haggard, the fine wrinkles about her eyes deeper than they were only a day ago. "Are you all right? Were you hurt?"

She smiles faintly, the story of her exhaustion written in her eyes. "I'm all right. I am not as young as I once was, nor as powerful. There is more than one reason each new generation must assume responsibility for the prophecy."

"How did you . . . how did you make them stop?"

She shrugs. "I didn't. Not really. I shocked your soul into reconnecting with the strand, with the astral chord, and then held them at bay with the little power I have, just long enough for you to escape their grasp. I *was once* the Guardian, you know." She says this with a trace of pride.

"So that is how it is, then? Once the next Guardian and Gate have been dispatched, their predecessors hold little dominion over the Otherworlds?"

She looks up, trying to find a way to explain. "In a manner of speaking, yes, though we all retain some measure of our gifts even after our time has passed. Some hold more power than others, but I cannot say why it is true. Your Great-Aunt Abigail, my mother's sister, was one of the most powerful Guardians in history. She was able to do things . . . to battle the Souls with strength that is still discussed today among those in the Otherworlds."

"What happened to her?"

"She left." Her voice is faint. "When your grandmother . . . when her sister passed, Aunt Abigail simply vanished."

I'm not sure what to say to such an odd piece of family history, so I turn to things more immediate. "I'm sorry you had to come, Aunt Virginia . . . that you had to put yourself in danger. I thought I was safe . . . the last time . . ."

A look of alarm settles onto her face. "The last time?"

I chew my lip, feeling guilty that I have not shared everything with Aunt Virginia sooner. That I have not trusted her as I should.

"The last time they came for me they stopped."

She shakes her head. "Whatever do you mean?"

"I didn't know I was traveling then. I thought they were giving chase through the skies of my dream. Sonia was the one who warned me. If not for her, I would not have stood a chance. Even so, they were near enough to detain me, but something stopped them at the last moment. It was as if they couldn't touch me, however much they desired it. I thought it might be the same this time. That's why I didn't make my way home with more urgency." I shrug. "By the time I realized my mistake, it was too late."

Her face goes very still. "You must be mistaken. What you have described . . . well, it could only be so through a show of forbidden magic."

"Forbidden magic?" The words make my skin grow cold. "I know no magic."

Her breath comes so fast I can see the rise and fall of it in

her chest as she stares at the wall behind my bed. She stands suddenly, looking at me with stark fear.

"Lia. Get up and help me."

❧

"Will you not tell me why we are doing this, Aunt Virginia?"

We have moved the small night tables aside to give us room and are on either side of my heavy bed, preparing to slide it off the rug.

Aunt Virginia meets my eyes over the bed cover, her hair falling loose around her green dressing gown.

"Not yet. I don't know if I'm right. Besides, we needn't move it all the way. Just a little. Just enough so that we can pull back the rug a bit."

"All right. Just enough. Let's go, then. You push and I'll pull."

It is not very heavy, not as heavy as I expect it to be with its great carved posts and headboard. We move it off the rug at a slant, giving us access to the corner. Aunt Virginia bends to it, reaching for the corner quickly, before she pulls her hand back as if reconsidering.

"What is it?"

She raises her face to meet my gaze. "I don't want to be right. Not about this."

She takes one audible breath, as if gathering her strength. And then she pulls back the rug, gasping when she sees the thing hidden there. I do not understand the symbol under the rug, the thing carved into the wood of the floor, but even still, the site of it brings goose bumps to the skin of my arms and the back of my neck.

"What is it?" I whisper.

Aunt Virginia does not take her eyes off the mark on the floor. "It is . . . it *was* a spell. A spell cast to provide a cloak of protection around you while you sleep." She looks up at me. "The circle is an ancient symbol of protection, Lia. If one is powerful enough, one can cast a spell that will ensure the protection of any within the circle's bounds or keep out those one wishes to exclude."

Her words ring in my ears. I have a sudden recollection of Alice, sitting within the circle of the Dark Room in the dead of night. I remember my own helplessness in the face of it, my inability to cross the line of the circle's edge. And then I hear Aunt Virginia's words when talking about my mother: *She was a Spellcaster.*

I tip my head to get a better look at the symbol. Even with only a portion of it exposed, it does not look like a circle to me. I say as much to Aunt Virginia, and she rises from the floor. She is trembling, shivering as if she is very cold, though the fire was stoked by Ivy less than an hour ago, and the room is warm.

"That is because it is not a circle, Lia. Not anymore. Someone has reversed the spell. Someone has scratched through the circle and broken the spell of protection with which it was cast. Someone who wanted to leave you vulnerable while traveling the Otherworlds."

I feel her eyes on my face, but I dare not look at her for fear

I will either weep or scream. The remnants of the circle itself are faded, carved by someone's hand long ago. But the gouges that cross it — the scratch marks that defile it — they are recent, as fresh as the circle carved on the floor of the Dark Room.

Aunt Virginia does not need to name the one who has done this, who has exposed me to so much danger. I focus my thoughts instead on the person who tried to protect me, on the one who would go to such trouble to ensure my safety.

"Could my mother really have cast such a spell?"

"She is the only one who had both the power to do it and nothing left to lose." Aunt Virginia pulls something from a pocket in her dressing gown, holding it toward me. "I have long held this for you. She wrote it before . . . before she died. Perhaps I should have given it to you sooner. Perhaps I should have taught you the ways of the prophecy sooner. I only wanted you to be old enough, wise enough, to let the truth make you strong instead of letting it ruin you as it did her."

A cynical laugh escapes my throat. "I feel anything but wise, Aunt Virginia. Anything but strong."

She reaches out and pulls me into an embrace. "You are wiser than you believe, dear heart. And stronger than you know." She looks back to the circle. "I am not a Spellcaster, Lia. And even if I were, I would not be permitted to reinstate the spell of protection."

"Then how did my mother . . . Wait." I stop, remembering something. "You said the spell was forbidden."

Aunt Virginia nods, her face solemn in the half-light of the fire.

"Who would forbid her to use the power that was hers when it seems I am prompted day by day to use the power I wish wasn't mine at all?"

She lowers herself to the bed, perching on its edge as she explains. "The Otherworlds have a system of justice, of checks and balances, just as ours does. Its rules might seem strange to those not accustomed to the unique aspects of that world, but they are rules nonetheless. Rules set by the Grigori."

"The Grigori?" The name rings familiar, but I cannot place the reference.

"The Grigori is a council made up of angels from Maari and Katla's time who did not fall. Now they preside over the Otherworlds, ensuring that each creature and soul there follows a set of guidelines established long ago. Using the magic of the Otherworlds anywhere else is cause for punishment, but I do believe your mother felt she had nothing left to lose when she cast the spell of protection around your bed."

"But if Mother would have been punished for casting the spell, can we not bring Alice to justice for breaking it?"

Aunt Virginia sighs. "I'm afraid not. As with our world, there are ways to work within the confines of the rules."

"I don't . . . I don't understand."

Aunt Virginia meets my eyes. "Alice did not cast a spell of her own, Lia. She simply negated the effects of the spell your mother cast long ago — a spell that in and of itself was forbidden from the beginning."

I stand up suddenly, my frustration getting the better of me as my voice rises into the room. "So there is nothing? Nothing

we can do to stop her? To hold her accountable for placing me in danger?"

She shakes her head. "I'm afraid not. Not this time. It seems Alice has somehow learned the full force of her magic and is well versed in using it within the Grigori's boundaries. For now, we shall have to hope she slips along the way." She shrugs helplessly. "There is nothing else to do."

I stare into the fire, my mind abuzz with this new, unwanted knowledge:

Alice has all the cards.

Alice has power I do not.

And worst of all, Alice knows how to use her power to her aid and my detriment without consequence.

"I am sorry, Lia, but we shall work through this together, I promise. Let us take one step at a time." She stands to leave. "Luisa and Sonia are at the breakfast table. I have arranged a trip into town with Alice so that you may search for the list without fear of interruption."

I look up at her, feeling the weight of the tasks in front of me. "And then what? Even if we locate the list, we must still find the two remaining keys. And even if we find them, we do not know what to do with them or how to end the prophecy."

She presses her lips together before answering. "I don't know. Perhaps we can locate Aunt Abigail. And then . . . well, there are always the sisters. . . ."

This mention of the sisters gets my attention, for it is the same term used by Madame Berrier. "The sisters?"

She sighs. "Let us just say that there are those in the world

with knowledge of the prophecy. Those with gifts that might be useful. Some are sisters of previous generations, and others . . . well, others simply seek to use their gifts for the good of us all. But we shall have to leave that for now, Lia. All right? Let us find the list. Let us find the keys. You shall have to trust me — if you call on them when the time comes, there *are* those who will help you."

I suppose I am a coward, for I am glad to allow the details of this new revelation to wait for later. "I trust you, Aunt Virginia. But . . ."

"What is it?"

"What of my night travel? How do I prevent myself from falling unprotected into the Plane while I sleep?"

Her face darkens. "I don't know, Lia. I wish I could give you an answer — some sure way to avoid travel. But with the power of the Souls so determined to call you to the Plane, it is all I can do to say you must try to resist."

I nod as she rises and makes her way out of the room, leaving me alone with my mother's letter. My hands tremble as I break the wax seal on the envelope. I unfold the paper to the slender, curving script that was my mother's, knowing that I may well hold in my hands the long-sought answers to her death — and her life.

25

My dear Lia,

It is difficult to know where to begin. The beginning of this tale stretches back centuries, but I suppose I shall begin at my beginning, as my mother did for me.

My beginning was with the medallion, found in Mother's bureau long after her death. It called to me even before I knew it existed. It must sound strange, but perhaps as you read this you are familiar with its temptation and the manner in which it insinuates itself into your thoughts, your dreams, your very breath.

At first I wore it only on occasion, as I would any other trinket from my dresser box. It was not until I woke to find the forbidding symbol etched upon my wrist that things began to change. I began to feel the power of the medallion seeping through me.

It spoke to me, Daughter, called to me. It whispered my name even when stuffed under the mattress of my bed, even when I found myself away at school or calling on friends.

Of course, I wore it. More and more, I am ashamed to say, I wore it over the mark. The Souls called me in my sleep, summoning me to the Otherworlds. At first I resisted, but it was not so for very long. I did not yet know the story of the prophecy or the stakes that lay in my continued resistance. I knew only that I felt most free, most alive, most myself, when traveling the Plane.

As I grew in the knowledge of my gifts — traveling at will while my body slept, speaking to those that had passed, casting all manner of spells — my life marched forward. I met your father and thought if ever there was a man who could love me even with the burdens of the prophecy it would be Thomas Milthorpe. And yet I did not tell him. How could I? He looked at me with such admiration, and as time passed the secret grew bigger and bigger between us until the thing I would have told him would not have been the truth as I had planned, but the lie I had kept for so long.

It was just before you and your sister were born that the sirens' call of the Souls became more insistent. As you and your sister grew in the darkness of my womb, the Souls brought to me my own darkness. They lured me to sleep in the middle of the day. They tormented me in my dreams with images . . . horrible images. Images that made me ponder doing terrible things to myself even as I knew it would mean an end to you and your sister as well.

The medallion found its way to my wrist even after I locked it away in the bureau. Even after I buried it in the ground near the stables. Soon, I woke with it encircling my wrist even when I had not put it on before retiring. I felt sure I was losing my tenuous hold on sanity.

Looking back on that time, I know not how I managed to survive it, though I feel quite sure it was due in large part to the careful attentions of your father and Virginia. They rarely let me out of view.

Once you were born, you and your sister, the softness of your heads, the rose blush of your cheeks, the deepening green of your eyes . . . they all served to make me believe that perhaps there was something worth fighting for in this world even if it meant holding the evil at bay. I thought perhaps I could manage, if only to stay and be your mother.

And for a time it seemed to work just that way. I still felt the pull of the Souls. I still traveled in my dreams, though not as often. But nothing very terrible happened. You and your sister grew, crawled, walked, and spoke. My family remained safe, and if I brought anything, anyone, back from my night travels it seemed no one was the wiser.

I know now, of course, that it was a kind of fairy tale, those years when the medallion, the prophecy, and all of us, lived peacefully together. And then I found out about Henry. I discovered that I would have another child, though the doctor had cautioned against it after the difficult birth of you and your sister. Still, what was there to do but be proud that I might finally offer your father a son?

And proud I was — for a while. But as Henry grew in the darkest part of me, another kind of darkness gripped me so completely that I became truly frightened. I wanted to escape, Daughter. I wanted to visit the Otherworlds every hour of every day, and I wanted to bring the Army back with me, as many Souls as I was able, though I knew it was for no good purpose. Their howl became a song I never wanted to stop hearing.

But even this was not the thing that frightened me most, that made me realize how far I had slipped into evil, how close to madness. No. It was the greed with which I began to view my travels, so that soon I was forcing myself to lie still on my bed at all hours of the day and night in order to will myself into traveling, forgoing food and sometimes company to sleep,

only sleep, for never did I feel as complete as when I traveled. It was this that finally made me afraid.

When Henry was born . . . well, it was another difficult birth as I was told to expect. The doctor could not do another operation, and Henry's feet were down instead of his head. His legs . . . I do not have to tell you, Daughter. You know what happened to his legs. The doctors pulled as gently as they could, but he would have died had they not gotten him out when they did.

I was very sick after he was born. Not just tired and weak, but sad and angry and hateful, as if all the good had seeped out of me during Henry's birth only to be replaced by everything mean and evil that the medallion embodied. I would have flashes of love for you, for your sister and brother, for your father, but they were all too brief, settling on me like a butterfly and gone a moment later.

I slept more than ever, and when I awoke I knew with a certainty both sick and joyous that I had brought the Souls back with me. It is this streak of satisfaction that has made me realize that I do not have the strength to fight the legacy that is mine.

I am weak. I know you shall think me a coward, but how am I to stop a circle that was begun at the beginning of time? How am I, alone, to fight a thing that has won battle after battle through the ages? And most of all, how am I to pass

this legacy, this curse, on to you? How am I to look you in those clear green eyes and tell you what awaits?

Virginia is wise — wise and clear-headed. She will surely give you better counsel than I, in my current state of despair, can offer. I cannot bear the thought of passing this burden, of all things, on to you, my beautiful Lia.

So along with it, I shall bequeath you every last drop of my protection. The Souls will come for you, of this I am sure, but I shall use every ounce of power, every spell that would see me banished from the Sisterhood, to see you safe while you sleep. It is all I can do.

Please know at this moment, as I put this letter in a safe place and make my way to the lake, I am thinking of you with love. I wish I had sage advice, but all I can offer you is my love, and the hope — no, the belief — that you are somehow stronger and braver than I, that you will take this battle to its end once and for all. And win it for all the sisters before you, and those yet to come.

There is nothing else. No answer. No guidance.

She *knew* it was I. That much is a revelation. Aunt Virginia may not have known at first, may not have pieced together the confusion of our birth, Alice's and mine, and the consequences it would have. But our mother somehow knew that there was no escaping fate, no matter how chaotic and random it sometimes seems.

It was she who carved the circle of protection into the floor around my bed. Though I was only a girl, I remember moving from the nursery, from the small room I shared with Alice, not long before our mother died. Now the separation seems less a random rite of passage than a calculated move on the part of our mother.

A move to protect me from my sister.

That Alice's rage and greed have led her to a place where she would sacrifice me to the Souls . . . it is beyond imagining. I cannot even reconcile that my sister could see her way to send me to my death, to something worse than death, by way of the Void.

My fury, my disbelief, is an itch I long to scratch. But it will only do harm to our quest for answers. The smart thing, the wise thing, is to let Alice think me still ignorant.

And to let her believe that she holds all the power.

26

It is later than usual when I finally emerge from my room.

The door to the guest room is open, Luisa's and Sonia's beds already neatly made, as I make my way down the hall. I have every intention of joining them, feeling badly that I have slept late and left them to their own devices.

But that is before I see the half-open door to Alice's room.

Though I can see only a small portion of her chamber from my vantage point, her room emanates an aura of emptiness. I know, even from the hallway, that Alice is not there.

Looking quickly down the hall to be sure no one is coming, I step into the room and close the door quietly behind me. I stand for a moment, surveying Alice's room. It has been years since I have spent any time in it. It is different. Older. I stop to remember the years when toy animals and fine porcelain dolls sat atop the bureau and writing desk. But remembrances are a luxury I cannot afford, and I move farther into the room with careful footsteps.

I don't know where the list might be, but the possibility that Alice has somehow found it ahead of me cannot be ignored. I begin with the bedside table, opening the small drawer identical to the one in my own room. In it are some of Alice's stationery, a quill and ink pot, and a jar of rose-scented hand cream. I continue searching, resisting the pull of disappointment as I search the wardrobe, the desk, and even under the bed.

The bureau is the only place left, the only remaining hope for finding the list in Alice's room. I begin with the top drawers, working my way down to the larger, deeper drawers at the bottom. My fingers slide between nightgowns and capes, feeling for a slip of paper that might have the names of the keys. Instead, my hand closes on something heavier, wrapped in cloth at the back of the largest bottom drawer.

I pull the bundle from the drawer, surprised at its weight, and rest it atop the bureau for a better look. The object gives me pause, for surely it is not the list. But curiosity gets the better of me, and I lift the edges of cloth one by one until a knife is revealed in its center. I draw in my breath at the sight of it. It is no ordinary knife, but a rather large one with many-colored jewels inset into its hilt. I reach toward it, pulling my hand back when I come into contact with the ornate handle. I touch it again, feeling the tremor of raw power that pulses through the handle and up into my arm.

I look at the door over my shoulder, knowing I must hurry. I grab the knife with authority, my body humming with new energy as I lift it off the bureau for a better look. What I see on its blade freezes the blood in my veins.

Wood shavings cling to the shimmering silver. They are small, but I know them for what they are, and now I know the knife for what it is: the knife used to reverse Mother's spell of protection. The knife used to defile the circle on the floor of my room.

Rage surges through my body. It is far more powerful than the energy that courses through the knife, and I carefully wrap the sharp blade in the cloth, putting it in my drawstring bag and closing the drawer to Alice's bureau. I do not feel guilty taking such a thing from Alice. A thing used for so dangerous and evil a purpose.

I make my way from the room without a backward glance, leaving the door wide open. Perhaps it is reckless, but the battle lines have been clearly drawn. There is no longer cause for pretense between my sister and me.

"You've been keeping secrets." Henry's voice comes to me from the parlor as I step off the staircase.

I take a couple of steps back to locate his voice. He sits near the window in the parlor, already bundled in his winter coat and scarf for the ride to town with Alice and Virginia.

Assembling a smile on my face, I move into the room. "Whatever do you mean, Henry?"

His face is somber. "You know."

My own smile falters. "I'm afraid I don't."

He lowers his voice to a whisper. "You're the bad one, Lia. Aren't you?"

I shrug. "I don't know, Henry. I don't *feel* bad."

His nod is solemn, as if this makes perfect sense. "Only time will tell, Lia."

"Only time will tell? And who told you that, Henry?"

"Aunt Virginia," he says simply. "She said there is no sure way to know who the bad one is, even with the mark. She said that only time will tell."

I am surprised by his knowledge, but there is not much to say in the face of such wisdom. "I do believe she is right, Henry. I suppose we must wait and see." I turn to leave.

"I love you anyway, Lia," he calls after me. "Until time tells, I mean."

I turn to him and smile, loving him more in this moment than any other. "Until time tells then, Henry, and beyond. I love you as well."

❧

"However are we supposed to find anything here, Lia? I've never seen so many books, not even at Wycliffe!" Luisa turns from the bookshelf, leaning against it and putting a hand to her forehead in exasperation.

I look up from Father's desk, sitting back in the leather chair. "Well, I don't know where else to search. If Father were to hide something, I feel sure it would be here. The library is where he spent his time. Everything that is dearest to him is in this room."

"And yet, we have searched every conceivable location here!" Luisa says.

Sonia stands suddenly. "Here. We've searched every conceivable location *here*."

Luisa shrugs impatiently. "Yes. That's what I said."

But I think I understand to what Sonia alludes. "Wait a minute . . . what do you mean, Sonia?"

"We haven't searched his chambers," she says.

I wave away the implication. "Yes, but the library was Father's sanctuary. And it's where the book was found."

Sonia nods. "Exactly. Is that not more reason why the list could be hidden elsewhere?"

I chew my lip, contemplating her words. I do not want to admit that it is a possibility, not because it isn't, but because violating my father's privacy by searching his room gives me pause, even now that he is gone. Still, I cannot ignore the merit of the idea.

"You're right, of course. If the list is not to be found here, his chamber is the next logical place."

Luisa levels her gaze at me. "So," she says. "What are we waiting for?"

Without the fire to keep it warm, Father's room is cold as a tomb.

Luisa and Sonia enter without hesitation, but I close the door behind me and stand with my back to it for a moment. I survey the room, realizing it is unfamiliar to me because I so rarely had occasion to enter it when Father was alive. He slept here, that is all. All of his living was done in the library and the rest of the house with me, Alice, and Henry.

And yet, when I finally move into the room, I cannot help but feel that an important part of father did reside in this room. Perhaps it was a secret part of himself. A part that he kept hidden away from the rest of us. But as my eyes light on the picture of my mother on the night table, the books stacked neatly next to it, I begin to realize it was no less important for its secrecy.

"Lia?" Sonia is looking at me from the center of the room, palms up in question. "Where shall we begin?"

It takes me moment to come back to the reason for our visit to Father's room, and when I do, I find I have no more idea where to begin than Sonia.

I shrug. "I don't know. The bureau, I suppose. Under the mattress?"

Luisa steps to the bed, kneeling before it and slipping a hand between the two mattresses. "I'll begin here. Lia, why don't you search the more private of your father's things?"

"I'm going to feel behind the wardrobe," Sonia says, moving toward the armoire in the corner of the room.

I stand in the center of the room for a moment, trying to overcome my feelings of guilt at invading my father's privacy, even for a reason as important as this one. Finally, I remind myself that the list will not present itself to me, and I set to work.

I have never so much as looked inside a man's dresser. I

don't know what I expected, but the neat rows of dark stockings and suspenders are a sharp contrast to the frilly lace and silk of my mother's things. With every step I take closer to the prophecy, I feel as if I peel back the layers of my parents, seeing them as the man and woman they were instead of my mother and father. It is a strange and oddly touching journey, and I endeavor to be respectful as I move Father's things aside in the drawers.

It doesn't take long. There are only four drawers and it quickly becomes apparent that there is nothing unusual in any of them. I spin to face the room, leaning against the bureau. Luisa sits on the bed and Sonia stands against the wardrobe, arms folded in front of her chest as she chews the corner of her thumb. They don't need to say a thing.

"Nothing?" I ask.

Sonia shakes her head. "I even opened the wardrobe and went through the shirts and trousers. There's nothing there."

Luisa sighs. "And I've checked between the mattresses, under the bed, and behind the headboard. I'm afraid I've had no better luck."

I fight the frustration that has become my familiar companion since discovering the prophecy and my place in it. With every step forward, it seems we take two back. We need some assistance, something to match the aid Alice has had from the Souls, thus far.

I look first at Sonia and then at Luisa. "There is one person who knew for certain where the list was hidden before my father died."

Luisa breaks in, her voice firm. "We cannot risk Sonia again to speak to your father, Lia. Not after last night. We shall have to find another way."

I do not intend to risk Sonia's welfare again. Her face is still wan, dark crescents shading the skin under her eyes. She has not said it, but it is clear that contact with the Beast has sapped her strength. Asking her to speak with Father was careless, but putting her at risk again is not an option now that I am fully aware of the danger.

But I do not have to say aloud any of these things. Sonia looks into my eyes and sees clearly the plan that is written there. "It isn't me she means to risk."

Luisa shakes her head. "I don't understand."

Sonia pulls her gaze from mine and looks at Luisa. "Sittings are not the only way to make contact with the dead."

"My father is in the Otherworlds, Luisa. Isn't that right, Sonia?"

She nods. "Somewhere. Yes."

And now Luisa understands. She shakes her head, her brown eyes wide. "No! No, no, no. You will not travel *willingly*." She jumps to her feet. "Didn't you hear what your aunt said just last night? It's dangerous, Lia. For all of us but most of all for you. No. It is simply out of the question. We cannot risk your discovery by the Souls. We'll have to find another way."

Sonia sighs as if feeling compelled to say something she does not really want to say. "Only . . . there might be a way . . . a way in which Lia could find her father quickly and avoid the Souls."

If there is a way to find my father and determine the location of the list, any way at all, I will do it. I meet her eyes. "Tell me."

"There are rules to traveling the Plane, and one of them is that no soul can occupy more than one of the seven Otherworlds at once, though all may travel freely among them. If you can locate your father in one world while the Souls remain in another . . . well, it may be possible to obtain the location of the list quickly before you are detected and detained."

Something she says makes me stand up straighter. "But why only seven worlds? I thought you said there are eight?"

"The last world is reserved for the dead. Once one's soul crosses into the final world, there is no returning to this one."

I shudder at her words. "Is it even possible, then, to meet my father in the Otherworlds since he is dead, and I am not?"

Sonia nods. "Your father has not yet crossed. We would not have been able to speak to him if he had. Those who wait willingly in the Otherworlds do so for a reason. Your father must be waiting to help you. Once he crosses, you will not be able to speak to him again until you join him in the final world. But the other seven worlds are . . . in-between places . . . in-between places in which you can meet." She stops, looking at me kindly as if wanting to ease my disappointment before the words are even spoken. "But . . . you are as yet untrained, Lia."

"I know, but this is our only hope. We *must* find the names of the two remaining keys. We cannot go any further without them, and the only way to find them is to first find the list." I ponder it a moment more before making my decision. "It is

the only way. You said it is possible to control one's travel, didn't you? That one can fall willingly into the Otherworlds? You can help me get there, Sonia. You can help me find my father. You can *tell* me what to do."

She doesn't want to agree. Her nod comes slowly and with effort. "But you will be taking a grave risk. The Souls are waiting. Samael himself is waiting. He is waiting for you, Lia. He will try to detain your soul in the Otherworlds. If he should succeed . . . if he should succeed, he will take you to the Void and you will be Samael's prisoner for eternity. Do you understand what that means, Lia? You will never be able to cross into the final world. Never." She shakes her head, coming to a decision. "No. You must not travel alone. Not yet. I will go with you. "

But her words do not sway me. I have made my decision.

I shake my head. "No. I will go alone."

A half hour later, I lie on the leather sofa in the darkened library, the drapes pulled against the afternoon light. Sonia kneels beside the sofa, her eyes earnest and worried.

"When I say, close your eyes and empty your mind of everything but the place you wish to go, the face you wish to see. We will count together until I say stop. Try to hear your own breath, to feel the beat of your heart. I know it sounds . . . well, it must sound mad! But that's what you must do. Reduce yourself to the workings of your physical body while you empty your mind of all but that which you desire to see." She pauses before continuing. "Be careful what you think about while traveling. Thoughts have power, Lia. Especially in the Otherworlds."

I store away this new rule for later use and feel a moment of panic as fresh questions arise. "Wait a minute. Must I travel through the worlds in some sort of order while searching for Father?" I remember the dead field where I met Alice. "And what if I find myself in the wrong place? If I cannot find Father, or worse yet, if I arrive in a frightening place altogether?"

"You may travel anywhere you like, though it will take some time to gain control over your destination. Because you are unpracticed, you must try to . . . to call your Father to you. He will feel your presence on the Plane. This knowledge, this . . . energy will bring you together in the right world. He will find his way to you if he can. And if he doesn't, you are in the wrong world and must leave immediately for another before the Souls detect your presence."

"What if . . . what if the Souls find me? Or Samael? How will I get away?"

Sonia chews her lip, thinking. "You will have to set your feet on solid ground at the first possible moment. We are always vulnerable on the Plane. It is not our natural place. But we are most vulnerable of all when flying. Those who live in the Otherworlds know its ways. They know how to navigate its terrain, how to locate the things they seek. And how to bring harm to those they view as intruders. If you become trapped by the Souls, or Samael, or anyone else —"

I prop myself up on my elbows in protest. "Anyone else?"

She places a warm hand on my arm. "The Otherworlds are full of spirit beings. Some will seek to help you, others to make simple mischief, and still others to do real harm. Even experienced travelers must be wary on the Plane."

This new knowledge serves only to spur me forward, anxious to have the deed done so that I may return to the safety of Birchwood. "All right. Tell me how I can protect myself then."

Sonia's brow wrinkles as she searches for words. "All living things give off energy of some kind, and this includes those whose spirits dwell in the Otherworlds. When they seek to cause you harm, they do so by harnessing the energy they have. To protect yourself, you have to do the same."

I nod, thinking of the Souls that swirled above Alice and me in the dead field, the force of them, the power that made me weak-willed and complacent. "How do I manage such a thing? To . . . harness such energy?"

She taps her fingers nervously on the sofa. "That is the part that's so difficult to explain. I've been doing it since I was small, so it isn't an easy thing to name, but think of the energy you harbor as a seed, a tiny seed lying at the very center of your being. The seed is small, invisible even, but within it is more force, more strength, more light, than you can imagine. When you feel threatened, you have to see the seed unraveling, opening to reveal the living thing within."

I don't want her to know that this seems very fantastical. That the idea of an invisible seed protecting me against the force of the Souls seems farfetched in the extreme, and that is putting it quite nicely. Instead I nod, opening my mind to her words, reminding myself that I would not have believed any of it — the mark, the medallion, the prophecy — a few short weeks ago. And yet it has all proven true.

She continues as if she can hear my disbelief. "You mustn't simply think it. You have to see it, all right? You have to envision the seed opening, allowing your energy to flow outward from it, creating a barrier that will allow you time to escape."

"Is that my only hope then? Escape?"

She nods. "For now. You've not the strength or skill for anything else. Just finish the task at hand, Lia. Find your father. Ask him where he hid the list. And then come back without delay."

27

"Eleven . . . twelve . . . thirteen . . . fourteen . . . fifteen . . ."

Our voices make ghostly music in the emptiness behind my eyelids. They work together — mine, Luisa's, and Sonia's — creating a whispery backdrop to the darkness into which I will myself to fall.

And then they fall silent, privy to some cue I cannot see.

"Lia, you will let this world go. Allow yourself to fall into the blackness toward the Otherworlds." Sonia's voice is deep and soft before it goes quiet, and I am left to the empty world of my mind.

At first it is difficult not to think. It is difficult not to wonder when Aunt Virginia will be home, whether the servants find it strange that I am behind closed doors with my friends, and whether I shall be able to find Father.

But my mind covers this small area quickly, and soon I am

left with nothing else to wonder. With nothing else to do but think of Father's face, hear my breath, at first shallow and then ever slower and deeper. I picture the soft and fragrant world of my sea flight, the endless sky stretched smooth above me. I smell the salty air of the sea and imagine Father's face.

All at once, there is a flash, a blinding light that leaves me not in the darkness of sleep but in blazing sunlight through which I cannot see. The sound of my heart beating is magnified, thudding insistently in the background as flashes of memory come more and more rapidly. Birchwood. The faces of Sonia and Luisa, Alice and Henry. The river, James lying by its side. And then I am let loose of the constraints of my body with a great, freeing tug, coming to consciousness flying over a wood I don't recognize.

The ground below me is dense with trees, a thick green carpet that looks smooth and soft from the air. As I move through the sky, the smell of salt becomes stronger, the trees below me thinning until they are lost completely to a far-reaching meadow swaying with long, green grass. I hear the sea in the distance. It grows louder and louder, and soon I am over a beach of sweeping sand, an azure sea lapping at its shore.

It is here that I will myself to touch the ground, remembering Sonia's instructions to avoid flight where possible. My feet sink into the sand. I feel the coarse roughness of it even through my boots and marvel at the sensations that seem stronger each time I travel.

I am not sure how to go about locating Father. According to Sonia, he will be looking for me, but even still it does not seem wise to stand so exposed on the beach. Especially since I cannot yet be sure that I am in the right world.

Spectral rock formations have created caves that make it impossible to see beyond the beach. I am relieved that I don't have to worry about protecting myself in an open space, but I avoid looking too closely at the darkness beyond the mouth of the caves. I focus on the path in front of me, picking my way along the stretch of sand and stepping around stray boulders as I go.

"Well, hello, there!"

I almost jump out of my skin at the sound of the voice coming from the caves, alarmed that I have company in a place so deserted. A gentleman walks toward me, avoiding the many craggy rocks as he goes. He is young, dressed in trousers and a waistcoat. The formality of his dress is comical on the untamed stretch of beach.

"H-Hello." I take a quick look around, wondering if there are others nearby.

The man comes closer, and I see that he is quite handsome. His hair is fair, like that of James, his face slightly tanned. He is not much older than myself, and the gleam in his eye is entirely friendly. I relax my guard just a little.

The man bows before me in mock seriousness. "Michael Ackerman, at your service, Miss. I thought I should wander the beaches all day without company, but I guess I'm in luck! To what do I owe the pleasure of such lovely company?"

"Well . . . Uh, Mr. Ackerman —"

"Oh, you must call me Michael. Mr. Ackerman is my father!"

"All right, then . . . Michael. I'm looking for someone, you see. But I'm not sure where he is and I don't . . . well, I don't know my way around as of yet."

He nods knowingly. "I understand. You're here for your father, aren't you?"

I tip my head, surveying him with renewed interest. "Why . . . yes. Yes, I am. How did you know?"

He waves into the salty wind. "Oh, it is not difficult to know things here. You might say it's a small world, eh?" He laughs at his joke.

"I suppose. Do you know where I might find my father, then?"

He nods with authority. "Yes, yes. Of course, I do! He sent me to find you, as a matter of fact."

"He did?"

"Yes, indeed. Told me to look for a lovely girl of about sixteen and to bring her to him at once." He takes hold of my arm, propelling me forward down the beach.

I pull my arm from his. "Oh, wait one moment, please! I'm not sure I should be leaving with anyone. You see —"

"Nonsense!" He takes hold of my arm, more firmly this time. "I know just who you're looking for, and I shall take you right to him."

But I only take a couple of steps before I see the strange shine in his eyes. It does not seem helpful anymore, but something more sinister, and I hear Sonia's voice across the worlds.

Some will seek to help you, others to make simple mischief, and still others to do real harm.

"Now listen here." I move to pull my arm from his grasp. "I do appreciate your help. Truly. But I think I'll stay here a moment. Surely my father will find me, if only I stay in one place for a bit."

His grip tightens, and I wince as his fingers dig painfully into the soft flesh of my upper arm. "No, no. I don't think so." His voice has changed. It is harder now. And something less than friendly. "We have another engagement, you see, one —"

But he does not have time to finish. All at once, a boy of perhaps Henry's age is standing in front of us wearing a strange shirt without buttons and short britches that reveal his scratched legs. His face is smudged with dirt.

"Time to shove off, now, chap," the boy says.

"Now, now, little man. You'd do well not to concern yourself with matters beyond your years. Run along." Michael Ackerman pulls me a step farther before the boy steps in his path.

"I'm not gonna tell you again. Let her go. I don't want to have to hurt you."

It is strange to hear the threat come from so small a boy, but looking into his steely eyes I feel quite sure he means it.

"Listen here." Michael Ackerman draws himself straighter and taller. "I don't think you know who you're messing with, you understand what I'm saying? The girl is supposed to be detained."

The boy shakes his head with resignation. "I tried. I tried to tell you." He looks at me. "Didn't I try to tell him?"

"I . . . I suppose —"

My words are cut off when the boy raises his hand and says something in a language I don't recognize. At first the air around us falls strangely silent. Even the waves breaking against the shore seem to be soundless, as though the energy of the elements has been silenced by the boy's incantation. Then, all at once, the ground begins to shake. There is a moment — a split second, really — when we exchange hurried glances, the boy's unexplainably satisfied and Michael Ackerman's both knowing and afraid. I don't understand why his hand on my arm releases its grip until I look down and see the ground opening up beneath him. The sand parts seamlessly underneath his feet until he sinks, swallowed bit by terrified bit, into the ground. It all happens in an instant, and when I blink, Michael Ackerman is gone, the sand as smooth as if he were never there at all, the waves resuming their hypnotic rhythm.

I turn to the boy. "But . . . What . . . Where...What have you done with him?"

He sighs. "C'mon, now! Don't be upset. I gave him plenty of warning, and you saw how easy he went down. Besides, he was gonna take you to the Lost Souls." His speech is strange and loose, without care for manners or proper grammar.

I take a step back. I don't have time to question his bizarre display of magic, which, cruel as it may seem, has just saved me. My concerns are more personal and far more pressing. "And how do I know you're any better? Perhaps you will take me to the Souls as well. After all, you're here in the Otherworlds just as they are."

"Yeah, but I'm not one of them. I'm only here because I haven't crossed over yet."

I narrow my eyes at him as if it will help me determine his honesty. "And why is that?"

"I don't know, but there are lots of spirits here like me. Sometimes we stay by choice, and sometimes we just . . . stay." He shrugs. "Anyway, you don't have to worry about me taking you to the Souls." He leans in, lowering his voice and looking around as if for eavesdroppers. "Thomas — er, your father — has been looking after me, see? Protecting me from all kinds of weird things. This place?" He looks skyward, affecting a low whistle. "It's crazy. Anyway, Thomas asked me to look for you. Thomas and your mother."

It is the boy's familiar use of my father's name together with mention of my mother that makes me believe him. "You've seen my mother? Here?"

He nods. "Of course. They're together! What did you expect? She's pretty, you know." He blushes. "A bit like you in the eyes."

I have to swallow the excitement that rises in my throat. "Can you help me? Can you take me to them?"

He presses his lips together, looking skyward and then along the beach, before leaning in, his voice low. "I can't *help* you, in so many words. The punishment for doing so would be . . ." He shudders. "Well, it would be bad, okay? But I can . . . *direct* you a bit, and if someone should *happen* to notify your father that you're here, wandering the Otherworlds in search of him, well . . . who's to know, if we keep it quiet?"

"Listen, I would greatly appreciate your help. I don't have a lot of time, and it is imperative that I find . . . you know." His paranoia becomes my own, and I lower my voice and look around before continuing. "How do you suggest I proceed?"

He leans in, lowering his voice to a whisper and touching my arm with fingers I feel only as the whisper of a breeze. "You have to think only of him. Don't even bother thinking of a place. You can't know where he is. Not really. But he will try and find you. Just not here."

I still fear listening to this boy with his strange speech and stranger attire. Suppose it is a trick? Then again, suppose it isn't? Suppose he is trying to help?

I have no choice, I decide. I shall have to trust that he means to help. Otherwise I shall be a gray-haired old woman, still standing on the beach in one world and lying on a leather sofa in another.

"So I shall have to travel to another world, then?"

He nods. "I'm afraid so. But trust me on this; if you just think of Thomas and nothing else, he'll find you. He's been trying to reach you for a long time."

He turns as a breeze blows off the ocean, bringing a chill to the air that makes me cross my arms and look to the water. The wind dies all at once, the suddenness of it reminding me that I am not in my own world.

When I look back the boy is gone. I am once again alone on the deserted beach. I look around to be sure, but there can be no doubt. The boy has vanished as if I never saw him at all. I hurry to a slab of rock near the lapping shore, arranging my skirts haphazardly about my legs. I am eager to find my father and get back to Birchwood, back to the world I know. Closing my eyes, I think of my father and begin counting, the numbers a prayer on the breeze off the water.

"One . . . two . . . three . . . four . . ."

I am off the ground but not flying. Not exactly. Instead, I am caught in a black vortex, pulled in every direction. This is not the swift and effortless journey from world to world, but a churning sea that makes me feel as if I cannot breathe. The panic that rises within me is instinctual. I wonder if the man I met on the beach has told the Souls of my presence in the Otherworlds, if they will try to take me to the Void.

In an instant, my feet touch the ground. I did not realize my eyes were closed until I open them to the world around me. It is almost colorless, ice reaching as far as the eye can see. The sky is white, stretching above and beyond, making it difficult to see where the ice beneath my feet ends and the bleached sky above begins.

Instinct tells me to run, to leave this world as swiftly as possible, to try to find my father in another, but I decide to wait, to give Father the time to find me if he is, in fact, searching for me here. Though there is nowhere to go, I don't like the feeling of standing exposed on the ice. I shuffle forward until a low, echoing call catches my attention. I stop, listening.

It is a voice, muffled and coming from a distance. Holding very still, I try to make out the words but cannot, so I make my way toward the sound. There are no landmarks by which to gauge my progress. But I know I am approaching someone,

because the voice grows louder. It is the strangest sensation, to hear the voice grow nearer and nearer though there is not a thing in sight — not a building or tree or cave. Nothing.

As I grow closer to the source of the voice, I feel certain it is calling out as if in need of help. I walk faster, though it is awkward across the treacherous ground, and I am uncertain of the kind of help I could provide. The voice is very near now, and I stop, looking around for the source of it before shuffling forward once again, feeling as I am playing the childhood game "Hot or Cold." I know the boy on the beach would tell me to be silent and wait for Father, but it is impossible to stand so near the moaning without inquiring after the person making the noise.

"Hello? Is someone there? Are you all right?" I feel silly, shouting into the emptiness.

The moaning stops, but only for a moment. It resumes soon enough, and now, at last, I make out some of the words. "Help . . . Help me . . . Please." It sounds like a woman.

I look around, trying to figure where the person might be calling from. "Hello? Where are you?"

"Help . . . me." The voice is at my elbow, almost on top of me. "Please . . . save . . . me."

This time there can be no doubt. The voice is not at my elbow, but under my feet. I bring my gaze to the ice, slipping as I see the figure frozen beneath it. I stifle a scream, the sudden movement causing me to slip, arms and legs flailing as I fall. I scramble on hands and knees, slipping and sliding to get away from the person entombed in the ice directly under me, though there is no reason why I should be afraid of her. The face is colorless, but perfectly preserved within the ice. Even her hair is frozen, stretched out in the ice behind her.

When she speaks, her lips move almost imperceptibly. "Help me. They . . . are . . . coming."

I am overcome with both terror and pity. I want to help, but truth be told, my desire to help wars with a powerful urge to flee, to run as far as possible from the gruesome image. My mind pages through the possibilities and comes to a quick conclusion; there is no time to help. If I am to find Father and locate the list, I must steer clear of the Souls. It will not do to stay in one place for long, particularly a place as frightening and dangerous as this one.

As I scramble to stand, the voice of the woman beneath me becomes the voices of many, all moaning, their voices stretching into the air around me, grasping and tugging until I feel as if their icy hands pull me toward the ice.

"Help . . . us . . . Lost . . . Die . . . Please . . . Release us . . . Child . . ." The voices morph together, warped, insinuating themselves into my mind until I hold my hands over my ears as I stand, gasping for breath, immobilized by fear and horror.

I remember my last thought as I left the beach. And I know I am in the Void.

28

I shake my head against the knowledge, but the truth cannot be denied. I was brought here, not by the Souls, but by my own fear . . . my own thoughts when traveling.

Thoughts have power, Lia. Especially in the Otherworlds.

The memory of Sonia's voice shakes me from my stupor. I close my eyes and picture my father. In my mind, I make room for nothing else.

Father, Father, Father.

I am lifted, the frozen landscape below becoming distant. As I rise, I see the faces . . . so many faces trapped under the ice, stretched as far as the eye can see. A multitude of souls, banished and frozen for all eternity.

And then I am back in the vortex. Back into darkness.

When I open my eyes, I am floating just over the grass, moist with dew. I know I am near Birchwood in the parallel plane of the Otherworlds, though there is nothing but fields and trees in every direction. It is evening, and when I look to the sky I see that it is not the gray sky under which Alice made her threats, but the deep and darkening violet of my first, invigorating travel over the sea.

I recognize the large oak that shades the clearing by the river. Father often brought me here when I was a child, reading to me in summer under the shade of the leafy giant. I lower my feet to the downy grass.

I am not afraid.

Walking to the tree, I have the greatest sense of expectation, as if I am waiting for something wonderful that I cannot quite name. When they emerge from the forest, I understand why.

Father appears younger than I remember, though Mother looks just as I have imagined, a young wife and mother. Her laugh travels to me on the breeze as they approach, hand in hand. She looks up at Father with adoration. I feel an intruder, as if this moment is theirs alone. But it lasts only a second. When they see me, their faces light with smiles.

In an instant they are standing before me. I throw myself into Father's arms.

"Father! Is it you?" My voice is muffled in the shoulder of his overcoat.

His big laugh surrounds us, reverberating through his chest. "Of course it's me, love! Who else would be walking, arm in arm, with your lovely mother?"

The mention of my mother is a reminder that Father and I are not, after all, alone.

"Mother. I . . . I cannot believe it. I cannot believe it's you."

She smiles, tipping her head in a gesture that reminds me of Aunt Virginia and a little of Alice. "I had to come. It seems you need us now more than ever." Worry colors her eyes.

I nod. "I have come to know the prophecy and my place in it as well. I must find the list of names, but I don't know where Father has hidden it." I turn my face to him. "Was it you? When we spoke through Sonia . . . through the . . . the Spirit Talker?" I remember the word used while Sonia was in the spirit trance.

He hesitates before nodding. "I tried to tell you about the list, but I couldn't hear you clearly. And then He came."

The words bring a chill to my blood though the wind is as soft as ever. "Yes."

"I was forced to leave or risk being held and taken to the Void. I would be there now if not for your mother's power. She intervened when the Souls tried to banish me there. We have been running from them ever since." He turns to look down at her, putting an arm around her shoulders and pulling her close in a gesture of deep affection that brings a lump to my throat.

He turns back to me. "I knew you needed me. That is why I haven't crossed . . . why neither of us has crossed." He looks around, lowering his voice. "Word has gone out across the worlds, Lia. Word that you are to be stopped if anyone sees you. Samael is feared above all else, and his Army ensures that the weaker spirits among us do his bidding. They have spies in every corner. We have allies . . . those who will help us if they can, but it will not be possible to hold the Souls at bay for long. It is not safe for you here, or for us."

I take a deep breath. "Then we must move quickly. Tell me where the list is, Father, so that I can find the remaining keys."

He leans forward, his lips near my ear, and whispers. "I left it in care of the one I love. In my chamber."

I try to decode his words as I remember our search through his room. "But I have —"

He holds a hand up then, as if to stop me from speaking further. Placing a finger to his lips, he looks around us. I understand his meaning; we may be spied upon, even now.

I shake my head, trying to tell him that the list is not there. That I have looked and looked, but the list still eludes me.

But he nods firmly, as if to say, Yes. It IS there. You must look again.

I repeat his words in my mind: *I left it in care of the one I love. . . . In my chamber.*

The image comes to me suddenly, as easily as if it were there all along. I look into his eyes and nod, feeling a welcome burst of hope.

He looks up as the sky darkens, casting shadows about us where before there were none. "We must go, Lia. Our time is nearing its end."

My chest tightens at the thought of their leaving. Against my wishes, I have grown accustomed to the responsibility of my role in the prophecy. I have grown accustomed to going without Father's comforting embrace, his steady hand. But being with my parents again, if only for a moment, has reminded me of all I have lost.

"I don't want to go. I want to stay with you." I am not ashamed to sound like a piteous child.

My mother steps forward, pulling me into an embrace. "Lia." She breathes into my hair, and I smell the jasmine on her neck. "I'm sorry I've brought this upon you. But you are the Angel, the one sister who can end the prophecy forever. And it is meant to be so, however much we wish it were not. It was always meant to be you. There are no mistakes, Lia. Not ever. For ages and ages, the sisters have been waiting only for you."

I want to deny her words, even now after all I have seen. But there is truth in them. And so I nod, staring into the eyes that are so like the ones I see every morning when I look into the glass above the basin in my room. I nod to tell her that I understand. That I accept my duty in the prophecy, the duty that she passed on to me. That I am not afraid.

Father looks up into the sky. It is still blue, but the cold wind has returned and with it the vaguest sense of danger.

He looks at me with apology. "We must go."

I lift my chin. "Yes."

I nod, already sensing the futility of trying to keep them with me. Even now they are less vivid, less *present*, than they were only a few moments earlier.

My mother gives me a last embrace. "I knew it was you, even in the beginning, but I saw something in your eyes, something that gave me hope. I'm only sorry I was not strong enough to fight it for you."

I shake my head. "Remember, Mother. There are no mistakes."

She smiles through her tears, leaning in to kiss my cheek. "No mistakes, my angel." They turn to go, more quickly than I would like. Mother turns back once more, her face clouding over with worry. "Watch out for Henry, Lia. Will you?"

She does not wait for my answer, but I nod anyway, shouting after them. "I love you. I love you both."

It is all I have time to say. And then they are gone.

❧

Emotion courses through me as I travel in the direction of Birchwood. There is great sorrow at the parting with my mother and father but great happiness as well. It fills me so totally that I feel as if their love pushes me through the sky.

I marvel at the control I have gained in the Otherworlds in so short a time, the new assurance I feel in the direction and speed with which I fly.

But that is before a distant crack sounds from the sky behind me.

It begins as a vibration, and I feel sure the ground shakes though I am not touching it at all. With it comes a low rumbling from the earth, as if it might break open from the sheer force of the thing that thunders toward me.

A looming mass lies ahead. I feel quite sure it is Birchwood, but when I look behind me I see the Souls roaring toward me in a great, black horde. From a distance they seem a buzzing cloud of insects, but I know they will be here all too soon and will be anything but easy to swat away.

The call of Birchwood, of familiarity and safety, is powerful, but I do not trust myself to outrun the Souls. I stop flying, having made the only decision that offers any hope of escape, and imagine myself hovering over the ground until I am doing just that.

And then I wait, watching the cloud get bigger, darker, louder, as it makes its way toward me. I shall have to face them here, in the skies of their own world. I would like to say that I am not frightened, that I stand brave and firm in the face of the Souls. But it would be a falsity, for who could stand without fear before the roaring legion making its way toward me? No, I am more than frightened. I am terrified to the point of shaking, even in my astral being. But I stand fast, forcing myself steady.

My plan is not clever, but it is all I have, and so I wait until the exact moment when the Souls will be near enough that I may call on the power of Sonia's instructions. I must time it carefully, early enough to stop the Souls' advance but not so soon as to waste what little time I may have to escape. I think of Sonia's voice in my head, counting.

One . . . two . . . three . . .

Not just yet.

Four . . . five . . . six . . .

They are close now, close enough that I can see their tortured, angry faces, their long beards vanishing over black waistcoats, torn and falling from their hulking bodies.

Seven . . . eight . . .

The howl that emanates from the mass is inhuman, a battle

cry belonging to a savage animal. As they come nearer, they spread out, over and above me, to either side, even under my hovering body until I despair that I have waited too long. Until I am sure they will devour my soul completely.

There is nothing to do but close my eyes and imagine the seed, tiny and closed in the deepest, most secret part of my body. I see the layers peeling back, revealing ever more layers, lighter and lighter in color until I reach the lush, living entity at its center. It breathes. It throbs. It *pulses* with life.

I still hear the Souls, but their shrieks are part of another place entirely, for I have retreated into a hushed and muffled world of my own. The only sound I hear clearly is the beating of a heart. At first I think it comes from my own chest, but then I open my eyes and see the red light pulsing at the center of the mass, the thunderous wings beating the air with an ominous *whoosh* from within the shadowed form of the Souls. From Samael at their center a red glow emanates outward, his heart beating in time to my own, his many, great wings spreading up and out over his Army.

I must force my mind back to the seed, to the thing at its center. I see it opening, unfolding, *bursting,* filling up every crevice of my body. When I look down, a lavender light spills from my skin, my eyes, my mouth, intensifying with every passing moment as a power I have never before felt or imagined undulates from my body, flowing outward in small ripples that grow to echoing waves.

If the Souls make any sound at all it is lost in the music of my own power and the still-beating heart that throbs between

Samael and me. I think this may be the moment, my only moment to flee to the safety of Birchwood while the Souls are held at bay with whatever authority I have managed to tap. But then I hear the voice.

"Mistress . . . Let chaos reign. . . . Open the Gate."

I shake my head by instinct, afraid to utter words that may shake whatever foothold I have gained with my small show of force.

"Power and peace will be yours. . . . Open your arms, Angel of Chaos, and let the havoc of the Beast flow like a river. . . . Open the Gate . . ."

The voice slithers to me through the Souls, through the silky sky. It makes its way through the lilac light as the Souls themselves cannot. It is only a voice. They are only words. But they call to me in a way that is both a warning and a caress.

The light still flows from my body, but my strength wavers as the words of Samael find their way past my ears, past my mind, ever deeper into some ancient place that has been waiting, only waiting, for their call. In the voice is the promise of release. Release from the fight that seems never-ending, though it has only been mine a short time. Release from a future continuing that fight, from a future that will not hold the things I most desire — security, love, hope.

But the seed unfolds ever more, past the point at which I think it can further grow, until it feels as if the power of it will split me apart, body and soul. And with that last burst of strength I find the resolve I need.

I do not take the time to look back. Instead, I turn within

the light and call to the mystical power that is mine. I call on it to hurry me home with as much speed as is possible. I call on it to see me back to Birchwood, to hold Samael and his Army at bay long enough for me to fall back into the body awaiting me on the sofa in the library.

I race on the swell of light toward the looming thing in the distance. It does not take me long to confirm that the building ahead is, indeed, Birchwood. There was a reason, after all, that Father wanted to meet me in the world closest to home. He knew they would come.

A great roar erupts in a mad screech behind me. I do not turn and look, though the urge to do so is powerful. I only fly, the fields racing below me as I near the house. It is only when I am close to home that I begin to lose strength. It does not happen all at once. Rather, it is a slow exhaustion that seeps into my bones, weakening the light that flows from my body. I am so near, near enough to make out the diamond panes in the leaded windows. Near enough, even, to see the glow of the lanterns as dusk fast approaches. But a resounding clamor resumes behind me, and when I turn I know why I have fallen just short of the time needed to make a complete escape.

Samael has come for me. He has risen to the front of the Souls, the still-beating heart growing louder as he makes his way to me. The strength of the Souls is nothing compared to that of Samael. His power, his fury, is primordial. It rises in a swell of evil that steals my ability to move.

I am hovering at the library window, my will leaking from

me like rain, when I remember something Virginia said. Was it just this morning?

. . . If you call on them when the time comes, there are those who will help you.

My body is too weak to continue. But my mind . . . my mind has just enough fight remaining to call for the help I need.

"Sisters . . . those of Sisterhood past . . ." My voice does not sound like my own. It is tinny and far away, but I continue anyway, closing my eyes and trying to block from mind Samael drawing closer, closer. "I call on you, Sisters, to help one of your own. To save me that I may save us all."

I cannot even feel the ridiculousness of asking for such help in the face of the thing roaring toward me. As the moments tick on — are they seconds, minutes, hours? — I resolve to close my eyes, to wait with dignity for whatever will come.

But then I feel a fierce, warm wind, followed by a crack that makes me look to the heavens. When the woman comes into view, Samael and his Souls seem to slow their progress. She stands a few feet away, somewhere between me and the swiftly approaching Army. There is something familiar about the stubborn set of her jaw, the green pools of her eyes.

The nameless woman stands between me and the Souls as other women appear from the sky as if out of nowhere, fanning out and forming a circle around the Souls and Samael. Ethereal gowns billow around their translucent legs as they raise their hands until they are almost touching. White-hot flames spark and burst from their palms, forming a circle of mystic fire between the Beast and me.

The first woman hovers nearest me, the weak lavender light that poured from my body a brilliant purple pouring from hers, extending, rushing outward until it echoes through the circle in which the Souls' steeds rear on panicked legs.

Her mouth does not move as her voice comes to me from a distance. It resonates in my mind, and I realize she is not speaking aloud at all. "Go, child. Gather your strength. We shall meet again."

Samael howls, raising a sword through the center of the circle. It glows orange, sparks hissing off its blade, crackling against the light of the sister's circle, and though they are clearly powerful, I've no wish to test their strength against Samael's for an extended length of time. I nod to the woman in acknowledgment of her words, pushing through the walls of the house in what feels like my last moment of strength.

Sonia and Luisa sit on the floor near the sofa, Sonia holding my limp hand with her eyes closed, her mouth moving in silent prayer. I drop into my waiting body with a gasp felt in both worlds, sucking in air as if I have been deprived of breath for a great while and have only just been revived.

"She's back! She's come back!" Luisa's voice bursts from the floor next to me.

I only vaguely feel Sonia's smooth touch on my hand, as if all of my senses have not fully re-engaged with my body. I try to speak, to tell them that we must go back to Father's room to look for the list, but what comes from my mouth is a series of noises and sounds that do not resemble real words. I shake my head in frustration as Sonia speaks harshly.

"Lia? Lia? Look at me, Lia. Listen to me." She takes her hand from mine, turning my chin so that I am forced to face her, looking into my eyes with such authority that I am forced to look back. In them is the peaceful sea of the Otherworlds. "You must be calm. It is natural. It is natural to be unable to speak when returning from such a journey, all right?"

I can only stare, not trusting myself to speak again.

"All right, Lia? You must trust me. Your speech will come back in seconds. The feeling in your body will come back in seconds. You must slow your breath and wait. You must allow your mind to process all you have done, all you have seen. You must allow it a few moments to return to its physical state. Look at me, Lia! And nod that you understand." Her voice is harsh. I feel suddenly like a child, but there is safety in the firm command of her words, and I look her in the eyes and try to nod.

"Good. Now, stay still. Just stay still and breathe."

I give myself over to the utter helplessness of my body. When I look at Luisa, the fear in her eyes frightens me further, so I force myself to turn back to Sonia, to look into the blue depths of her eyes until I am breathing more normally.

I test my fingers, commanding them to move and am grateful when they do as ordered. I follow the same procedure with the rest of my body, making small demands of it until it seems all is in working order. Only then do I try to speak. Sonia and Luisa are held in rapt attention as I try to form the words.

"H-h-his chamber. The list is in his chamber. Behind the picture of my mother."

29

"Are you certain this is where it is?"

Luisa hands me the photo of my mother after retrieving it from Father's room. I have been forced to stay on the sofa, as Sonia has informed me that weak limbs are one of the unfortunate side effects of an especially long and difficult journey on the Plane. As if that is not enough, my head is pounding, giving me new sympathy for the trials of Sonia's life as a spiritualist. Though it has not been said aloud, the darkness beyond the windowpanes tells us that our time alone runs short. Aunt Virginia will return with Alice and Henry at any moment.

"Not entirely, but as certain as I can be under the circumstances."

I stare at the image of my mother. Her eyes are no less intense for the black-and-white photo, and I remember their vibrancy during our brief visit on the Plane.

"Would you like me to do it?" Sonia asks softly.

I shake my head. "No. I'll do it."

I turn the photo over in my hand, laying it facedown on my lap. The thin metal clips at the back slide easily out of the way, allowing me to lift the thin piece of wood from the frame. At first I think there is nothing there. I can see the back of the photo, and am preparing to lift it, too, from the frame, when something catches my eye in the corner of the frame between the glass and the ornate metal.

As I lift the frame closer to my face, Luisa breaks in. "What is it? Is there something there?"

"I'm not sure. . . ." But it does not take long to realize that there is, indeed, something there. I pluck it from the corner of the frame with shaking fingers, though whether they tremble from excitement, fear, or my recent visit to the Plane I cannot say.

"But . . . it's so small," Sonia says. "Surely that cannot be the list!"

It is just a scrap, a minute piece of paper that has clearly been torn from the corner of a larger page, but I am not as disappointed as I might have imagined. It is the closest we've come yet to the list. Although it is no longer hidden in the frame where my father left it, of one thing I am certain; it once was.

Sonia and Luisa are as quiet as I. The disappointment is audible in the silence of our breathing, the lack of words spoken between us. It is I who finally speaks, who finally breaks with one word the heavy quiet in the library.

"*Alice.*"

I pace the floor in my bedroom, trying to gather my thoughts before confronting Alice. I could not do so amid the flurry of activity as Aunt Virginia and Henry shared their purchases and recounted the tales of their day. I had time only to meet Alice's gaze in a searing glance before she retired to her room. Dinner followed, a tense though grand affair with guests still in the house, though Thanksgiving proper has passed.

Luisa and Sonia offered to accompany me when I confront my sister. But this part of the prophecy, this part of the battle, is mine. I have waited through the evening with growing fury.

Alice, working in concert with the Souls who would see me dead.

Alice, exposing me to harm by undoing Mother's spell.

Alice, taking the list.

By the time the house settles into sleep I am more than prepared to retrieve the list from Alice, and I leave my chambers with a purposeful step that is not as silent as it should be given the hour. I knock when I reach her door but open it before she can answer. She will not have the choice to deny me entry.

On her face is a look of true surprise that I have never seen before. Her hand flies to her bosom, her mouth forming an O of bewilderment. "Lia! Whatever —"

I march toward her, and for the first time in all the years we have been sisters, in all the years we have been friends and

confidantes, my sister looks afraid of me. She takes a step back as I come within a foot of her face.

"Give it to me, Alice." I hold out my hand, wanting her to understand that I will not leave without the list of names that is my passage to freedom.

She shakes her head, making a good show of false confusion. "I don't . . . I don't know what you mean."

I narrow my eyes. "Yes . . . you . . . do, Alice. You have it. You stole it from Father's room."

She pulls herself up straighter, eyes blazing, the look of fear receding behind her own indignation. "I tell you, Lia, whatever it is that you think I have, I don't. Though from the look of things, it is must be very important to you. I quite wish I had it now, whatever it may be." Her eyes take on the wicked shine that always makes me fear what she will do or say next. When she continues, I understand why. "Especially since you have something of mine."

We stare at each other for a moment, our breath shallow and audible in the quiet room. I do not intend to confirm my possession of the knife, nor do I intend to return it to her. Instead, I force a calm into my voice that I do not feel. "Give it back, Alice."

She tips her head, meeting my eyes without flinching. "I still don't know what you mean."

Frustration threatens to boil over. She knows to what I refer. I am sure of it. But I have no choice but to spell it out further unless I should like to stand in Alice's room playing word games all night.

"The list. Father's list of names. It was on his night table behind the photo of mother. And now it's gone."

She turns, wandering casually back toward her dresser, pulling pins from her hair as she looks at me in the mirror over her bureau. "Ah . . . Now I see. You have finally become wise enough to realize the importance of the keys." She turns around then, clapping her hands together in applause as if she is at the theater. The sound erupts into the quiet room. "Well, good for you, Lia. You must be so proud. Nevertheless. I don't have the list. Oh, I wanted it. I even went into Father's chamber to retrieve it. I looked behind the picture of mother, but the list was not there even then."

I cannot hide the confusion I feel spreading across my face. "But how did you know? How did you know where it was when I've been looking all this time?"

She laughs aloud, and there is genuine amusement in it. "Oh Lia! You still don't understand, do you?" She spins to face me once again, her long hair spilling onto her shoulders in a riot of curls. "I don't need Father to tell me things. I never have. I learned early on that I was of no interest to him. Not when he had his precious Lia. No, I didn't need him in this world, and I don't need him now that he is in the next. I don't need Virginia. And I don't need you. I have my own ways of finding things. I'm only sorry I didn't find the list in time."

"What do you mean? You found it too late?"

She sighs as if having to explain something very simple to a small child. "The frame was empty save for our dear mother's

picture." Sarcasm drips from her words. "I knew it was there at one time, so I assumed you'd simply found it and had hidden it elsewhere."

Facing her, I cannot think of a single thing to say. My anger has been replaced with a deep and unsettling confusion. If I don't have the list . . . if Alice truly doesn't have it . . .

Who else would have use for such a dark and dangerous thing?

The Angel, guarded only by the gossamer veil of protection, fragile and worldly, easily torn.

I open my eyes to the words, whispered in some lost recess of consciousness. I have slept fitfully, full of dreams that I sense are, for once, only that. Dreams. When I wake, it is not with the answer I need, but with the familiar words echoing in my mind.

The Angel, guarded only by the gossamer veil of protection.

Guarded only by the gossamer veil of protection.

Guarded only by . . .

Veil of protection . . .

. . . of protection.

. . . of protection.

The words repeat as if there is a scratch on one of Father's Gramophone disks.

As if someone is trying to tell me something.

And then there are Father's broken words, spoken across the Worlds, *Henry is all that is left of the veil. . . .*

And all at once, I know what it means.

30

I descend the stairs at a dead run. I don't give a thought to the commotion I make as I reach the bottom, but it must be considerable because Luisa and Sonia emerge in a fright from the dining room.

Sonia holds a napkin in her hand, looking at me with surprise. "Lia! Whatever is the —"

"Aunt Virginia?" My voice is a bellow through the house, desperation seeping deeper and deeper into my bones.

Luisa and Sonia stare with wide-eyed shock at my behavior.

The click of shoes on marble makes me turn. Relief fills my body and then leaves just as quickly when I see that it is not my aunt but Margaret, looking at me as if I have gone around the bend, yelling through the house like a child.

"Why ever are you shouting, Miss Milthorpe?"

"I'm . . . I'm sorry, Margaret. I must speak to my aunt at once. Have you seen her?" My shaking voice betrays my fear.

She smiles. "Why, of course, dear. She's upstairs. In bed."

"In bed?" Margaret might as well say Aunt Virginia is grooming the horses for all the likelihood that she would be in bed during the day.

"Yes. In bed. She's not feeling herself. She has been un-usually tired of late, and I have sent her to bed for added rest. Nothing to worry about, I'm sure. Just a little under the weather." She smiles, as if this alone can quell the turmoil rac-ing through my veins. "Check on her later, dear. After she has had some time to sleep. I'm quite sure she'll be fit as a fiddle."

I nod, remembering Aunt Virginia's weariness after in-tervening on my behalf in the Otherworlds. Tipping my head into the parlor, I see that it is empty and turn back to Margaret.

"Margaret?"

"Yes, Miss?"

"Where are Henry and Alice?"

Uncertainty crosses her normally unflappable features. "Well, that is a matter I wanted to discuss with Miss Spencer. . . ."

I raise my eyebrows. "Well, perhaps you should discuss it with me."

She shifts nervously from foot to foot, and I think that this may be the first time I have felt myself mistress of my own home. "Well, Miss . . . Alice took Henry to the river."

My mouth drops as I look beyond the window to the steely

sky. "To the river? Now? Why, it looks as if it will pour at any moment, Margaret!"

She has the grace to look sheepish. "I wanted to tell Miss Spencer, but she was unwell, so . . ." Her voice trails off, and she looks away.

"But how could you let her? How could you let Alice take Henry? He is only a child!" There is no hiding the accusation, though I know it is unfair. Alice is, after all, Henry's sister. Why should she not take him out for some fresh air, even on a forbidding day such as this, if that is what he desires? Why should Margaret have reason to doubt that it is only sisterly love and duty that would cause her to do so?

Her face hardens. "Well, if you must know, it was Alice who insisted she wanted time alone with Master Henry. And she made no secret about the fact that it is she who is Mistress of Birchwood, not Miss Virginia. And that I have no business questioning her activities. That's exactly what she said, Miss: 'You have no business questioning my activities, Margaret.' I *am* sorry, but there was no stopping her."

I turn to Sonia and Luisa. "Remain here. Whatever happens, do not leave this house." I grab my cloak and open the door, and then I am out into the biting cold.

I make my way around the house and see them standing by the river's edge as the first drops begin to fall. Pausing, I tip my head upward as a cold drop falls onto my cheek.

And then I run.

My skirts swing heavily around my ankles as I race down the stone path. In the distance, Alice stands just a few feet

from Henry. Nothing seems amiss, and for a moment I think perhaps I am mistaken. They seem to be doing nothing more ominous than conversing.

But then the sky opens with a thunderous crack, and the rain begins to fall in earnest. In moments my hair is plastered to my head, my soaked skirts heavier and harder to manage. And yet Henry and Alice remain on the riverbank as if they are standing in bright sunlight, unmoving and seemingly unaware of the torrent that surely soaks them as well. Now I know that I am not mistaken, and I will my legs to move faster.

They are off the stone terrace entirely, on the dirt near the bank. Too near the bank, I think. Neither turns when I reach them, though they must notice me, panting and trying to catch my breath not five feet from them both.

"What are you doing?" I shout it over the furious roar of the rain, though I believe I know quite well why Alice has brought Henry here.

For a moment, neither answers. They simply stare at each other as if only they two exist.

It is Alice who finally speaks. "Go away, Lia. There is still time for you to stand aside. Let me speak to Henry alone. I will settle this thing here and now."

I look at Henry — really look — and am livid with rage. He sits in his chair appearing smaller than ever, as if the rain has somehow made him shrink to look like the barn cat we once tried to bathe in a tub behind the stables. His teeth chatter with cold. He is not wearing so much as a coat.

"This is every bit as much my business as yours, Alice. Have you no shame, bringing Henry out into the rain?" I move toward him, meaning to return him to the warmth and safety of the house. Everything else will be addressed later.

But Alice steps between Henry and me. "Henry will not be going anywhere, Lia. Not yet. Not until he gives me the list."

I want him to deny it. I want him to protest, to say anything that might save himself the torment of standing between Alice and me with the one thing we both want more than any other. But that is not what he says.

"She was going to take it, Lia. I saw her looking. It is my place to protect you. Father said so."

"Father . . . is . . . dead, Henry!" Alice shouts it into the wind, raising her arms to her sides. "There is no one left to whom you must answer. No one but me and Lia. And you can *free* her, Henry. You can free her forever by *giving me the list.*" Her voice is full of new power, and it rises even over the river's swift rush and the pounding of the rain.

"Henry! Look at me, Henry!" I want him to see that I am not afraid, and I try to hold his eyes through the will of my thoughts alone. "I'm not afraid, Henry. There is no need for you to protect me, all right?"

His lips have turned a morbid shade of blue, purple around the edges. He can hardly speak, can hardly get the words out for the cold. "Father told me to keep it safe. F-f-for you, Lia."

And then I see what I most fear. Henry's fist, closed tightly around something limp and white. I curse myself inwardly.

Demanding the list from Alice only proved to her that I did not have it. It only gave her cause to look elsewhere.

"Put it in your pocket, Henry. Put it away until we are back inside." I step toward him with every ounce of authority I can muster. I will take him in. Let Alice try to stop me.

Except that she does not. She does not, in fact, come anywhere near me. Instead she steps toward Henry, grabbing hold of the handles on his chair as she turns sideways, turning her face to look at me.

"Don't come one step closer, Lia. I told you to step aside." And then to Henry. "Give me the list, Henry. If you want to protect Lia as you say, as Father wanted you to, you will give me the list. If you don't, Lia will never be free of the burden that is hers." She needn't threaten me with words, for her hands on Henry's chair so near the river are threat enough.

Henry shakes his head stubbornly. "No. I'm only doing as Father asked." His lip quivers, belying the fear and cold that he tries to hide behind his steadfast refusal.

I have had enough. I step toward Henry, trying to affect a confidence I do not feel. "This is ridiculous, Alice. Let go of Henry at once. I'm taking him inside."

I have just reached her shoulder when Alice spins, faster than I think possible in such rain, so that she and Henry are facing the river as she looks at me half over her shoulder.

"Don't come any closer, Lia. Don't."

I stop, holding very still. Thinking. Thinking as fast as my mind will carry the thoughts forward. The look on her face is indecipherable — a mixture of anger and fear and sadness so intermingled it is difficult to determine where one ends and the others begin. She looks half-mad, her eyes wild. I do not trust her with our brother. It is wisest to get Henry away from her grasp as quickly as possible. I take one step toward her, feigning a confidence in her rationality that I don't really feel.

"Don't." Her eyes are pleading, begging me for something I don't understand and cannot grant. "Please, Lia."

It is this final plea that makes me feel safe stepping forward once again, that makes me believe Alice does not want to hurt Henry.

But I am wrong, so very wrong, for I have only taken one step when she gives a small shake of her head, heaving Henry and his chair forward toward the river as simply as if he is a stone.

It seems strange that I should hear the sickening creak of Henry's chair over the downpour, but I do, and the wheels inch forward across the rocky riverbank, not very quickly at first but picking up speed as it hits the incline.

In what seems the oddest thing of all, everything happens slowly. Somewhere within the logic of my mind I know things are pressing ahead much too fast, much too dangerously, but in this moment it seems that everything has slowed down, the time passing in a strangely twisted version of itself.

I lunge across the wet earth, flailing desperately for his leg, the spoke of his chair, anything at all, as Henry rolls closer and closer to the river. Sprawling across the mud, my fingers catch on the spoke of one wheel, and a spark of pain runs up my

wrist as the backward movement of the chair is stopped with my fingers.

Henry is painfully silent, clinging to the arms of his chair with all the strength his small body can muster. I try. I try to hold the chair, but it is so very heavy, my fingers are not nearly strong enough to stop the force of so much steel. It pulls loose from my hand in a last, excruciating tug.

And then Henry is falling, falling, down the bank of the river. Amazingly, he stays in the chair until it hits a rock near the bottom, tipping and spilling him out of it.

Straight into the rushing water.

31

"I-I-I didn't —" Alice's voice is a stutter over the rain in the moment before I race to the river's edge.

I give no thought to anything but Henry, helpless without the use of his legs in the rushing water. I cannot get to the river fast enough. I dive headlong into the center of it, knowing it is deepest there and will carry me more swiftly toward my brother. The water hits me with the cold shock of surprise as it closes over my head, taking me downstream even as it pushes me under its surface. I struggle against the current before finally letting go, allowing the force of the water to push me to and fro, to throw me painfully against the bottom, scraping my body against the rocks that lie there.

It is only as I begin losing my breath that I come to my senses, making a desperate bid for air by pushing off the rocky riverbed with all the force I can muster. I long ago learned to swim in the calm water off the island where we vacation in summer, but my violent tumble down the river has nothing in common with the gentle rocking of the ocean. My head emerges from the murky depths, but the river tugs at my skirts, threatening to pull me down once more. I believe I see something dark floating downstream just before my head is again pushed beneath the roiling current.

This time I fight, thinking Henry may not be far out of my grasp. I kick and stretch, reaching for the surface until I break free, gasping for air while I am able. The rain still falls, making circles on the surface that fold quickly into the rapids. I look and look, scanning the churning river for any sign of my brother, but the water is muddy, the rain incessant, and I see nothing that gives me hope before I am slammed to the bottom yet again.

My bones are weary, numb with cold and the constant abuse of the rocks at the bottom of the river. Tossed through the water like discarded baggage, I feel the alluring tug of eternal sleep. Something within me wants to let go. To open my mouth and let the water flow to every inch of my body, if only to complete the struggle that is the river, the prophecy, the burden that is mine.

It is my mother's voice that forces me to a moment of lucidity. *Watch out for Henry, Lia.* It is an echo in the half-dead part of my mind, the part that has nearly given up, and with it I kick to the surface, fighting for my life and the life of my brother.

"Lia! Over here! Come this way!" At first I think I imagine it, but the voice is real and calling to me from the riverbank.

I lift my head over the rapids, scanning the shoreline until I see her. It is Alice, standing at the river's edge with a long, thick branch in her hand.

"Come on, Lia! You must try! Try to make your way to me." I can barely hear her, though she must be shouting with everything she has in order to be heard at all from such a distance.

She is far enough downstream that I may make it if I paddle furiously and with all my might. But Henry . . . Desperation makes me frantic, and I begin to sink once more as I scan the river. There is no sign of him. No sign of the chair, so heavy it has surely sunk somewhere along the length of the river.

"Lia! Over here!" Alice is still waving. Still calling. Looking only at me. Who will search for Henry?

I decide to try and grab onto the branch, if only to give myself a moment to be still while I scan the water and the riverbank for Henry's dark head. The river pushes me along with such force and at such great speed that working against the powerful current takes every ounce of strength left in my battered body.

Against every odd, I begin changing direction, slowly turning toward the bank on my right. As my body settles more fully into its new direction I am able to use the current to my advantage, and by the time I am near to Alice and the proffered branch I am moving so fast I fear I might pass them entirely with one sweep of the river's great arms.

"Ready, Lia? You must grab as you pass, all right?" Alice's voice is a command up ahead of me, and I find myself nodding in agreement despite everything that has happened.

I am rushing, rushing toward the spot where the branch dips into the water.

"Be ready, Lia. One . . . two . . . wait . . . Now, Lia! Now! Grab it!"

She is leaning so far out over the river that I think she will topple in after me, but as I rush by, I reach out a hand and grapple through the water. I am nearly past it, nearly past the point where I might find salvation, when I feel the crackly, rough branch on my palm. I close my fingers around it quickly, before it is too late.

In an instant my body stops its journey downriver. I still feel the pull of the current. I still feel my skirts, heavy with water, tangling against my legs and weighing down my body. But for now, at least, the branch and my sister serve to keep me above water.

"Lia! Lia." Alice is panting, out of breath and soaked to the skin as if she, too, has nearly drowned in the river. She extends one hand with effort, keeping the other on her end of the branch. "Take my hand, Lia."

I hardly hear her at all. My eyes scan the length of the river, taking it in until it disappears in a curve around the bend. *He may have grabbed a low-lying branch*, I think. *He may have become stuck on one of the shallow stretches of river. He may have found a rock to cling to until help arrives.*

I tick the possibilities off in my mind as if counting down the options for tea. As if every one of them is just as possible as the last, despite the fact that there is no sign of Henry. No

sign of his chair. Looking at the river, it is easy to believe that Henry was never there at all.

"*Now*, Lia! You must grab my hand. This branch will not hold you forever." Alice is angry, and I am surprised that her anger can still gain my attention.

"H-h-henry." I am so cold I can no longer feel the branch beneath my palm, though I see it still enclosed inside my fist.

"We shall get a search party for Henry, Lia. But you must come out of the water now before the branch gives way."

I am still thinking. Still thinking. Trying to think of a way to save Henry.

"Lia!" Alice is shouting at me through her tears, and I notice for the first time that she is sobbing, sobbing so hard she can hardly speak. "You will come out of the water *this instant*. Do you hear me? *Do you?* Because you will be no good to Henry dead at the bottom of this river."

There is no time to question her offer of help. Something in her voice, in her tears, in the stark fear on her face, makes me nod. She is right. Only too right. I must get out of the water to help Henry properly, and right now, there is only one way out.

One of Alice's hands holds onto the branch. The other reaches for me.

It takes me a moment to muster my courage, for I am so cold and the river so fast that I fear falling back into the current. I will not survive it again.

I wrap one hand tighter around the branch. And with the other I reach for Alice.

She grips my hand so tightly with hers that I do not doubt for an instant that she will come into the river with me before letting me go. She pulls with a strength I didn't know she had until she falls backward into the mud and I am lying half in and half out of the water.

She scrambles to her feet, slipping in the mud, and turns me onto my back.

"Lia? Lia? Are you all right?" Her face is pale and wet. I don't know if it is the rain or her tears that fall to my face as I sink into darkness.

❧

The room is warm, but I feel it only as the absence of the cold that seemed to sink deeper into my bones in the hours since Alice pulled me from the water. I am still numb. Whether from cold or fear I don't know. Ivy and Aunt Virginia have been bustling about, piling extra blankets on my bed, forcing me to drink tea so hot it scalds my tongue.

"There, now. Are you warm enough, dear? Is there anything else I can get you?" I feel Aunt Virginia's gaze on my face, but I cannot meet her eyes.

I shake my head, studying the fine needlework strewn across the coverlet on my bed. The search party is still out looking for Henry. Sonia and Luisa are downstairs, somewhere in the silent house. I know these things, but cannot harness the energy to think about any of them.

A knock at the door forces Aunt Virginia's eyes to slide toward Ivy, standing near the washstand over a bowl of steaming water. Ivy makes her way to the door, opening it a crack before closing it and crossing to Aunt Virginia.

When she leans in to whisper in Aunt Virginia's ear, I know they think me so close to madness that they fear sending me around the bend completely when, in fact, I feel nothing at all.

"I shall be right back, Lia." Aunt Virginia smoothes the hair at the top of my head before leaning in to kiss my forehead. Her lips are cool on my hot skin.

I steal a glance at the doorway out of the corner of my eye, registering a roughly dressed gentleman standing with his hat in his hands in the hallway. It takes only a second to lower my eyes back to the safety and predictability of the coverlet.

It is impossible to say how long Aunt Virginia is gone, for time seems to have no measure in the warmth and security of my room. I am half disappointed when she returns to sit gently on the side of my bed. I should like to stay in the quiet of my room without anyone speaking to me for a very long time.

"Lia." Her voice is at first gentle, but when I do not answer it becomes only slightly more insistent. "Lia. I must speak to you. About Henry. Will you look at me?"

But I cannot. I cannot break the spell of the quiet room. This room where I have lain since Alice and I were moved from the nursery so long ago. This room where I have wrapped gifts for Henry at Christmastime. This room where I have dreamed of James's lips on mine. Surely nothing too terrible will happen here.

"Lia." Her voice cracks, and the sadness there is so unbearable that I almost obey. I almost meet her eyes.

But I cannot. I turn my face to the wall, lifting my chin in a stubborn refusal to hear the thing I know she will say. The thing that will make it impossible to go on.

32

I listen for a moment before closing the door quietly behind me and stepping out into the cold night. I want to hear the silence of my home, the only home I have ever known, before I commit this last treacherous act. I have been wise enough to put my boots on before leaving. They look odd, visible in the light of the full moon and peeking out from the bottom of my delicate white nightgown.

My senses are heightened as I climb the hill to the cliff overlooking the lake. The air is crisp and clean, the smell of winter's imminence obvious to me in a way that it was not even a few days ago.

I try not to think. I do not want to think of my mother. I do not want to think of Alice, of the terrible combination of greed and love at the bank of the river.

Most of all I do not want to think of Henry.

I have to stop to catch my breath when I reach the top of the hill. My legs are still weak from my time spent in the river. When I am finally able to breathe without the spread of searing pain through my chest, I continue to the edge of the cliff. Even now, it is hard not to marvel at the lake's beauty. Who can deny the lovely shimmer of its water? It is not such an awful place to die, and in a morbid moment of clarity I have some small understanding of why my mother chose it.

I shuffle slowly to the edge — closer, closer — until my toes are nearly hanging over the rocky face. The wind whips my hair back from my face and rustles the leaves in the trees behind me. I feel my mother here more than anywhere, I think. I wonder if she stood in the same place I am standing now, if she saw the same ripples on the same water. For the first time in my life, I know with certainty that I am connected to her, that she and I are one, with each other and all the other sisters.

But I have failed those sisters. My father spent over a decade compiling the list that would set us free, and even with such help, more help than was offered any sister before me, I have failed. The list is gone, and with it any hope of finding the keys, of ending the prophecy. Starting again would take years — years in which Sonia's and Luisa's lives would be in danger. Years in which I would be subject to the constant torment of the Souls. Years in which I would not even be permitted to fall into the peace of sleep without fear of letting in the Beast that would destroy the world.

And then there is Henry. If I were born with the desire to fulfill my role in the prophecy, Alice would not have trapped

Henry at the river to gain possession of the list. In another life, another world, perhaps Alice and I could have shared the prophecy with one purpose. Instead, Henry was made a pawn in its cruel game.

Watch out for Henry, Lia. My mother's words bounce off the walls of my mind until tears track down my face, slowly at first and then fast enough to wet the collar of my nightdress. I sob into the wind, wanting to let go, to open my arms and fall. But then she speaks to me again.

There are no mistakes, Lia.

I cry harder. "I don't want it to be me," I scream at the water below. "Why does it have to be me?"

The water does not answer, but the wind does. It kicks up in a forceful burst, sending me reeling backward from the cliff until I scramble the ground some distance from the edge.

The wind dies, not a little at a time, but all at once. The leaves in the trees fall quiet, the only sound the gasp of my own labored breathing. I sit there for a time, not feeling the cold, though my breath makes white smoke each time I exhale.

There will be no quick and easy end to my part in the prophecy set in motion so many ages ago. Wiping the tears from my face, I stand and turn from the lake without a backward glance.

I will not look over that precipice again.

❧

The blue sky mocks me, a cruel joke played by God on this of all days.

Henry's funeral is not the wet, gray occasion of Father's

burial. Instead the sun is warm on our shoulders, and the birds sing as if they, at least, are happy Henry is with Mother and Father. And I have no doubt that is where he is. No doubt at all that he walks with them, laughing under that velvet sky. But it does not make it easier to bear.

I feel Alice's stare from across Henry's grave as the minister recites the Twenty-Third Psalm, but I do not meet her eyes. I have not met her eyes since the moment after she pulled me from the river. In fact, I do not think I have looked at anyone since, though Luisa and Sonia and, of course, James have all come to call several times. I feel badly about sending them away, but I can hardly stand my own pain at the loss of Henry. I could not bear seeing it reflected and multiplied in the eyes of those around me.

"Ashes to ashes, dust to dust," the reverend says.

Aunt Virginia steps forward, opening her fist over the hole in the ground and letting the dirt fall from it onto Henry's grave. Her face is drawn and pale. If there is one person who knows my pain, it is Aunt Virginia.

I have begun several times to tell her about those last moments at the river with Alice and Henry, but something prevents me from saying the words aloud. It is reason, in part, for without proof or witness the story would be told differently by Alice and me, of that there can be no doubt. But it is something else, as well; the vacant expression in Aunt Virginia's eyes. The realization that even she can bear only so much. And if I am completely honest, even with only myself, it is a fierce and violent fury burning me up from the inside out. A fury that desires retribution in my own time.

My own way.

I look away as Alice walks toward the grave, lifting her hand and letting the dirt fall onto Henry's small coffin with a dull thud.

Aunt Virginia looks at me but I shake my head. I will not be responsible for one particle of the dirt that covers Henry in the ground next to Mother and Father. I already bear my share of the blame.

That is more than enough.

My aunt nods, looking to the reverend in a silent gesture he seems to understand. He closes his Bible and says a few words to her before nodding and muttering something unintelligible to Alice and me. I can hardly stand his black-suited presence, so full of death and despair. I nod and turn my head, grateful when he moves quickly along.

"Come, Lia. Let us go back to the house." Aunt Virginia is at my shoulder, her hand on my arm. I feel her worry but cannot bring myself to look at her.

A shake of my head is all I can offer.

"You cannot stay here all day, Lia."

I have to swallow hard in order to use the voice I have not used in so long. "I'll be along in a bit."

She hesitates before nodding beside me. "All right, then. But not too long, Lia."

She moves away, Alice trailing behind. It is only Edmund

and I now. Edmund stands silently by, his hat in hand, tears streaking down his rough, lined face as if he is no more than a child. I find comfort in his presence and feel no need to speak.

I stare into the emptiness where my brother's body will spend eternity. It frightens and saddens me, his boyish smile and bright eyes being left in this ground. This ground that will grow colder and harder as winter progresses before bursting forth with the wildflowers I will not be here to see.

I try to imagine it, to fix a vision of Henry's grave covered in violet flowers. To commit it to memory so that I can call it up when I am far away. And then I say goodbye.

&

Despite my exhaustion, it is impossible to sleep the night of Henry's funeral. But it is not my grief that keeps me awake. It is something else, something on the very tip of conscious thought. I know it is important, though I know not how or why.

It is the story from childhood I hear in my mind. The story Father used as proof of his identity when speaking to Sonia before the Beast began speaking instead. I remember it. I remember Henry, trying to be brave but unable to hide the tears that leaked from his eyes as his small boat pitched jauntily down the river. I remember Alice, not wanting me to build the ill-fated raft, not even wanting to help me *try*. And I remember myself, sweaty with perspiration and cumbersome in my pinafore, sloppily nailing together the mismatched boards because we surely could not just stand there, could not just watch Henry cry as his most cherished toy bobbed farther out of reach.

It is the memory of Henry that takes me to his chamber. His eyes, his face, his brilliant smile. Perhaps I need only to be near him one last time before I leave.

His room is quiet, his things just as he left them. I close the door behind me, wanting to take as mine alone this final moment near my brother. I sit on the edge of his bed and pick up his pillow. It still smells of him. Of books, the house that was his refuge and prison, and the faintly sweet scent of sticky little boy fingers. My chest tightens with such force that I fear I shall not be able to breathe.

I put the pillow back on his bed, turning it over and smoothing the surface as I did when he was small and I would tuck him in or read him a story before bed. I make my way over to the bookshelf, for Henry was so like Father and me in his love of a good story. The books go on and on, every beloved tome I read as a child and more. My eye is drawn to the spine of *Treasure Island* as I remember his bright-eyed enthusiasm for the tale we sometimes read together. I pull it from the shelf, enjoying the weight of it in my hand, the feel of old leather.

The book is as I remember, complete with engravings depicting various scenes from the story. In one of them men work on the beach, digging for buried treasure, and it is this that sparks my memory.

Father told me to hide it. He told me to keep it safe. For you, Lia.

My mind wants to deny the possibility, but my heart has already skipped ahead, wondering if the aimless drift of thought is perhaps not so aimless after all.

I scan the bookshelf, knowing it has been here since Henry

lost his boat down the river. At first I do not see it. It has been pushed to the back of the shelf between a bookend and the interior of the shelf. But when my eyes light on that particularly vibrant shade of red, still so vivid after all these years, I know I have found it.

Standing on tiptoe to reach the glass case, I remember the hours Father worked with Henry to build the replica. Father, with no real interest in using his hands beyond holding his beloved books, spent days and days with his head bent to Henry's, carefully nailing together the tiny pieces of wood. Carefully painting them the exact colors of Henry's original boat and then taking it to the glassmaker to have it sealed so Henry would always have a reminder of the beloved toy.

The glass is cold and smooth in my hand, and I try to separate it from the base on which the boat rests. It is tightly sealed, and though some small part of me feels ashamed to take apart Henry's model, another more powerful part feels that I was led here for just this reason.

Turning the case over in my hand I realize that there are a limited number of places in which to look, and I turn my attention to the wooden base. It is square and finished with a dark lacquer. I give it a stronger tug, but it still does not budge from the glass enclosure. It is the depth of the base that gives me pause. At least three inches high, it looks out of place at the base of such a small boat. Of course, it could have been built that way simply as a way to give Henry's boat a place of honor, my father's tribute to his only son.

Or it could be hiding something.

Holding the glass top securely in my hand, I inspect the bottom of the base for a ledge, a lip, anything that might give me a place to pull. When that does not work I try twisting, but I quickly realize how utterly ridiculous it is to twist something square. Its perfect angles, the clean angular lines, suggest something even simpler, even more elementary, and when I place both thumbs along the very bottom and push, the thin piece of wood at the bottom slides effortlessly away, as if all this time it has been waiting only for me.

The folded paper inside the small cavity makes me suck in my breath, and chills rise along my arms and neck. My hands shake so dangerously that I cross back to the bed, removing the paper and setting the glass case on the coverlet.

However much I thought I might be right, I cannot help but be in awe of my small brother when I see the names. They travel like a line of ants down the page, one after the other.

Sonia Sorrensen   London, England
Helene Castilla   Barcelona, Spain
Luisa Torelli   Rome, Italy

Philip Randall — Investigator
428 Highgrove Avenue
London, England

I fall onto the bed, shaking my head. He never had it at all. The crumpled paper in his hand was only that — a piece of paper, likely blank or full of fake names. Perhaps he meant to

throw it in the river so Alice would not continue searching. Perhaps he meant to give her a false list in order to waylay her on a journey without end. Whatever his motive, his gift will allow me to follow the prophecy, to seek its end, without delay. I wonder if the name at the bottom of the list is the person whom my father entrusted with finding the keys. It will be easy enough to find out.

And now I know. Only three of the keys were identified before my father's death.

Three, not four.

Even still, it is a start.

33

As I lift my hand to knock, I cannot help remembering the
last time I stood on this threshold. Then, the prophecy and
my part in it were still a mystery.

This time, Aunt Virginia is decidedly more surprised to
see me.

"Lia!" She reaches for my arm, pulling me into the room
and shutting the door behind us. "Are you all right? Is something wrong?"

I want to tell her that, of course, everything is wrong. That
Henry is dead and will never come back and that Alice will
stop at nothing to bring forth the Beast. But Aunt Virginia
knows this. Repeating it will only waste time we do not have
to waste.

I shake my head. "No. I just . . ." I look down at my hands.
"I must leave, Aunt Virginia."

When I look up, she nods simply. "What can I do to help?"

I take her hands in my mine. They are soft and dry and light as a feather. "Come with me."

She looks into my eyes with a small smile before reaching out and embracing me. "Oh Lia. You know I should like nothing better."

"Then say you will."

She shakes her head. "It isn't yet time for me to leave."

"But Henry is . . ." I nearly choke on the words. I think they will kill me on the way out of my mouth. But I force myself to say them. "Henry is gone, Aunt Virginia. There is nothing left for you here."

"There is Alice."

I cannot hide my surprise. "Alice?"

"I know it is difficult to understand, Lia. But I made a promise to your mother. A promise that I would look after *all* of her children. I cannot help feeling that I have already failed her."

Her eyes grow dark. I know she is thinking of Henry, but her guilt and sadness only bring forth my anger. "Alice? You will stay to care for *Alice*? And will you train her in the ways of the Guardian as well? Will you give away the secrets of the sisters to aid her cause?"

"Lia." Her voice is soft. It is not scolding. Not exactly. But I hear the admonishment in it. "I would never do such a thing. Alice is beyond my help. Beyond my intervention. I will not train her in the ways of the Guardian, because she doesn't wish to fulfill the role, but neither can I simply abandon her."

I want to scream, *What about me? Shall I be abandoned to make my own way in the prophecy with nothing at all to guide me?*

Aunt Virginia continues as if in answer. "And neither am I abandoning you, my dear. You shall have the support of the keys and the guidance of the sisters, and I will join you when I can. You have my word."

I shake my head. "Join me where, Aunt Virginia? I don't even know where I shall go. I need time. Time to refine my knowledge of the Otherworlds and the gifts I can still scarcely control. I need a place where I can feel safe, if only for awhile."

"Not to worry." Her eyes meet mine. "I know just where you'll go. There are no guarantees, of course. But it is as safe a place as any."

C/

"Edmund." My voice cracks as I say his name.

He polishes the carriage in long, slow strokes, his back to the door of the carriage house. He stops when he hears my voice, hand still raised against the gleaming flank of the carriage that appears as if it has been polished every moment of the three days since Henry's death. When he turns to meet my eyes, I wish he had not, for there is such grief there, such naked anguish, that I almost lose my breath.

I move toward him, stopping to place a hand on his shoulder. "I am . . . I am sorry, Edmund. For your loss."

The words hang between us, and I wonder for a moment if

he is terribly angry. If he shall ever forgive me for losing the boy he loved so dearly.

But when he looks at me, it is with surprise and a kindness of his own. He nods. "Thank you. And I for yours."

I hesitate, before asking for the favor I have no right to ask, least of all now. Even still, there is something I must do, and I cannot do it without Edmund's help.

"I need a ride to town, Edmund. I . . . I need to see James. And I need to see him tonight. Will you take me?" The barriers have fallen between us. I am not asking our servant to transport me to town. I am asking Edmund. The nearest I have left to a father.

He nods without hesitation, reaching behind him for his hat. "I'll do anything you ask, Miss. Anything at all." And with that, he opens the door of the carriage.

❧

The light coming from the bookstore is dim with the coming evening. Edmund stands patiently and without prompting in the open door to the carriage, as if he knows how difficult the next moments will be and seeks to give me the time I need.

I have tried to practice what I shall say, how I shall explain to James the prophecy, my role in it, and why I must leave, if only for a while. Even still, nothing I have practiced brings with it the guarantee that James will see fit to love me still, and so I have decided on nothing at all. I shall have to tell him in whatever way I can, allowing things to unfold as they will.

Stepping from the carriage, I march quickly to the book-shop, unaware until he speaks that Edmund is right on my heels.

"I'll wait right here, Miss." He leans against the building near the door in a way that tells me there will be no argument, and I smile faintly before stepping into the warmth of the shop.

Breathing in the smell, I stand for a moment trying to commit it to memory. I don't know when I will return. I have become used to these small moments of melancholy, these moments when I realize all I will be leaving behind. There is no use fighting them.

"Lia!" James emerges from the curtain blocking the back room. He crosses to me quickly, the worry evident in his eyes. "What are you doing here? Are you all right?"

I look down at my skirt for a moment, bracing myself for the difficulty in the words I know I must say. When I finally look into his eyes, I want to throw myself into his arms, to lose myself in the comfort I know I will find there, to forget the thing that stands between us.

"I'm . . . I'm bearing up. I suppose you could say I am as well as can be expected." I try to smile bravely, but it must not be very convincing, for James sweeps me into his embrace.

"Lia . . . Oh Lia! I've tried to see you. I've come calling every day. Did Virginia tell you?" His voice is a fierce whisper in my hair.

"Yes. I'm sorry, James. I . . . I simply couldn't speak to anyone. Not to anyone."

He pulls away, holding my shoulders as he surveys my face. "Of course. Anyone would feel the same. But why? Why have you come all this way? You need only send a message, and I will come to you. You shouldn't have troubled yourself to come in the dark and cold." He leans toward the window, seeming satisfied to see Edmund leaning against the wall outside.

I take a deep breath. "I . . . I had to speak to you. Tonight. I needed to ask you for something." *That's it*, I think. *Just like that. A little at a time.*

"All right. But come get warm, Lia. Come and sit by the fire." He takes my hand, already pulling me to the warmth of the back room.

I shake my head, remaining with my feet rooted firmly to the ground. "No!" It comes out harsher than I intend, but I must not be lulled to the comfort of the fire and the back room, for once there I shall never leave. "I can't. That is, I . . . Let us speak here, James. Please?"

His eyes seem to darken with the desperation in my voice. He nods reluctantly, but when he speaks, his voice holds such determination that I cannot deny his words. "You must know that whatever it is, whatever you need, I will do it for you. I will give it to you if it is in my power to give."

I feel his gaze on me as I focus on the books over his shoulder. His words should bring me comfort and courage. They should serve to remind me that James will do anything I ask, give me anything I need. But somehow they do not. Somehow his resolve only seems to prove that which, somewhere inside, I have suspected all along: James will not turn his back. He will insist on accompanying me to London, to the ends of the earth if necessary, rather than see me go alone into harm's way.

When I look back into his eyes, the untruth I tell is the hardest lie I shall ever utter. "It is . . . it is nothing, really. Only that I fear it will be some time before I can go on as before. Before I can . . . overcome what has happened." My words become softer and softer as I speak them, until the end is but a whisper, and I find it is not an untruth after all. For I know now that there will *never* be a time when I will go on as before.

He breathes deeply, as if relieved, smiling softly into my face and taking my hands. "No one expects it to be otherwise. Least of all me. I'll be right here waiting, however long it takes."

Returning his smile, I stand on tiptoe to kiss his smooth cheek. "Thank you, James. I pray that is true." I turn to go before I change my mind.

"Lia?"

When I turn back he is holding his hand to his cheek, as if trying to keep my kiss from floating away.

"I love you." He says it as if he knows he will not see me again, though surely he cannot. "I love you, Lia."

"And I you, James." My throat closes with emotion as I say the words.

And then I am out the door, closing it firmly behind me and turning to Edmund. "Thank you, Edmund. I'm finished here."

34

This time when I knock on Alice's door, I wait for a reply. The saving of one's life does elicit a strange sort of politeness, no matter the things that have come before it.

"Come in." Alice's voice sounds small behind the giant door, like it did when we were children.

I open the door slowly. I have avoided this conversation, the last true goodbye I must make. And by far the most difficult for the finality it brings.

"Alice." I stand formally at the end of her bed while she maintains her own position by the bureau.

"Lia. Are you well?" Her eyes are kind, her voice sincere.

I shake my head as her eyes grow large with new concern.

"What . . . what is it? Have you spoken to the doctor?"

My throat hurts when I swallow, and for a moment I wonder

if I shall begin to weep, if the tears I thought I had used to extinction can be back so soon.

"No. There is nothing the doctor can do for me. He cannot bring back Henry, can he?" In my voice I hear the plaintive question. Not a question at all, really. And yet my voice allows for an answer other than the one we both know to be true.

Alice shakes her head. "No."

I grab on to her bedpost, rubbing my thumb across the warm wood if only for something to do with my restless hands. "I'm leaving early tomorrow."

"Aunt Virginia told me. You'll be in London, then?"

I nod. Aunt Virginia and I discussed the merits of keeping my destination a secret, but the truth is, I fear Alice far more in the Otherworlds than I do in my own. And then there is the matter of my position as Gate. Alice is most certainly in a quandary, for though she might like to see me out of the way, she also must acknowledge, if only to herself, that she is better off hoping to change my mind than doing away with me altogether.

At least, this is what I tell myself in my darkest moments. In the moments when I force myself to acknowledge that my life is in jeopardy at the hands of my own sister.

She takes a deep breath before continuing. "Lia. I did not mean . . . that is, I don't know why I . . . why I did what I did. It all happened so quickly, did it not?"

I should be angry. I should be beside myself with rage. And yet I find a strange numbness in my heart. My anger is as help-

less and weak as my cold limbs after I was pulled from the river.

"Yes. It happened very quickly." It is a whisper, the memory of those moments a ghost that will not let me rest. "But you have placed yourself firmly on one side of the prophecy. The other side."

"We have been on opposite sides since the beginning of time, Lia. We never had a single chance to be anything but adversaries. Don't you see it, even now? Do you seek to blame one or the other of us still? Can we not simply accept that this is our destiny? That no fault lies with either one of us?"

I lean my head against the bed, staring at the reeded carv-ing in the slender post. "It is true that our names were written in the prophecy long ago, Alice. But there was a choice. For us both. There is always a choice. You have made yours. And I have made mine as well. It is only too bad they are not one and the same."

She walks toward me, smiling her real Alice smile, and I know I shall remember it always when I think of my sister. That shining smile that makes one willing to do almost any-thing to feel its warmth. When she reaches me she puts her hand on the post near mine, leaning in until we are touching foreheads as we did when we were girls.

"I will miss you, Lia. Whatever happens."

Her skin is cool on mine. "And I as well." I straighten up, afraid that if I stay close to my sister for too long I shall forget who she is. I shall forget what she wants, what she has done. "But we will meet again."

She takes a step back, reaching for my hand before dropping it just as quickly. "Yes."

I look into the bottomless green of her eyes, a mirror to my own. "You will not reconsider your position, then? Even now?"

She shakes her head. "Especially now. Abandoning our cause for one destined to fail would be foolish." Her gaze, unwavering, turns as icy and empty as the lake in winter. "And I am anything but foolish, Lia."

I can only nod. With her words, the battle lines are more deeply etched. The next time we meet, we will not look so kindly upon one another.

There is nothing left to say. I turn quickly, filled to overflowing with such regret, such sadness, and finally, such anger. I leave her room without a backward glance, closing the door behind me. Closing the door on the sister I once knew.

❧

I return to my room to find the door ajar, but it is not this alone that stops me. It is that singular sensation of empty space that is difficult to define but that so often follows the leaving of one from a room.

I look around, trying to determine if anything is amiss, but the windows are closed, and everything is as I left it.

Except for the piece of paper lying on my writing desk.

I cross the room warily. Though I'm quite sure I am alone, it is disconcerting to know that someone has been among my private things. When I come to the desk, I reach down and lift the paper from its surface. The room is dim, lit only by the soft glow of the fire. I must hold the paper very close to my face in order to make out the words, and even then it takes me a moment to focus on the curving script, though the message is simple and short.

*To find the book's end,
cross the ancient wood to the mystic isle.
Until then, prepare yourself for the coming battle. . . .
And trust no one.*

I drop to the desk chair, still holding the piece of paper in my hand. The hopelessness that has been my familiar companion in the days since Henry's death lifts just a little. In its place is a sense of purpose.

I look back down at the note. It bears no signature, but it doesn't matter. It is a clear sign of how very much my life has changed that I know well the meaning behind the cryptic words, if not those responsible for its delivery.

The missing pages of the book are still out there.

I must find them and use them to bring an end to the prophecy.

And then try to begin again.

❦

I pause with the quill over paper for some time, trying to find the words. Despite our conversation in the bookshop, it would be unfair to leave without telling James some measure

of the truth, for is not James my oldest friend, my dearest ally, my truest heart?

And yet, there is no place in the prophecy for love. Not now.

Involving him would be nothing but selfishness, but neither do I want to hurt him. I must try to explain without telling him too much. I must try to make him understand the time I require. Time away from him, from Birchwood, from Alice. From all the things that only keep me from the answers that will bring an end to the prophecy once and for all.

I don't know if it will be enough — my small words, my meaningless platitudes, my empty apologies. But it is all that my mother left to me and all I can manage under the weight of my grief and with the knowledge of the fight ahead.

Dearest James,

I will not say goodbye. For this is not the end of our love. How can it be, when your heart has beat next to mine almost since our hearts began beating at all?

No, we are two sides to the same coin. We belong to one another, have always belonged to one another.

I think of your warm lips on mine, of your words on Thanksgiving, and I tell you "yes." Yes, I will be yours. Yes, I wish to spend my life with you. Yes, I long to feel my hand in yours for all of eternity.

338

But these things cannot come to pass until I find the answers to a question I have only just been asked. A question both dangerous and dark, and as I search for its answer, I do not wish to involve you, though I know you would argue this decision if you could.

I write this letter instead of speaking to your beloved face because I know you will try to stop me. I know you will demand answers. I know you will not let me leave without your help, your counsel. And the truth is, I do not trust in my own strength to resist.

And yet I shall. You must trust me if you have ever trusted me, if you have ever loved me. You must trust that I would never leave you if there were another way. And you must trust me to come back to you. For I will, James. I will. You have the promise of my love, and you must carry it close to your heart until I can bring to an end the things that would keep us from one another.

You have always kept me safe. And now you must believe that it is my task to do the same. To keep us both safe so that someday we might be together as one.

I endeavor to be true to you, James. And I pray you will wait. If you will wait, I will return. You have my word and my love.

Yours,
Lia

35

The train rattles under us as we speed through the night. There are windows, but there is no point looking through them. I have already tried, and it is as black as pitch.

At first I worry that I will be sick, the way I so often am in the carriage when I cannot see out the windows, but this time the rocking and swaying bring me comfort. I think if only we can stay on this train, rocking and swaying forever, everything will be all right. Not the way it once was, but perhaps all right just the same.

A warm hand reaches over, covering mine. When I look up, I am met by Sonia's smile, at once excited and concerned. Convincing her to accompany me was not as hard as I expected.

My only bag is stuffed under my seat. In it are an extra gown, a few essentials, and the knife from Alice's room. The rest of my things have been sent ahead to London. Aunt Virginia has arranged everything, writing to let the staff there know that I am coming. Milthorpe House, like Birchwood, has been in the family for ages. We shall be comfortable, Sonia and I, while Sonia teaches me the ways of our gifts. While we contact Philip Randall and seek out the remaining keys. While I become strong enough, in this world and the others, to fight the battle at which I am the center.

Luisa will join us at a later date, when she has found a way to have herself removed from Wycliffe with a minimum of suspicion and disappointment to her father in Italy. Saying goodbye was difficult. But it is written in the stars, and on the marks of our wrists, that we shall meet again.

Sonia squeezes my hand, and when I look down I see the medallion, gleaming taut and flat against her wrist. This is the bargain we have struck. I do not know if the medallion will remain on her wrist, or if it will find its way back to me the way it has in the past. It is my hope that it will be secure, that the power of the soul entrusted with its care will keep it from traveling back to me. Sonia is not the Gate. Samael cannot come through her, though she has warned me that the Souls will attempt to trick her, to frighten her, to harass her in any manner of ways until they succeed in their quest to get to me. But she is stronger than I in the ways of the Otherworlds. If anyone will hold them at bay, if anyone will give me the time I need to prepare for the battle ahead, it will be Sonia.

Will it work? Or will the medallion find its way to my wrist during some fitful night, carrying me to the Otherworlds and the Beast that will use me as its gate, as a conduit to the battle that will begin the Seven Plagues?

I do not have the answers. Not yet.

It is all I can do to travel forward into my future, that dark and shapeless shadow that lies in wait. Into the future my mother never quite reached, hoping for a way to fulfill my own part in the story. For a way to find the missing pages and the remaining keys. There are those who will always be with me — my mother and father, Aunt Virginia, James, even Alice.

And Henry. Henry is my talisman through every dark night.

I recall his somber eyes during that last, private conversation. His eyes and his words, far too wise for a boy of ten: *only time will tell, Lia.*

In the end, I suppose it will.

 ## ACKNOWLEDGMENTS

The journey to publication of this book includes five unpublished manuscripts and more amazing people than I can name. I'll try, though, by first saying thank you to my agent, Steven Malk, the sincerest advocate for children's literature I know. Your instincts and talent are golden. To my fantastic editor Nancy Conescu, who somehow manages to strike the perfect balance between hand-holding, vision, and editorial tough love. It's a gift. To Amy Verardo and the Subsidiary Rights department at Little, Brown for helping the Prophecy conquer the world (heh) and to the entire Little, Brown PR and Marketing team. A more enthusiastic and talented team of people does not exist. To readers and friends extraordinaire Madeline Rispoli, Beth Helms, Karen Barton, and Jackie Lynch. To my friends Karla Galazzo, Eileen Cole, and Kathy Strucker. Life would be so much sadder without sweet potato fries and crazy diner conversations. To Maddi Collier, my first YA fan who has a bright future as a poet and writer. To all the young people who so generously allow me to be a part of the magic and joy and humor and pain of adolescence; Morgan Doyle, Jake Marks, Mike Strucker, and Conner Raymond. Knowing you all is a privilege. A special thank-you goes to Anthony Galazzo, whom I love like a son. I'm in awe of your intellect, insight, and creative mind. Your enthusiasm for life, reading, and writing is a constant reminder of why I love what I do. I can't wait to see what happens next! To my dad, Michael St. James, for the writing gene. And most of all to the hearts of my heart; Kenneth, Rebekah, Andrew, and Caroline Zink, who sacrificed uncomplainingly for my elusive dream. You inspire me every day.

DATE DUE

APR 0 1 '1			
APR 0 7 '7			